The Ups and Downs
of
Miss Margaret Landings

Patti R. Albaugh

Rudin Press
2013

Printed in the United States of America

First Printing, 2013

Cover Design by Cheryl Carter
Cover Photo from Shutterstock.com
Interior Design by Charli Jackson
Editor: Lois Taylor

ISBN 13: 978-0-9895530-1-8
Library of Congress Control Number: 2013912603

Rudin Press
Tucson, Arizona

www.margaretlandings.com

Dedicated to all women who wonder
who they are.

Acknowledgments

I am sublimely grateful to: my beach friends who contributed to the birthing of the novel's plot (Connie, Elizabeth, Georgene, Linda, Lynn, Mary Lou, Nancy, Sue, Suzanne, Suzie, and Teri—especially Mary Lou, my roommate who laughed in the dark with me over story elements); my cousin Kathy Rudin who helped me remember the details of small-town retailing; my brother Walter Rudin, who helped with police scenes; Lois Hanson for being my writing cheerleader; Charli Jackson for volunteering to read the first draft and kept on reading many more versions and did the formatting; her daughter Cheryl Carter for insightful reviews and the gorgeous cover design; Mary Anne Butler for being my first SaddleBrooke writing buddy; fellow writer Barbara Berg for the term "special mourners' row;" Roger Salls for photo editing that made me appear younger; Bill Muto for careful reading and editing; Angie Muto for medical information; Gloria Kempton, my first writing coach and the other writers in Finish Your Novel; my Prague buddies Victoria and Allene who kept asking "What would Margaret do?;" the Roadrunner Saturday breakfast group, including Vivian, who gave me ideas for Margaret's story titles; Carol Hanthorn and the Unit 48 Book Club for reading an early draft; Lois Taylor for careful editing; Meg Files, teacher and mentor extraordinaire in the Pima Community College writing program; Shawne Cryderman for enthusiastic contributions to my book launch party; my husband Tom who tolerated my writing obsession; and my children Amy and Justin, who encouraged their mother's passion to write. Finally, I would like to thank all my friends and acquaintances who patiently listened to the joys and travails of my writing journey.

The Ups and Downs

of

Miss Margaret Landings

There are only two people who can tell you the truth about yourself—an enemy who has lost his temper and a friend who loves you dearly.

—Antishenes

June 1955. My life was about to change, again, and I was avoiding the question whether it would bring me more trouble or less.

Packed boxes labeled "important stuff" and "not so important stuff" lined the walls in my one-room Pittsburgh apartment, just big enough for a single girl like me with little money and big questions. A breeze whispered through the open window and carried the sounds of caged animals from the nearby zoo, trapped like I was going to be. A barely audible laugh track played from the Philco television, the *Honeymooners* maybe, providing me distraction from next week's move to Liberty, the town where I grew up but had outgrown. And I was returning unmarried. Criminy.

I sat at the dressing table, the only cleared surface in the room and the stage for my night's escape. I hungered to become a person I wasn't, if only for a short time. The vacancy in my gut demanded a hefty portion of make-believe. The soothing cream and crunchy squiggle on top of a chocolate Hostess cupcake would have lessened some of the physical pangs, but the cupboards were empty.

I used to play dress up with my mother's evening gowns and costume jewelry. I made Father escort me around the living room, and my mother would pretend to photograph us, the famous couple making their way down the red carpet. Then I was Vivien Leigh, and I stood on Father's shoes so he could waltz me around the room. He crooned "Daddy's Little Girl" to me, and I was the happiest daughter in the world.

I still played dress up. Everyone had clandestine oddities, didn't they? In the mirror before me was a woman defined by the people I knew, "good cheek bones" my grandmother would say, "bird legs" my cousin Tommy teased, "strong, straight teeth" our dentist announced.

The thinness of my silk slip revealed a pointy bra. Lace panties covered the Yangtze River-like scar that traveled down my belly. Mother's voice whined in my head, "Foundations mold a lady's body for a proper impression." The outside was easy to fix, thank you very much, Mother—it was my insides that were resistant to change.

I opened the drawer that held makeup, reserved for the times when I couldn't stand being Margaret Landings anymore and yearned to take on the glamorous world of my current idol and mentor, Miss Bette Davis, star of *All About Eve*. Her brilliance as Margo Channing fighting against the ambitious ingénue Eve gave me hope for surviving in a world of competitive females, wolfish men, and judgmental acquaintances. My obsession with Margo Channing wasn't my only secret, and I was determined to keep her hidden along with the other parts of myself that the world didn't deserve to know.

Tubes of bright lipstick, black eyeliner, and rouge sat in the shiny compartments of a rescued TV dinner tray. It was a silver container of many saviors, and I worshipped their powers to heal me, or at the very least, keep bad memories at bay.

My skin was bare, cleaned down to the pores. I applied moisturizer, letting the cream sink into my skin. I took the bottle of tinted foundation and shook a small dollop on my forefinger. Using a Catholic friend's chant, I dotted my forehead, chin, and both cheeks to the rhythm of "In the name of the Father, the Son, and the Holy Ghost," careful to smooth the four dots together into a seamless tinted veil that covered my freckled skin. I gave my cheeks a fertile flush with a small bit of rouge. I saw life in my face.

Like the planchette on a Ouija board, the eyebrow pencil moved into my fingers, and I drew strong arches onto my own thin straggles. Eyeliner, false eyelashes, and smoky shadow finished the sultry appearance. Each layer of artificiality brought me closer to a world I craved. I nodded to Miss Davis in the mirror, who watched from the poster on the wall behind me.

The lipsticks lined up like soldiers in the square compartment, probably where buttered corn had been, and my hand hesitated over the choices. I chose "Where's the Fire?" and filled my lips with the bright, deep red.

With a wig of dark auburn tresses placed over my pinned hair, I was ready for the dress. An off-the-shoulder taffeta gown, dark red, cinched at the waist and full skirted, called from my closet. I stepped into the sensuous material that evoked power in me even before I strapped on the high heeled shoes. My final touches were a large rhinestone brooch, pinned on the bodice, and a pair of dangling Hollywood-esque rhinestone earrings. I twirled before the mirror and imagined what my high school friends would say if they could see me so fashionably dressed. I had been a bystander more than a participant during high school forays into Graham's Department Store, and I missed out on the fashion education that teenage girls exchanged. And so my daily clothes were woefully dated, influenced by a mother who was still living her sorority days from three decades before.

I took out a tortoise shell cigarette holder, placed a Lucky Strike in the vessel, and held it in my manicured hand like the movie stars do. I never lit the cigarette—one afternoon of eye-crossing nausea in the basement of an eighth-grade friend convinced me never to smoke again. In my other hand I cradled a gin and tonic. Looking in the mirror, I tilted my chin downward just a bit and gazed upward with a haughty, pouty expression.

After a pretend puff and an elegant withdrawal of the cigarette holder, I batted my heavily lashed eyes and gestured toward the Bette Davis poster. "It's such a bother," I said to her. A sip of my gin brought me a moment of luxurious illusion, and downing the rest gave me utter control over my world, a world that had changed into a Hollywood spectacle. Light bulbs flashed, calls of "Miss Davis, Miss Davis" demanded I face the photographers' hungry lenses. My agent shuttled me through the throngs, under the marquee emblazoned with *All About Eve*.

I twirled a couple of times in front of the mirror, but there was nothing else to do—my play acting had nowhere to go, no one to impress. I had no father to escort me down an imaginary red carpet and no mother available to take photos.

I pulled off the wig and placed it back in its cabinet, took off the dress that no one ever saw and put it in the closet beside the clothes that could be worn into the real world. Tomorrow it would all be packed. Back at the dressing table, I used cold cream to remove the eyes and lips that weren't mine. Star for such a short time.

Miss Davis and I were not going to like Liberty, Ohio.

2

Holding a want ad for a reporter at *Liberty News*, I stood on the sidewalk outside the building, trying to muster up enthusiasm for a job. After a decade of independence and judgment-free living in Pittsburgh, there I was back in Liberty.

Seeking employment in a town where I was so well known was much more frightening than taking anonymous leaps of faith I did as a stranger in Pittsburgh. And I had no motherly advice in my head for the journey I was about to take up the concrete steps of the newspaper office. Mother never worked, never had to promote herself, her skills, or pay for food and rent. Her only quest had been to find Mr. Right, which she found before she graduated from college, and she had plenty of advice for me on that subject.

"Of course I will come back for Mother," I told the minister who called me. Then I cried for her and for me. Our relationship hadn't been easy. I had been a trial for her as much as she had been for me, but I loved her, and I wanted to do the right thing. It wasn't her fault that her heart was failing.

Taking a deep breath, I started up the stairs, tripped on the last step, and nearly sailed into the lobby when someone opened the door. I composed myself and approached the receptionist who had cat-eye glasses and a cigarette in her mouth.

"May I speak to the General Manager, please?"

She took the cigarette out of her mouth and squashed it in the bean bag ashtray next to the phone. The smell of stale ash made me gag. "Sure, honey."

I sat in one of the shiny steel chairs and picked up yesterday's paper. June 10, 1955. The headline read "Chicken Stolen

Off Grill." Only in a small town, I thought. Admittedly, I scanned the chicken article to find out who and when rather than reading the story about China providing aid to Hanoi, wherever that was. Grilling thefts or any other personal news in Pittsburgh never piqued my attention, so why here? The name of the wronged poultry owner came into focus. Darryl Boston. Didn't know him.

A large man came and introduced himself as Dale Carpenter, the managing editor. "You probably don't remember me, but I played poker with your father." He motioned for us to sit in the chairs in the lobby. I didn't even rate an office interview.

I remembered Mr. Carpenter as part of the group of loud men who commandeered our dining room table once a month. Father's right to play poker was one battle he had won with my mother. When they played at our house, Mother and I hid in her bedroom doing crossword puzzles. After they left, Mother spent an hour or two cleaning up ashtrays and beer bottles. It was my job to open the windows to air out the house.

I stood up and held out the want ad, by then slightly damp from my perspiring hand. "You have a reporter position open. I was an English major in college, and I worked as an assistant for a magazine editor in Pittsburgh."

"Heard you weren't an English major very long," he said.

What else had the big ears of Liberty heard about me?

He studied me from head to toe and added, "But I'd say you've grown up, young lady. I don't hire girls as reporters, though, and I don't have any secretary jobs." His cigar and bushy eyebrows popped up and down with each syllable. "Why would you want to be a reporter anyway? There are plenty of sales clerk jobs. Try Graham's."

The words "sales clerk" sent a shock through me. Anybody could be a sales clerk. I swallowed my indignation at the mention of my short academic career. Coming home to care for Mother should have given me some points for good luck, but I realized my point count wasn't high enough to avoid begging for a job from a Neanderthal newspaper manager.

He cocked his head toward a phone ringing in an office on the other side of the lobby. "I'll be right back," he said.

I found myself standing alone. I inspected my flats and noticed they weren't polished. The scuff marks screamed, "Lazy, lazy." The Peter Pan collar of my blouse was making my neck itch, but if I undid the little elastic band that fastened the top button discreetly under the collar, I would, as I heard my mother say, "look sloppy." I tried to ignore my scuffed shoes and itching neck by watching the newspaper staff through the door Mr. Carpenter left open. Everyone was typing, scurrying from copy desk to copy desk, picking up the news stories from the reporters—all men.

"Where were we?" he asked when he returned. "Oh, yes, I don't have any jobs for you." He waved me away. "Good luck."

On the way out of the newspaper office, I stopped at the large plate glass window and studied my reflection in the dust-covered glass. Superimposed on my discouraged countenance was a smoky apparition of my ex-boyfriend Howard, shaking his pastoral finger of shame at me. I shook my head free of the image and walked down to Main Street.

People scurried about their business, men in suits and fedora hats, women in shirtwaist dresses, children dutifully holding their mothers' hands. A little girl, skipping to keep up with her mother, reminded me of my own youthful shopping excursions.

"Margaret, is that you?"

Neither the voice nor the face was recognizable.

"Long time no see," said the woman, hatted and gloved with a shopping bag in one hand. Waving as she swept by, she said, "I'm so sorry to hear about your mother."

Criminy. I had flunked the small town code of knowing everybody, yet I was relieved I got away with it. I longed for the anonymity of Pittsburgh's crowds. A person could have a cold sore and just be a person with a cold sore. In Liberty, my wounded lip would be connected to my name, remembered, and perhaps spoken about. "Did you see that volcanic eruption on Margaret's lip?" the observer would ask of a mutual friend. As soon as my obligations to Mother were over, I planned to go back where there were no spying eyes and prying words.

I crossed on the green light and stopped in front of Graham's Department Store. Maybe I could find employment at Graham's— where housewives, spinsters, and teenage girls fancied themselves as fashion consultants or office managers, or even, as sales clerks. The lucky ones had respectable jobs that paid a little, gave them shopping money, and didn't threaten the authentic work of men who were the real family wage earners, as I had heard the poker gang say between bets. They may not have known about, or ignored, women like Mrs. Charskey. I heard her husband drank up the grocery money so she worked in the basement at Graham's to buy food for her kids.

Me? I had my pride, and I wasn't willing to depend on my mother for food and Kotex.

The large glass display windows held mannequins dressed in shirtwaist dresses, pearls, and gloves. Traditional dark furniture, not the metal and curvaceous light woods displayed in Pittsburgh, was placed in a scene so the still models appeared to be in someone's living room.

The glass door was heavy, and I saw the polished linoleum tiled floors and inhaled the lemony wax of the wooden display cases. Money canisters whooshed overhead as they traveled through pneumatic tubes to the office and back with receipts and change. I walked down an aisle between cases of cosmetics and hankies. Sales clerks glanced up from their stations and each said, "Good morning" in genuine tones that made me think they really were glad to see me.

My eye caught a display of embroidered cotton hankies, arranged in a glass and oak case. I pondered their lace edges and embroidered initials. Mother would like one, but Kleenex was my preference—blow your nose and throw the thing away. Wish I could do that with parts of my life—blow mistakes out my nostrils and toss them into a trash can.

I was gulping water at the white porcelain fountain when the elevator doors next to me opened. A handsome man stood at the controls. It was John Graham—community leader, sturdy

Methodist, and a member of the Liberty Country Club where his father and mine used to play golf. John had also been my classmate at Liberty High. Unavailable John, football captain John. He kept his sights on the pretty girls, not the brainy girls, even if they were attractive.

He stepped out to greet me, and he did a quick look over as men were wont to do, but not as leering as Mr. Carpenter. He pointed to my chin, and I reached up to feel dripping water. I brushed the drops away, but I didn't know what to do with my wet hand so I let it hang by my side and hoped it would air dry, quickly.

John had again caught me in an awkward situation. In high school study hall he once alerted me to a gigantic piece of spinach in my braces. Another time he happened upon Roger Overholt and me in the empty band room. Roger was trying to unbutton my blouse, to which I was happily yielding. It could have been a humiliating situation except that behind John was Sally Munchkin, probably about to give John her blouse to explore.

Casting my eyes upon him ten years later, the electricity still shot through me like when we would brush shoulders in the crowded high school hallways. I put the visceral tug back into my mind's "don't enter" space. John was married, last I'd heard.

"Well, hi, Margaret. Missed you at our class reunion last year," he said. "Ten years." He took a step closer to me.

I didn't answer. I wanted to keep those ten years locked, inaccessible to inquiring minds.

He brushed a hand through his thick black hair. "I heard you were coming back to Liberty, small town you know. I'm looking forward to hearing your famous hiccups again. Do they still sound like a rodeo star coming out of the chute?"

Heat crawled into my face. "Thanks a lot."

He stopped and scanned me again. "But wait…is that a cloud hanging over your pretty head?"

"Perceptive as always. You caught me stewing over my need to get a job. I'm here to be with my mother."

"Yeah, sorry about that." He cleared his throat and gave me a weak smile. "And how about you? You gave up quite a bit to come home and help out. Are you staying at your mother's house?"

"I'm now a homeowner. She gave the house to me. She thinks I'll be making a new life in Liberty, but I'm pretty sure I'll go back to Pittsburgh as soon as…" I couldn't finish the sentence.

He checked the elevator over his shoulder. "I heard she wasn't too happy about you breaking up with that minister fellow."

Did my mother keep nothing sacred? "She was overjoyed I was dating a Presbyterian minister. She said she could hear a chorus of Calvinistic ancestors applauding their approval from heaven."

John laughed. "You have such a way with words."

"Yeah. Back to my task. Any job openings here?"

I steeled myself for his response. Worse than sales clerking, what if he offered something like cleaning restrooms, selling shoes for stinky feet, or unpacking boxes of plastic tablecloths and men's underwear?

"I hear you had a job with a magazine. I'd like to hire you to do the advertising copy, but the job isn't open yet. Mr. Beals, the advertising manager," John leaned closer to me and lowered his voice, "is getting pretty long in the tooth as they say, and should retire soon."

"So?"

"Well, Miss Left-Town-to-Become-Famous, we need someone to run the elevator. What do you think?" He looked at me with that captain-of-the-football team gaze that led men and seduced women.

Elevator operator? Every elevator operator I had known was a spinster. At least it wasn't clerking, I thought. What could be so bad? It was a job. "If it's temporary—the advertising job sounds intriguing."

"Fair enough. One caution, though," he said. "We may be friends but here you have to call me Mr. Graham. I can't show any favoritism." He glanced at the nearest clerk who was watching us. "Morale is good, but the hawks hover, if you get my meaning," he whispered. "This is temporary. Mr. Beals will retire soon, if you're worried about that."

Sure. Nobody retired in Liberty, Ohio. People stopped breathing at their posts or died of natural causes in their beds with their work clothes set out for the next day. But John's word was trust-worthy. I smiled my consent.

"Welcome back to Liberty," he said and shook my hand.

The warmth spread from his strong grip and sped along my arm and up my neck. Almost thirty and still reacting like a school girl.

I almost forgot. "What do you pay?"

"For you, fifty cents an hour."

I gulped. "Fifty cents?"

"Small town retail, small town money."

"What happened to minimum wage?"

He laughed. "You're kidding, right? This isn't Pittsburgh, and you won't have full-time hours. You'll get a raise when you get the advertising job. Are you still willing?"

My mental balloon, filled with the hot air of a new job, deflated rapidly. "I guess so."

"It will be nice to have you as a Graham's Associate. Come in tomorrow at eight, and I'll give you a little training. It's really simple." He gave me a wink. "Anyone who runs the elevator calls it the Monster, but I'm sure you've conquered monsters before."

I winced.

The elevator buzzed behind him.

"Duty calls." He smiled that smile. John got in the Monster and waved before he closed the doors. Then he was gone.

Mother would be impressed I found a job, but it wasn't a job that came with bragging rights. What had I gotten myself into?

3

The theater billboard announced a repeat engagement of *All About Eve*, but Mother was expecting me. After I left Graham's Department Store, I walked up Main Street, past the theater toward Sisters of Mercy Hospital. The orange brick walls of the hospital reminded me that here was a place where lives took shape or lost form. I forced myself to climb the wide stone steps.

The doors opened to a world that reminded me of Mother's failing health and the accidental revelation of a family secret. I had been avoiding telling her that Howard took back an engagement when he learned about the baby. When he heard my Very Big Secret—the son I gave up for adoption—he jerked the ring box away before I had a chance to take the small diamond out of its velveteen slot. My mortification was public to the stunned restaurant patrons who witnessed his retracted proposal, a proposal sprung much sooner than I had anticipated and before courage had allowed me to share such an intimate corner of my past. It was a past that I swore to my parents I would never reveal.

My son was a family secret, classified information. "No one needs to know what you've done," my mother told me that evening at the kitchen table when I tearfully told my parents of the pregnancy. Mother hid her face in her hands and cried. From behind her hands she wailed, "Where did I go wrong?" After she became calm and resolute, she said, "No one is to know. You understand? We will tell people that you enjoyed college so much that you didn't want to come home for Easter." My father said nothing and avoided making eye contact with either of us.

Mother's solution meant that my college career was down the sewer, along with each breakfast and dinner I threw up for the next three months. Even before I started to show, my mother exiled me to my cousin's in Pittsburgh and then to a Florence Crittenden home, the refuge of choice for unmarried women. Mother made the long drive each week to visit, but not my father, who had been, before my downfall, the conqueror of house rodents and shoo-er of boogey men from my childhood closet. He told Mother I would be embarrassed for him to see me "in a family way."

For five months I hid out with other young women who had "gone all the way" and simply disappeared for a few months. We lived a structured, orderly life of early wake ups, early bedtimes, and assigned chores that would give us the tools for living a productive, virtuous future after childbirth, and each without child. We all returned home to extoll the supposed virtues of camp, college, or trips abroad (lost the photos, sorry).

All of us had something in common besides being pregnant—we shared plans to leave some memento with our babies that would be a signpost to their birth mother's existence. One of the nurses at Florence Crittendon encouraged the tradition and helped sneak the remembrances into the baby's bunting. We were comforted to think that when the child grew up, he or she would finger the relic and magically sense the birth mother's love and regret.

My token was the most treasured item I had—a mustard seed encased in a clear bauble that my grandmother gave to me. I always wore it, even on the night I conceived my son. When the nurse prepared my baby for his new parents, I made sure she included a little card with the bauble, the card with my Gram's shaky handwriting, "If you have the faith of a mustard seed, all things are possible." I couldn't believe I would never see my son again, and that little seed carried the hope that I would.

My best friend at the "home" was Bethany, whose due date was close to mine. We were also roommates, so we had plenty of opportunity to share experiences unmentionable to the outside world. Bethany was also a caught-on-the-first-time girl. We lamented our bad luck and anticipated going all the way again, but with more consciousness and forethought…and fun.

My stomach knotted. Criminy, ten years of pretending I never gave birth. Ten years of packaging my embarrassment. Ten years of seeing Mother's face with *rescuer* written on her forehead. If I told her why Howard dumped me, I'd hear again that I should have thought about that ten years ago.

Inside the hospital the cool, pharmaceutical air assaulted my nostrils. Sister Agatha, in her white habit and starched wimple, sat at an oak table that held a cardboard box of little recipe cards with patients' names and room numbers. Her wimple surrounded a round face that beamed an angelic glow. The large cross that hung upon her breasts—certainly there were breasts under those many layers of pure cotton and starch—drew my eye toward her trimmed and spotless nails. Sister, a.k.a. Michael the Archangel, guarded the doors that led to the elevators. There were several people in line and like a dutiful student I waited my turn for a visitor card.

Patient for my own moment with Sister Agatha, I revisited my secret within the secret. The knot tightened. I would have hell to pay if my mother found out I had betrayed the family trust by divulging our secret to Howard. My mother would rise up from her deathbed and give me that "How could you?" expression. My cousin was in on the secret. I lived with her in Pittsburgh after my son's birth, but she was family, right? But Howard wasn't family, and he was good friends with Mother's pastor.

Sister Agatha glanced up.

"Why, Margaret," she said. "It's nice to see you." She smiled with that peaceful presence that eluded me and probably always would. "I prayed with your mother this morning. She's such a good soul." Almost as an afterthought she asked, "How are you, dear?"

"Oh I'm fine."

A young volunteer bedecked in a pink and white apron picked up mail from Sister Agatha's desk. The nun asked, "Say, didn't you used to be a candy striper?"

"Don't remind me. I was…for one day."

"Oh. Well… God bless you, child."

"Uh, sure, God…" I couldn't finish it. Saying "God Bless You" was like kissing strangers on New Year's Eve—so automatic for some people and so unnatural for me. Sister Agatha waved me toward the elevators that gave access to an inner sanctum of rooms where patients gained strength or ebbed away.

Waiting, I recalled my candy striper debut. My pink striped apron gave me status even above the well-dressed girls at school, and I set out to deliver mail and magazines to the patients as I had been trained to do. But strange tubes snaked out of the patients' bodies and frightened me, and the sickly sweet perfume of flowers invaded most rooms. Mysterious metal-bound charts hung on hooks at the foot of each bed, and I imagined what secrets those pages held. "Read me, read me," they called.

In the fifth room the patient was sound asleep—and snoring—and I saw an opportunity to peek inside one of those secret laden charts. Coughing to test the patient's unconsciousness, and getting no response, I looked toward the door. No one. I quietly moved to the bed and lifted the metal cover to peek inside. I heard a "Harrumph!" and saw the patient staring at me, wide-eyed and blue in the face. He made horrible phlegmatic sounds. I ran out of the room and grabbed a nurse. Once she was at the patient's side, I ran again, out of the hospital and to my home a mile away. I was sure I had killed poor Mr. Cummings with my surprise intrusion. That evening I buried my pink apron in the backyard.

I shuddered at the memory. My experience with hospitals always included death of some sort, like dying inside when I gave up my son. And what if talking about the baby made Mother bug-eyed and blue like Mr. Cummings? Just to clear my conscience? I cleared my throat to change my focus.

The elevator finally arrived, and a parade of people got out—people in wheelchairs, people with crutches, and finally a beaming couple with their new baby. Jealousy stabbed me. Once inside, I saw the push buttons. So impersonal. There was no operator to greet you and no operator to ask which floor you wanted.

A pair of women boarded with me. They had the same eyes and nose, although the chubbier one was blonder than the other. Sisters? They took a position behind me.

"Should I tell her?" asked one.

I leaned a tad closer to them, directed my gaze to the ascending numbers over the elevator door but turned my left ear in line with the women's faces.

The other woman clucked her tongue. "What difference would it make?"

"Isn't the truth always better?"

"Not if it's hurtful. What would it accomplish? She'll be gone soon."

They got off on the second floor and left me with my conscience reeling for another two floors. What force of fate put these two women in my life? I considered my own choices. Tell Mother that Howard knew about the baby or let her die without knowing, as the ladies on the elevator were wont to do? But Mother may find out from someone else and our last days together would be spent in her increased disappointment and my guilt.

I exited and proceeded to Mother's room. She was sound asleep, and a nurse sat watch in the corner.

"Shhhh." The nurse put her finger to her lips. "She's had a dreadful day. I don't think you should bother her."

"She insists that I wake her whenever I'm here."

"Try not to upset her. She was a little agitated after your last visit."

Oh, yes, yesterday's visit. Mother had scolded me about being single. What about me? I was far more agitated. Why didn't mothers understand that when we leave the nest we want to fly in the direction of our choice? No, no, I pictured telling my bird mother…I'm going out the other side of the nest.

The nurse got up from her chair. "Let me know when you leave," she instructed from the doorway. Her judgmental frown gave me chills.

Mother was a lump on the freshly made bed, her pale cheeks visible through the plastic of the oxygen tent that surrounded her. My mind clamped down on preparatory grief—the grief before the death, the grief that a person knows is coming. Even though there were many days growing up I couldn't bear another day as her daughter, I could hardly stand the thought of life without her.

At the hospital she was surrounded by people who took care of her with steady, skilled attention. She had clean, pressed sheets and attentive nuns who prayed with her—not a bad place to be when on death's watch list.

Sitting on a wooden chair next to my mother, I slipped my hand under the synthetic barrier that separated us. I thought it odd I would be spending my time encased in a steel elevator car while my mother spent her last days encased in a plastic tent.

She took care of me as best she could. I could never count on when the "best" days were going to be. We had had a teeter totter relationship—memories of warm cookies, cuddled storytelling, and hugs after broken dates mingled with flashbacks of her cutting up my favorite teddy bear when I left it on the floor after many warnings to pick it up, the slap I received when I pouted about going to church, the week of silence after I talked back to her. Father was always the go-between. He would hold me when I cried, but he didn't interfere with Mother's rants.

After Father died, we declared a truce, but The Very Big Secret was to stay that way and was non-negotiable. "You wouldn't want to ruin our reputation, would you? Your father insures many people in Liberty. They look up to the Landings."

The mother I came back to was weaker and a little kinder. Lack of oxygen must have killed off some of her judgmental brain cells. Maybe my sense of impending loss made her personality quirks less irritating, or perhaps I had developed armor around my heart to protect me against her biting comments. I had to admit that I began to enjoy her sense of humor.

"Mother?"

Her eyes opened, and she smiled.

"Hello, Mother, how was your day?"

She licked her dry lips. "It's been exciting, fighting off old geezers with no teeth." She took a big breath and tried to laugh but all that came out was a muffled "ha."

"That's my mom."

I stroked her papery hand, crisscrossed with bold blue veins that stood out against the pale skin. Her eyes were still clear and piercing.

"You seem to want to tell me something."

I had a fleeting moment of courage. "I have a job at Graham's Department Store."

"That's great, honey." She took a breath. "I'm glad you're doing more than sitting here every day staring at me while I sleep."

"I got a job as an elevator operator."

A slight frown crossed her face.

"Later, you can find something better." She brightened. "Watch it, that cute John Graham is already taken." She gave a weak cough that made her choke, and her gagging made me wince.

"Oh, Mother. There are other men to watch out for." I paused. "Remember how we used to make fun of men saying stupid things in hope of some action?"

She gave a little air-deprived giggle. "You're the only one I've felt this way about," my mother mimicked, and she tried to flutter her eyelids.

I laughed and offered, "I've never met anyone like you."

"Speaking of men," she took a breath, "have you heard from that minister friend of yours?"

I stared out the window and watched the dancing leaves, hoping their motion would signal something acerbic to say. Facing her, I said, "No."

"That's too bad, dear. He sounded," she inhaled the helpful oxygen, "like such a nice young man. I don't understand."

"He was too religious," I said with my eyes averted.

"Good grief, Margaret, you can't be serious." She took another gulp of air. "I think you're being silly."

The knot in my belly tightened. "Criminy jeez, Mother, let me decide that—"

"There you go, using those awful words again. You know that's just a sneaky way to say Jesus Christ without really saying it. We didn't raise you to take the Lord's name in vain," she gasped for some air, "… and don't let the nuns hear you either." She closed her eyes and turned her head on the pillow. "You're not getting any younger, you know." She then drifted off to an uncomplicated place of elderly sleep.

Even though I had no intention of staying in Liberty, two factions pulled at me. One team, the Small Towners, had enticed me already with hearty welcomes, comforting sights such as Graham's dark oak shelves, and familiar sounds like the noon factory whistle and the Sunday church bells. The other team, the Independents, reminded me with each tug that I liked the autonomy of Pittsburgh, or any city, where the name "Margaret Landings" didn't connect me to the Landings of Liberty, and I could try new behaviors and ideas without fear of being reported.

But returning had reintroduced me to the pleasures of being greeted by name and feeling like an integral part of a small town's entwined life. Score one for the Towners—until the Monster and people in my past I might encounter in the elevator, that is. Score one for the Independents.

I watched her rest, her breathing steady and without struggle. As I held my mother's hand and studied her sleeping face, the events that brought us to this point swirled in my head. Soon after I went to the Crittenden home, Mother became pregnant with a change of life baby. We each lost our surprises. I gave mine to people who couldn't have their own children, and my mother yielded hers through miscarriage. My mother hinted that the Pittsburgh trips put too much strain on her and that was why she lost the baby.

In spite of suffering similar losses, we were unable to help each other. We shared the silent anguish of separate and empty wombs—the babies outlawed from our conscious lives. Mother's baby, my unborn sister, disappeared in our conversations as wind blows away fog—what couldn't be seen did not have existence, and I tried to do the same with the memory of my son's birth. We also had one more tragic coincidence in common—neither of us could have any more children. The children we lost took our wombs with them. My mother's miscarriage resulted in a hysterectomy, and my son's birth ruptured my uterus, and I also lost the organs of motherhood. I put that painful history into a box whose contents mysteriously leaked whenever I didn't have the strength to keep the lid sealed tight.

Mother's eyes opened again.

"I'm not going to get any better, you know."

"I—"

"So I hope you find a nice young man."

"Mother, I—"

A voice from the door startled me. "Oh my gosh, Margaret, is that you?"

I looked up to see Adele, high school classmate, now a nurse, holding a shiny metal tray of medications. She had been a cheerleader. I had been, well…at the games.

"Are you back for good or just visiting your mother?"

I hesitated, doing a mental check of Adele's appearance. Her lustrous hair was tucked neatly under her nurse's cap, and she had a spotless and shape-revealing uniform, as well as porcelain skin. She put me in a state of petty jealousy. No gray, either. Did she pluck out strays like I did or hide the scourge of reaching thirty with hair dye?

"Well, answer her," my mother said. My eyes traveled heavenward for patience.

Ignoring Adele's question and my mother's demand, I replied, "What a surprise…when did you move back?"

"About a month ago… started this job last week."

Adele put the tray on the bedside table and spoke in that too cheerful voice of nursing staff who assumed that all sick people were deaf and depressed. "Good evening, Mrs. Landings. How are we feeling?"

"Are you in this bed too?" Mother shot back.

Adele's smile faded a little but quickly brightened. "We are feisty tonight, aren't we, Mrs. Landings?"

Mother rolled her eyes.

"Did I see you roll your eyes, Mother? You've always told me they'll stick that way, you know."

"I've earned the right."

Adele started straightening the sheets. The nursing routine would take a while, so I kissed my mother's hand and slid it back under the plastic curtain.

"I haven't seen you since graduation," Adele said as she straightened Mother's bed. "Remember health class, trying to peek in Tommy Rankin's book to see what he drew on the skeletons?"

The memory of Tommy's altered illustrations made me laugh. "That was part of my sex education." In the corner of my eye I saw my mother grin.

I signaled Adele that I was ready to leave. "Good night, Mother," I whispered. How many more nights would I be able to say that? And how many chances would I have to break down this wall of silence about my son? Once in the hallway I glanced back and saw that my mother's eyes were closed again. I walked toward the elevator.

"Margaret, wait a minute." Adele hurried to catch me. "Say, are you free to go to the movies tomorrow night? It would be fun to get re-acquainted, and *All About Eve* is playing again. I haven't seen it yet." She looked at me, brows raised.

A movie, my favorite movie, was so tempting, and renewing a friendship would be a bonus. But there would be the strain of filtering out events of the last ten years that weren't suitable for Liberty and its news mongers, especially for a successful Liberty High graduate like Adele.

Like any cheerleader, she had a "ah, come on and join the fun" expression. All she needed were pom poms.

"Sure. Meet you at..."

"Seven."

"Seven it is."

4

He led the way to a corner alcove to the time card machine, which resembled an altar for productivity. There sat a brand new card with "Margaret Landings" typed on the top, and John showed me how to punch the card each time I came or left. I put the card in the slot and clunk, I was officially an employee. The time read 8:07 a.m. in little purple letters.

We walked toward the middle of the unoccupied first floor. The store teamed with the ghosts of customers past. The sound of coins and people's chatter hovered in a phantom collection of activity. I wondered who had been witness to the sacrifice of other virgin elevator operators? I thought of Fay Wray being tied up as bait for King Kong. She escaped, but I wasn't hopeful about my outcome. John turned on the first-floor lights and pointed to the subject of instruction.

"Are you ready for training on the Monster?"

"Yes." But I was distracted by John's cologne, a manly aroma of spice and forests. According to Mother, his wife was an alcoholic, their marriage rocky. His domestic unrest was a caution sign for me. One, unhappiness cracks open the marital door for illicit experimentation, and two, a single woman knows the door is open and unlocked. *Down, Margaret, down.*

"If the elevator has been named the Monster, I'm not sure this bodes well," I said. I surveyed the iron mesh doors, the wire stool in the corner of the steel elevator cage, and the brass control that dared me to take it on.

John waved me into the creature's yawning mouth and closed the doors. "If you close the outer doors and not the mesh doors, the elevator won't go, no worry of crushed fingers here. Of course,

since you didn't become the famous writer our class book prophe-
sied, maybe you don't need all your fingers."

I glared at him.

He took on a mock grimace. "I'm sorry, I always thought that
was high school dream talk. We all talked big."

"Forget it, John. I'm too sensitive, at least that's what my
mother tells me all the time. Now, about taming the Monster."

"Right." John pointed to a brass plate that had a black knobbed
handle, which followed a curved track. "The position of the handle
determines if you go up, down, or stop." He pushed the handle
forward, the motor came to life, and the car moved upward. He
gently pulled the handle back to the center position and the car
stopped. "You try it. Continue to the second floor."

"Seat belts, everyone."

"Huh?" John asked.

"This reminds me of a movie."

"Which movie?"

"*All About Eve*. Remember the scene where Margo tells everyone at the party to fasten their seatbelts because it's going to be a
bumpy ride?"

"Didn't see it."

"Oh."

I took the handle and moved it forward with confidence—too
much confidence. The motor roared and we sped by the second
floor opening.

John yelled, "Stop! The middle, pull it back to the middle."

I jerked the handle back, past the middle, and the elevator gears
screeched as the car changed direction. John grabbed the control
and brought the handle to the center stop. His carefully groomed
hair had fallen over his forehead, his eyes were wild, and a waft of
overheated oil seeped into the elevator. We were finally still.

"This is harder than I thought," I said. "As kids we laughed at
elevator operators who overshot the floors."

"You'll get better. Let's try this again."

On my next try, I pushed the lever forward more carefully and
the elevator began to climb. In a corner mirror I saw that my lipstick

was crooked, and I used the pinky of my free hand to straighten my lip line.

"Margaret!" John screamed.

The third floor landing whizzed by. Thunk! The elevator came to a sudden stop.

He took a deep breath. "Try moving the handle backwards to see if we can go down."

"Sure."

The elevator groaned but didn't move.

"It's stuck," John said. "It sticks if you take it too far above or below." He shook his head. "I have to climb into the shaft and loosen the gear." He took off his suit jacket and put it on the wire stool, popped open the roof of the elevator car, and pulled down a little ladder. He climbed up a couple of steps and turned back to me. "Don't touch anything!"

He disappeared, and I could hear creaks and thuds. The elevator shuddered a bit, and I heard something pop back in place.

John's feet appeared on the ladder, and followed by his legs, his tight backside…*careful, Margaret.* He dusted off his hands and put his coat back on.

"I don't think I can do this." My eyes watered. I hadn't felt that stupid since my falsies floated out of my bathing suit into Lake Erie and drifted by Billy Ebberts' astonished face.

"Don't be silly. It happens once in a while, but usually I'm outside the elevator and I can get to the motors from an access door. It's less dangerous too. I hope you've learned a lesson."

I hung my head.

"Shall we continue?"

Motivated by shame, I used each attempt to control the Monster for smoother takeoffs and landings, inch-by-inch, foot-by-foot. John's eyes went from rounded terror to crinkled approval. I was on my way to taming the elevator, but dreaded tomorrow when the customers and I would be unescorted and at the Monster's mercy.

5

The marquee shimmered with the title of my favorite movie. "Return engagement! *All About Eve* with Bette Davis," and the bright billboard made my skin tingle. I looked forward to hearing Bette Davis recite those magical words of Margo Channing's conflict, survival, and resolution. An infusion of her wit and glamour would lighten the anxiety about my new life in Liberty.

Adele was late. What if she didn't show? How naive of me to think that a long-lost classmate really wanted to spend time with me. The movie was starting in ten minutes and she was nowhere in sight. Then I saw her. She waved madly from down the street as though the flapping motion would propel her faster.

"Margaret, Margaret," she called as she approached within hearing distance.

I shook my head.

She was breathless and apologetic. "I hope I'm not too late." Her eyes were bright with enthusiasm.

"No, no," I said. "Let's get our tickets."

We stood at the box office window, and I slid two quarters under the crescent opening in the glass shield between the booth lady and me. "One, please." I marveled at how many hands, how many coins it had taken to wear the brass coating down to the bare, gray metal underneath. I sympathized with the worn tray. Too much use wears a person down.

The gum-chewing attendant said "Sure thing, honey" without seeing me, and she passed the ticket back through the worn tunnel.

"Same for me," Adele said in her cheerful nurse voice.

The attendant looked up, still chewing and popping her gum. "Oh, hi there. How's things with your doctor friend."

"Oh he's the cat's pajamas." Adele winked and gave a little Doris Day curtsy.

Tickets in hand, we walked toward the double brass-handled doors. I paused at the poster of Bette Davis, arm-in-arm with her co-star Gary Merrill. Their eyes bore into us, inviting us into their world. "I have that poster," I told Adele.

She looked at the poster and read the line, "*All About Eve…* all about women and their men!" She cocked her head toward me. "Oooh, men…I like that subject."

I laughed. "Me too. But Bette Davis is my favorite actress, and this is the best movie I've ever seen."

"Why?"

"The glamour, the wit…I really relate to Bette Davis' character. She's vulnerable, but tough, a crazy mixture of personality that makes me feel more normal." I pulled Adele off to the side to let a couple pass.

"I think this movie is going to teach me a lot about you," Adele said.

I held up my ticket. "Let's go see a movie."

We walked in, the overhead electric bulbs leading us to entertainment, fantasy, and I hoped, escape.

As soon as we were inside, my heart filled. For me a movie theater was a cathedral—promising redemption from a defective world. I inhaled the intoxicating aroma of popping corn, reveled in the comfort of the plush maroon carpeting with grey art deco swirls. "I have to have popcorn," I said and headed to the concession stand.

"Me too."

Armed with sodas and popcorn, we started down the aisle. I led the way and headed toward my favorite vantage point—eight rows from the front, middle seats. I hurried to get ahead of a couple who were heading toward *my* seats.

"Whoa," Adele said. She dodged a couple I had already passed.

I stopped at the eighth row and pointed toward the prize—the middle seat. As I got closer I saw that someone had spilled a drink on it. I stopped in my tracks.

"What's wrong?" Adele asked.

"My favorite seat is wet. Some idiot spilled his drink."

"Just sit in the seat next to it, no big deal."

"Then I'm off center."

"Yes, you are off center. Sit down."

So I sat, and my world was about twelve inches right of perfection.

I turned to Adele. "I can't believe you haven't seen this movie. Wait 'til you see what Bette's character has to put up with." I settled back and munched on the salty, buttery popcorn. I couldn't have been any happier, until I remembered one of the reasons I needed distraction.

"By the way," I said. "I have a job now—elevator operator at Graham's. How's that for fulfilling a life's dream?"

"A lot of people would kill for that job."

"That's easy for you to say, you're a nurse, a professional."

"Think of it as temporary. It's better than spending hours staring at your mother while she sleeps in a hospital bed. A lot of patients tell me that drives them crazy."

"That's exactly what Mother said. Anyway, I'm supposed to get the ad copy job when Mr. Beals retires."

"See, things work out."

"I hope." We both went back to munching on the crunchy bliss of popcorn.

"So," Adele asked, "what is this movie about, besides women and their men?"

"Gosh, where to start." I shoved more popcorn into my mouth and chewed noisily. "It's about a self-proclaimed waif, that's Eve, who worms her way into the lives of an accomplished but aging actress, that's Margo, and her theater friends." I took a breath. "Eve isn't honest about who she really is or what she really wants. She does a lot of damage to Margo's reputation, and Margo gets railroaded but eventually comes out on top. She's so elegant and witty."

"After the movie, I'll tell you whether she's a worthy mentor for you," Adele said.

"I have no doubt."

The lights dimmed and the heavy velvet curtains parted. The film reel rolled, and the clickety-click of the projector calmed me and excited me at the same time. I could sense the other movie patrons settling in as they sank into their seats.

"I wish you could see yourself," Adele said. "The reflection off the screen is almost as bright as the happiness on your face."

Self-conscious, I shifted in my seat a little away from her. "The newsreels are always interesting," I said. But Adele was already transfixed by the announcer's baritone voice intoning "Survival Town Test to measure the model village in the Nevada desert against the awesome power of nuclear energy…"

Adele grabbed my hand. "Oh no, how awful."

We watched the mannequin families poised in the living rooms and kitchens in the staged houses, and we sat in silence through the blast, the tearing apart of the houses and the incineration of the fake people. At the end of the newsreel there was a collective exhale of the audience, as though they had been holding their breath through the massive destruction created before them.

"Woo, I'm glad that's over," I said. "I'm ready for the cartoon."

"Me too."

Mickey and his friends cavorted their way through a long animation. Finally the coming attractions stopped rolling. The screen darkened and lit up again with the title image *All About Eve*. The deep voice of the narrator began, and I leaned forward. "There she is," I whispered. I pointed to the larger than life Bette Davis, elegant in her satin dress with her shoulders bare and a diamond brooch at her breast.

Adele glanced at me. "You are practically caressing the screen with your eyes."

"She's the cat's meow," I answered.

A "shush" sounded near us. We squelched our giggles with hands on our mouths.

The narrator in the movie described Margo Channing's star status, and I mouthed the words like a parent who followed every line of her child's play, at least that's what my mother said she did at my school functions.

"Oh my God, do you have the movie memorized?" Adele stared at me with wide eyes.

"Shhhhh, I won't be able to hear the next line."

For the next twenty minutes, I tried to say each Bette Davis line without moving my lips. From the corner of my eye I could see that Adele was glancing at me from time to time. She was starting to annoy me.

I moved my lips less and less, to no avail. "Why aren't you watching the movie?" I whispered.

"You're the movie," she replied.

I elbowed her. "Come on, let me enjoy it."

The story unfolded in front of us, and when Eve batted her eyes and lied about her theater experience, I muttered, "Treachery, treachery."

Adele tapped my arm. "Shhhh."

"Oh, here comes a really good part, the cocktail party. Margo is getting tired of Eve being so servile." I watched Margo down another cocktail with dramatic zest. My own nostrils flared when Margo turned to Eve and told her to stop treating her like royalty. I tilted my chin up and tossed my head slightly.

Adele poked me. "You're better at it than Bette Davis."

"I've had a lot of practice."

A few more lines of bitchy dialogue and Adele leaned over. "I think Margo is kind of a nasty person."

"No, she isn't. She's frustrated. I wished I could think of things to say like that, don't you? Those things we think of in the night hours after someone has humiliated us?"

"Hush," someone warned.

We watched the next forty minutes in silence. I wanted to feel what I came to feel but nothing was happening. Was Adele blocking Margo's spirit?

I prepared myself for the coming scene. I closed my eyes so that I didn't have to see Margo's maudlin face as she complained about being single. She whined about not being married and that was all that mattered.

"She sounds like my mother," I said to Adele.

"She wants what's best for you."

"That's easy for you. You're going to be a Mrs. Doctor some-day," pronouncing "Mrs. Doctor" a little too loud for people and several shushes followed. Even in the dark I could see Adele frown.

I stopped reciting the lines, put down the popcorn I no longer craved, and slouched in my seat.

When "The End" appeared, I said, "Slow curtain, the end."

We exited our seats and walked up the aisle. Disappointment draped over me. Instead of sharing my enthusiasm for the movie, I had offended a friend and revealed too much about me.

On the way out of the theater, a man was staring at me. He tipped his hat off his slicked-back black hair. "Who's that?" I asked Adele and tried to discreetly point to him.

"Oh, that's a traveling salesman who comes to town every month or so. Not much to write home about, is he? I think his name is Pete. Why do you ask?"

"Maybe I'm imagining it, but he seems to be ogling me."

"I've seen several men lay their eyes on you tonight, but don't encourage this one. He's not the type to bring home to your mother, but I hear he wants to be brought home, if you get my drift."

"Oh." I looked at him again and we locked eyes. Something stirred around the edges of my consciousness that did not feel right. Even so, I had to tear my eyes away from his.

"So," I asked Adele, "is Margo a worthy mentor for me?"

She glanced away at nothing for a moment. "Good question. I had a mentor in nursing school. She helped me become a better nurse. Is Margo helping you be better at something?"

"I don't know. For such a cheerful person, you sure can stir up some pretty heavy thinking."

She studied me with a Doris Day grin but with the wise eyes of an old soul. "We all have two or more sides to ourselves, don't you think?"

We said our goodbyes but she turned back and gave me a hug. "Thank you for sharing this movie with me." And she walked away.

On my way up Main Street toward home, I snapped off a leaf from a privet hedge and picked at its edges while I considered what I got from all those hours watching and being Margo. Did she help me be better at something like Adele asked? I wasn't even sure what I wanted to be other than a wife, or my son's mother, or my mother's daughter.

And two sides of ourselves? That night I had seen Adele as both painfully cheery and maddenly thoughtful. I wouldn't have guessed that while Adele had been jumping up and down at high school games and shaking pom poms she was taking in the world's mysteries. All I saw of myself was a jumbled mess of unrelated stuff, like my junk drawer. My conflicted brain screamed for a truce. I needed my soft bed, cuddly blanket, and the anesthesia of some sleep. I threw down the mangled leaf and quickened my pace for home. I had a date with the Monster tomorrow.

6

I used to think that running an elevator was simple, like sex. You go up and down a lot, and the quality of the ride depends upon the operator. Silly me.

My anxiety about my new job was evident in the state of my bed. The blanket draped more of the floor than the mattress, and the sheets lay crumpled at right angles from where they should have been.

I went to my closet and pondered what elevator operators wore, and all I could picture were their sensible shoes. I chose a green shirtwaist dress and white flats. When I tried to eat a bowl of Rice Krispies, the noisy cereal was like firecrackers to my ears. Though swimming in milk, those irritating rice kernels were still snapping, crackling, and popping when I put them in the sink.

An hour later I stood in front of the elevator, hesitant to enter.

"It's not going to bite you," John said.

I spun around and saw him watching me.

"Scenarios of me versus the Monster are running through my head... kind of like a Tokyo creature film," I said.

"Very dramatic. Take me up to the third floor and back, just to get you warmed up."

I took a deep breath, entered the elevator car, and grabbed the black handle. John walked on, turned to face the front, and we both stood there, going nowhere. I tried to push the handle forward but it was like a car with a dead battery. Nothing happened.

"Uh, first you have to close the doors."

"Oh, right," I said, the heat climbing up my neck. I closed the inner and outer doors, took my station at the control and pushed it forward for the ascent up to the third floor. The stop was a little bumpy, but not bad. The descent was smooth, although I stopped the car a couple of inches too low. John had to step up some to get out, but he patted me on the shoulder.

He rang the opening buzzer, and I worried who my passengers would be. I missed Pittsburgh, where people were strangers and would have no reason to be surprised to see me, would have no questions as to why I was there. My father used to say that it was better to be a big fish in a little pond than a little fish in a big pond. Well, this fish didn't want everyone watching me swim in circles against the confines of a steel elevator car.

The first passengers of the morning were the third floor furniture manager, Mr. Concord, and a mother towing a disgruntled preteen. She glared into space.

"Good morning, Margaret," said Mr. Concord. "Welcome to Graham's. I'm feeling a little lazy today and thought a moment of your company would be uplifting. Lovely dress, it brings out the green in your eyes." His clichéd flirting and his comb-over didn't impress me. My mother and I had once been victims of his less-than-honest salesmanship. We learned that his lifetime guarantee on carpet assumed you weren't going to have a long life.

The mother-daughter duo stood toward the front. In my peripheral vision, I saw the girl roll her eyes.

"Michelle, for heaven's sake, don't do that. They'll stick that way," the mother admonished, which only caused her to rotate her eyes in the other direction. My mother always told me eye rolling tempted fate. I would be looking at people sideways for the rest of my life. My eyes were quite straight, thank you very much, Mother.

I maintained my friendly Graham's smile and tried to ignore the horror of the five long hours ahead of me. I did think of a story title, however— "The Comb-Over Companion." I wanted to write stories and novels, but I could only think of titles—titles that made people smirk but not titles I could expand into tales worth reading.

"Which floor, please?" I asked of my passengers.

"Second floor to lingerie. My little Michelle here is getting her first Lollipop bra. Aren't you, dear?" I glanced back and saw the poisonous glower Michelle threw at her mother.

I deposited the mother/daughter duo on the second floor and Mr. Concord on the third. More of the same trooped in and out of my steel world for the next hour. My confidence grew with each customer who didn't have to climb over a misplaced threshold. During each break in the traffic, I sat on the little wood-topped wire stool, exposed like a zoo animal on display.

"Hey, Margaret, didn't expect to see you here." I jumped off my stool right into the path of an old classmate, Susan, the homecoming queen and wife, I heard from Mother, of a bank president. Did I really see her smooth her eyebrow with her ring finger—the finger with the really big rock? "Housewares, please. My cousin's daughter is *finally* getting married, and I'm getting her a shower gift. I thought she'd never find someone, why she's almost twenty-five."

I swallowed my envy of brides-to-be.

"Say," Susan continued, "I never thought I'd see you back in Liberty." She looked at me, at the elevator control, and back at me. "This is the only job you could find, huh?"

Smug Mrs. Banker Wife smoothed her eyebrow again.

"I'm just filling time. I'm here to help out my mother, and then I'm going back to Pittsburgh." I prompted the Monster to speed up so I could get rid of Susan and her giant ring.

A call back to the first floor revealed John Graham.

"Third floor, please," he said.

"Hello, again."

He stepped lightly onto the elevator. "I forgot to mention your appearance. Very smart dressing."

He calmed me and aroused me at the same time. "You are quite handsome yourself. We could be king and queen of the elevator."

"Take me to my castle on the third floor. I have dragons to slay."

"Yes, Sir Graham." We both laughed, and my insides tingled, yes, tingled.

I brought the elevator to a gentle rest and unloaded Sir Graham. I closed the doors, sat on the stool in the corner again (a dunce chair?), and shut my eyes. My feet hurt from standing the past two hours, and my shoulder ached from the tight grip I kept on the Monster's handle.

The buzzer again. I warned the Monster, "You be careful who you bring into this elevator." I took hold of the Monster's nose and pushed it backward to descend to the first floor. Smooth landing—yes, I was quite the woman.

"Good afternoon," I said in my best Graham's voice to the entering customer, whose face I didn't recognize. She was a woman about fifty. Her coppery hair obviously came from a bottle—a bottle from the drugstore, not the beauty shop, and I couldn't decide whether the stranger was cheap or practical. A title like "Copper on the Outside, Tin on the Inside" popped into my head. I overshot the floor a little, and it took several back and forth maneuvers to line the elevator up to the landing. The copper-coiffed lady's eyes grew a little larger with each jerking correction. I opened the elevator doors to the third floor, and she walked toward Mr. Concord, who brightened beyond friendly when he saw her. In Pittsburgh I gave copper heads, blond heads, fat heads, and bald heads hardly a thought. Here it was entertainment.

There was a buzz from the first floor, and I closed the doors and maneuvered the car downward.

The outer doors stuck a little and I could barely see the customer—he was waiting with his back to the door. He turned a little and I caught my breath. It was Howard. I slammed the doors shut.

He called through the steel doors. "Hello, hello?"

I waited a moment, hoping he would go away, but he rang the buzzer again. I braced myself and opened the doors.

"Uh, hello, Howard." I stood with my hands still on the partially open mesh door.

He hesitated, his mouth dropped, and his eyes widened. He recovered from seeing me and tried to sidle through the narrow opening.

"Could you open the doors a little more?"

"Oh, sure."

He went to the back of the elevator and turned around. His English Leather aftershave wafted around us.

"What are you doing here?" he asked in a low voice.

I closed the doors with care, counteracting the urge to slam them. I turned toward him. "What am *I* doing here?" I asked. "What am *I* doing here? What are *you* doing here?"

"Your mother called me. She said you worked here, but she didn't say you were an elevator operator. I thought you'd be in the office or something."

"My mother called you? She can barely talk." My hands shook.

"A brief call for sure, but she wanted to know if there was any way for us to get back together. She sounded so pitiful. I decided to make a pastoral visit." He focused on something away from me and cleared his throat.

"She's not even in your congregation." I steadied myself by holding onto the control.

"We had a nice conversation. She said you were working here. But, you told her I was too religious?"

"You are, or you wouldn't be so judgmental."

"I—"

"You didn't tell her I told you, about…you know, did you?"

"No, heavens no." A trace of hurt crossed his face.

"And you didn't tell her about putting the ring box on the table and taking it back five minutes later?" I glared at him—at least I hoped I glared. "And what did you tell her about us getting back together?"

"I told her it was complicated. Say, aren't you just a little glad to see me?"

"Are you kidding? I was hoping you were lying in a ditch somewhere with buzzards hovering over your putrefying body."

He hung his head. "I guess I deserved that."

"Yes, you did."

He paused. "Margaret, I've been thinking…rethinking, actually. I reacted pretty strongly about your son. I don't like the man I see in the mirror every day. I miss you. Could we talk sometime today?"

"No." I clenched my jaws and hands.

The buzzer rang.

"What floor do you want? I need to answer this call," I said in my most non-Graham's tone.

"None. I wanted to see you."

"You've seen me. Now go back to Pittsburgh." I opened the doors and gave my best "this way out" gesture.

He looked at the floor. "I suppose I will. Goodbye."

He waited for a response, but I didn't give him the satisfaction. He straightened his shoulders and stepped out. He hesitated a moment but continued his exit. I closed the elevator doors and leaned against the wall, ignoring the buzzing of the call button and the stinging in my eyes.

7

My mother told me, "If you don't have a man, you might as well have a snazzy car." And so she gave me one for my birthday—an aqua blue Chevy that I'd had since spring. It was the only aqua blue white top Chevy in town, and she turned heads when I drove. I tried to suppress the smile on my face when I drove the circle around the "Square," a roundabout that spewed autos down North and South Main Street or east and west onto High Street. Even the bronze Civil War soldier standing perpetually at parade rest in the center of the Square's small park had to notice my beautiful car. I nicknamed my token of Detroit dreams "Aqua Bella."

After work I walked to the parking lot and grinned when I spotted my Bella. I ran my hand over the satiny finish of the rounded hood and took a handkerchief to wipe fingerprints off the chrome door handles. Aqua Bella's job that evening was to give me a queen's ride home to my castle of quiet. My day of elevator stimulation, and especially Howard's intrusion, had drained me of energy.

Not having a garage, I parked Bella in front of the house and walked up the sidewalk to my front door. I focused on the positive ambiance of my home, a place where I had started to nest regardless of my vow to return to Pittsburgh. The trail of yellow marigolds guided me to the entrance, and I took in the energy of my refuge—the purple front door, white clapboard siding, and the massive elm trees. When I put the key in the door and twisted it, the click welcomed me to the three-bedroom house my mother had given me. I stepped into the entryway and took a deep breath to inhale the clean, polished wood aroma. I was home and away from prying eyes and rumors. A bit of energy flowed through me.

I hung my jacket in the hall closet and saw my mail that had been stuffed through the brass opening in the door and lay scattered on the floor. A water bill, hospital bill for my mother—that one can wait—but one envelope stuck out, *Guidepost* magazine. My fingers stumbled as I opened the envelope, too thin I thought for anything but a rejection. "Dear Miss Landings," it read. "We are sorry to inform you that we are unable to publish your story 'My Mother's Prayers.' Sincerely…" No explanation, just a "sorry." I was unsuccessful, again, this time trying to write from my Presbyterian side rather than my tawdry imaginative side. My third rejection met the same fate as the others—the bottom of the wastebasket.

I went into the kitchen and headed straight to the bottle of gin that sat half empty on the counter. I poured myself a short one and added lots of ice and a splash of tonic. I swirled the libation and held it up against the ceiling light as if the sparkling contents would purify my day. I took a sip and let the cool liquid slide down my throat on its journey to dull my brain.

Home from my first official day as an elevator operator, I stood at the door of my den with gin and tonic in hand and needing to shake off the day's tensions and Howard's reappearance. My feet ached, and the up and down motion of the elevator replayed over and over in my body. Growling gears vibrated in my ears. I think the score was Margaret 1, Monster 1.

I surveyed the room I had made into a retreat. Good north lighting, and on my desk was a Lady Head vase, her eyes gazing at me under long, ceramic lashes. With her black hat and black gloves, she epitomized Hollywood and resembled Margo Channing—my gutsy heroine of the silver screen. The vase had held flowers sent to me by a girlfriend in Pittsburgh when I moved back to Liberty. The card, still propped up against the vase, read "You are a class act. You will survive." The ceramic lady was my inspiration.

Stacked on the desk were bills, lots of bills, and I set down my drink and searched for stamps and envelopes. I opened the desk's junk drawer where I had put Howard's photo the night of his non-proposal. He had been a good date, and fun even though he didn't drink. He laughed easily, kissed passionately, and he was magical on the dance floor. The minister part I could have adapted to. A bonus was that he tolerated my passion for Bette Davis movies, even the recitations of her lines that I memorized from *All About Eve*.

Shuffling through the junk, I retrieved the stamps. I could still see little round water marks on the drawer liner from my tears the night Howard rejected me.

We had gone to dinner at one of Pittsburgh's finest restaurants, and we drank a toast with umbrella'd virgin mai tais. Howard was fishing in his pocket, his face flushed above his minister's collar.

"Margaret." His hand found the treasure buried in his coat pocket. He gently pushed aside the water glasses and put the small black jewelry box on the table in front of me.

He looked up at me with the sureness of a man who was presenting the moon and the stars to a desirable woman who wanted him and would adore him.

"Margaret," he began again. "Remember when we met in Kauffman's elevator? I was so taken by you that I couldn't help myself." He smiled sideways at me. "Here I was a man of God flirting with the most beautiful brunette I had ever seen."

His compliments were welcome, but his intent was not—a common quandary for a single woman who wasn't sure if the man in front of her was Mr. Right.

"I said to you," he continued, "'Surely you are the angel I've been looking for.' You smiled so shyly, and I asked, 'You don't have any boys in your life, do you?' And you said, 'No.' That was my lucky day."

He pushed the box a little closer to me. "Here, take a look."

I didn't want to touch the box until he knew the real me— the Margaret with The Very Big Secret.

"Go on, open it."

I kept my hands in my lap and didn't dare look at the ominous box. He was so handsome, so kind. "Howard, there is something you need to know."

"Darling, I know everything about you that's important. You're good-hearted, you come from a respectable family, and, gosh, you're such a good kisser." He kept smiling that earnest grin as though the world was his. "You're the answer to my prayers."

"There's something important that you don't know."

He looked at me, confusion washing across his face.

"You've been making an assumption about me, and the truth may make you feel differently about things."

"I can't imagine anything that would make me love you less. What is it, darling?" He leaned in closer and took my hand.

I took a deep breath. "The question you asked in the elevator, about having any boys in my life, my answer wasn't quite honest."

He let go of my hand and pushed the box forward even more. "Thank goodness, you had me scared there. I don't care if you had boyfriends as long as I'm the one you end up with." He pulled himself up straighter in the chair and puffed out his chest a little. "You had to experience some duds to recognize a prize, right?"

Criminy. Weren't ministers supposed to have some humility?

"Howard, I'm not talking about men, I'm talking about a young boy, a baby." I thought my head was going to explode from the pounding in my veins. I looked at him for clues to how he would take the revelation of my past.

His smile disappeared and a frown crossed over his once delirious face. "I don't know what you mean." He sat back in his chair. The box sat abandoned on the table, ignored, and suddenly out of place.

I didn't dare look at him. I focused on the cross lapel pin on his jacket. Help me, Jesus. "Ten years ago, I was a young and stupid girl who went to college and discovered freedom." I lowered my voice. "But I found myself trapped instead by…" I took a deep breath for courage. "Howard, I had a child out of wedlock."

Now that the words were out and threatening my future, I longed for a life with him—our children playing on the swing set, the casseroles I would take to church picnics, and the Christmas tree that would light up our modest but comfortable life. I changed my gaze from the cross to Howard. His mouth was hanging open and he wasn't smiling. His face had turned to an ashen grey. He clasped the edge of the table with both hands.

"Are you telling me what I think you're telling me?" His eyes bore into me with judgment—a side of him I had not seen before.

"I'm telling you now because it's obvious that you have plans for us. It wouldn't be fair to keep a secret like that from you. I care for you deeply, but I didn't know when to tell you, and all of this has come up rather suddenly. Please forgive me."

"Forgive you." Howard looked up toward his God and sighed. "I had no idea that you were..." He stopped and looked down.

"A fallen woman?"

"I've saved myself for the sanctity of marriage, and I expected my wife to have done the same for me." He didn't look at me in spite of the silent challenge of my stare. He folded and refolded his napkin as though he could solve the situation by rearranging anything in his reach. "I have a congregation that expects me to be their moral leader, with a wife whose own life reflects those morals. What if people found out?"

"No one needs to know." I startled myself with Mother's words from so long ago.

"Nothing stays secret forever. I would be embarrassed if my congregation found out."

"It's all the same package, Howard. The beauty you admired, the good family, the dancing, and... a child given up for adoption. I know love. I felt it when I handed my son to a family who would love and care for him. It was the hardest thing I have ever done."

"That must have been a very difficult time for you," he said, sounding more like a counselor than a friend.

"Don't good people make mistakes?"

"Margaret, I'm so sorry. I can't." He reached for the box, hesitated, and put it in his pocket.

We sat in silence. My face burned.

Howard pushed his chair back and stood up.

"I'll see that your dinner is paid for. I need to go. I'm so sorry. I hope you understand."

He did a small bow from his waist, and then he turned and left. I wanted to throw my fake cocktail at him.

That night I sentenced his photo to the darkness of my junk drawer, but I realized its resting place should not be in there but in the trash can, eventually buried with other people's banana peels and bird cage liners. And that's where I had put it, in the garbage. Somewhere in Pittsburgh his image was decaying in a landfill.

* * *

Forgetting about the bills, I set my drink on the desk, sat down and stared at the typewriter for a few minutes. The keys pulled at my hands, and Margo's voice said, "Get off your butt and do something."

Certainly I was capable of more than making up silly story titles. What about all those multiple pages of teen anguish and imagination that I had written in my diary, protected from nosy parents by the key I kept hidden in the box of Kotex?

I put in a sheet of paper, rolling it onto the platen with that brrzzzz sound it made. And I sat—waiting—I didn't feel like a writer at all. Nothing was happening. I closed my eyes and focused on sounds of the room, hoping the typewriter would talk to me. I heard the wind-up clock on my desk ticking—each tick a reminder of the wasted seconds, minutes, and hours of my life.

The copper-coiffed lady and that loathsome Mr. Concord floated through my mind, and Howard projected his Calvinistic image in my brain. His aftershave burned in my nostrils. Howard was the one to write about.

What should I call him? Horace? Sam? Claude—someone weak or lame—I remembered that tidbit from Latin class. He'd be like Mr. Concord a.k.a. Mr. Comb-Over. What about the woman? She would be the copper-hair-in-a-bottle person. I tapped my teeth as I considered her name. Oh yes, Diana… goddess of the hunt, the protector. Claude didn't have a chance. I would make him the victim, not me—every woman's dream revenge.

I typed each word as a deliberate act, and the words flew from my brain and out through my fingers.

Diamonds Don't Lie, by Margaret Landings

Claude fumbled in his pocket and removed the treasure. He pushed aside the water glasses that Diana wished held gin and tonics, and he placed the small and foreboding black jewelry box in the center of the table. Other restaurant patrons seated nearby began to poke each other and point demurely to them.

Claude looked at Diana as the woman who would provide him several well-behaved children. Nervous, Diana's hands swooped to fluff out the strata of material of her favorite dress—a maroon taffeta affair with a full skirt draped in layers. Her mother would have been proud of how the narrow waist and angled bodice helped compensate for lack of much "upper interest." Her coppery hair shone in the ballroom lights.

"God answered my prayers, Darling. Of course, it doesn't hurt that you resemble Lauren Bacall, either." He chuckled.

"Oh Claude—" Diana was flattered by the Lauren Bacall reference, but she couldn't return the favor. Claude was beginning to bald, and his comb-over started at a ridiculously low point on his right temple just above his ear. Though he was an excellent dancer, he was a little too religious for her. He was always talking God this, God that. Diana sighed.

"And what do you think this is?" he insisted.

She took a breath. His quizzes were so annoying; his need to test her memory always felt like an opportunity to have one up on her.

I stopped typing. It was true, I didn't miss Howard's one-upmanship game.

"Is it jewelry?" God, I hope it's not what I think it is, she thought.

He looked as triumphant as a game show host. "You're close."

Oh gag. I stopped for a moment and stared at Margo in the poster for more inspiration. "Fasten your seat belts, Howard, I'm in control now."

He pushed the box a little closer. "Here, for you."

She hesitated and opened the box. Claude asked, "Will you marry me, Diana?"

Diana stared at the contents. She was speechless. Embedded in a thin band of white gold was a tiny flicker of shiny. It was the tiniest diamond she had ever seen. She sensed the other diners looking their way with big smiles on their faces—they couldn't see the ring, of course.

"Let me put it on you," said Claude. He reached over, took the sad little ring out of the box, and slipped it on her finger before she had a chance to withdraw her hand.

She stared at the ring that looked like it came out of a Cracker Jack box. Is that all I'm worth? she wondered.

"What's wrong?" Claude asked.

"I can't." She took off the ring and put it back in the box.

"Why...why not?"

"Oh, yeah," I thought.

"I'm not the pure woman you're counting on." She examined him for shock value. "You won't be the first."

Claude loosened his pastoral collar, and he looked around to see if anyone overheard what she said.

"But Diana, I thought you were— "

"What? Untouched?" She looked at him defiantly, daring him to challenge her goodness.

"But—"

"You're judging me already...before you know the whole story. Not only are you cheap, but you are also self-righteous. Diamonds don't lie, you know. If you're that cheap with an engagement ring, you'll be cheap with your love too."

Claude clenched his jaw and put the ring box back into his pocket.

At the end of the page, I whirled the paper out and rolled another in. My hands were beginning to cramp so I intertwined my fingers, turned them inside out to stretch like I pictured Hemingway doing.

Claude pushed his chair back and stood up.

"I need to go. I'm sorry."

He did a small bow from his waist and left.

"You're not such a good deal yourself," she said to his back.

Diana sensed a stare and turned toward a woman who was gawking at her.

The woman removed the long cigarette holder from her lips and said, "Don't settle for just anybody, honey. I saw that ring. Good riddance." She raised her gin and tonic in a salute.

Diana gave her a thankful nod.

The woman did a double take. "Say, aren't you that author that was on the *Today Show* last week? You look awfully familiar."

She smiled. "Why, yes, I am. Have you read my book?"

"Oh yes, I couldn't put it down," the woman said.

"Please come sit with me." Diana gestured to the seat where Claude sat a few moments before.

"I can't believe I'm sitting right here next to Diana Broadstreet."

Diana summoned the waiter. "Bring each of us a tall gin and tonic, please."

Done and exhausted, I gathered the sheets of paper and re-read the story. Not the best story but each paragraph was a vindication of what Howard did to me.

I straightened the pages and folded them in thirds. At the top of the first page, I wrote "Dear Howard, you once made fun of my dream to write. See what you think of this. Margaret." Grabbing an envelope, I wrote Howard's name and address on the front, placed the papers inside, and licked the gummy flap. I wished I had had a skull and cross bones stamp.

I took the letter to the front door mail box, deposited it with a flourish, and pushed up the red flag. The letter would ripen overnight for tomorrow's mail.

8

On my way to the car, I glanced at the flag on the mail box. Howard's come-uppance would soon be making its way to Pittsburgh.

At Mother's bedside I yawned so hard that my jaw popped. I rubbed the soreness out of my face and hoped she hadn't seen me so open-mouthed. But she did.

"Do you have to open your mouth like a barn door? Owls could nest in there," she said. Mothers, God bless them.

"Late night, Mother. I hope my yawn showed off the beautiful fillings you and Daddy paid for." I straightened the sheets around her.

"And I hope you were on the phone with Howard, begging him to forgive you for your pettiness."

I jerked up.

"Sorry, darling. Perhaps we should put aside our hopes."

"Good idea." And I gave her a kiss. "On my way to transport customers on the Monster."

"The Monster"?

"It's such a temperamental machine. It's me against it."

"You're a Landings. You'll win."

* * *

"You seem a little tired today, Margaret," John observed.

"Oh, I was up late last night, watching Jack Paar," I lied. "Great show, don't you think?"

"Never can make it past ten, you know. Kids, wife, job. My day ends early." He studied me for a moment. "Impatient for the real job, I suppose."

I avoided saying what I really thought—the job was as fulfilling as filing invoices, work I tolerated for two days one summer.

"Feeling miscast, a little above being an elevator operator?"

"The days flew by where I worked in Pittsburgh. Here the only things that fly by are the bricks and doors." I waited for John to laugh at my clever analogy. Silence. "I guess I didn't anticipate the strain of staying put all day in a five-foot-square space—gives me new respect for elevator operators."

Again, silence. My mother would have said, "Want some cheese with that whine?"

He walked toward the buzzer that would announce the store's opening, but he hesitated and rotated back to me. "I'm glad you're here."

Was he glad to have Margaret the woman there, not just Margaret an elevator lady?

Standing at the elevator and waiting for John to ring the opening buzzer, I recalled my writing marathon the previous night. The copper-haired lady and Mr. Concord the comb-over man gave me the characters. I pictured readers smiling and enjoying my prose. And the story was a two-for-one—I gave Howard his comeuppance too. The letter was on its way to Pittsburgh by then, flying on wings of revenge.

I never questioned why I liked writing, but I had plenty of questions about the kind of stories I wrote. When I showed some to my cousin Penny her response was, "Your stories are certainly imaginative. Aren't there other things you can write that aren't so embarrassing? I mean, whew." She turned her eyes upward and fanned imaginary heat from her cheeks.

Publishers didn't like them either. An editor from one romance magazine—the only appropriate audience for my imagination returned my first submitted manuscript with "NO" scrawled across the top. No comments, just "NO." It was easier being the editor's assistant in Pittsburgh where I was the rejecter— once to a questionable author who wrote an article about aliens visiting Mamie Eisenhower, another for a "no we don't want your article" letter for a poorly spelled introduction ("She was a deer friend"). But with these and others, I avoided using the white hot branding iron "NO"

and tried to write encouraging words to the author—especially difficult to do with the writer who was trying to eliminate Mamie via
slime green creatures. I even wrote acceptance letters that bestowed
just reward on people who were doing what I dreamed of doing.

But I woke this morning with an image of the elevator car as
a movie stage, and I would be a witness to all those people's lives
that I could harvest for stories worth writing.

The buzzer rang, and another day of elevator attending began.
In a big department store, I would have a uniform, maybe even a
jaunty little hat to signify my importance. But no, I was dressed in
my own Madras plaid shirtwaist, fashionably belted at the waist,
showing off my thankfully trim waist.

"Morning, Margaret." Mrs. Remington waved me over to her
counter in leather goods. "Look at these billfolds that came in."
She pointed to the Buxton leather products arrayed in orderly fashion in their little boxes under the glass. Where her forefinger rested,
a missile from above splatted beside it. A gelatinous blob of spittle
bubbled beside her well-manicured finger.

Mrs. Remington's eyes bulged, her nostrils flared. She looked
up through the open atrium. "Someone spit on my counter! Someone spit on my counter!"

Mrs. Remington pointed at a little girl leaning over the wooden
railing three floors up. She had the countenance of a horrified crim-
inal who had been caught in the act. She stood frozen with her hand
over her mouth.

Stair people. They got up there without me.

Mrs. Remington grabbed a cleaning cloth and stormed to the
elevator. Her sensible shoes and flowered rayon dress accentuated
her take-charge demeanor. She was on the elevator in less than four
strides. "Take me up there," she ordered. "Nobody's going to spit
on my counters."

Steam from the enraged woman gave the elevator additional
speed. The movie cameras in my head were rolling. Sales clerks like
Mrs. Remington protected their stations as ferociously as lions did.

By the time we got there, the little girl's eyes were red and
swollen from crying and her mother was holding her by one arm

while she spanked her none too gently.

"How could you do something so awful? How embarrassing."

"I wanted to see how far spit would fall. I'm sorrrrrrry."

The mother saw the red-faced and furious Mrs. Remington, and her face revealed how horrified and repentant she felt. "I'm so sorry, Mrs. Remington, I don't know what made Sarah do that."

I stood by the elevator, relishing every moment of the drama—the flaring nostrils, the wide-eyed horror of getting caught, and the juxtaposition of accusation, guilt, and repentance. I envisaged the title "Momma's Devil Child."

Mrs. Remington ignored the mother and shoved the rag into little Sarah's hand.

"You come with me, young lady, and clean up the mess you made." She took the offender's other hand, and all three got on the elevator.

"First floor, Margaret." Her tone was brusque, but the adventure was worth it.

The mother, the prisoner, and executioner all stood facing the front, and no one said a word. An occasional sob escaped the girl.

I pinpointed the landing, opened the doors and the troupe marched out, led by Mrs. Remington. A couple of yards in front of the elevator lay the oaken and glass counter with a glob of spittle. Its shiny marble edged by little bubbles sat on the glass right over the billfolds, so artfully arranged on the shelf below. Mrs. Remington pointed to the rag in Sarah's hand and to the offensive glob.

"Wipe that up."

"Y-yes, ma'am."

Mrs. Remington's face softened, and she knelt to the girl's eye level. "You won't do that again, will you? My customers deserve clean counters, don't you think?"

"Oh yes, ma'am, I'm very sorry." What her mother or the clerk couldn't see was the little girl's crossed fingers she had hidden behind her back.

Mrs. Remington gave the quasi-repentant Sarah back to her mother, who looked relieved that she had somehow escaped the clerk's wrath.

But Mrs. Remington studied the little girl with the eye of a parole officer. "If you need to do more shopping," she said to the mother, "I can keep Sarah with me and she can help me dust the wallets. Would you like that, Sarah?"

Her eyes popped at this turn of events, and she begged her mother, "No, Mommy, no, I don't want to."

"I think more cleaning might remind you to respect people's property." She gave Sarah's hand to Mrs. Remington.

Sarah's mother re-entered the elevator, but I caught Sarah sticking her tongue out at her mother's back. No, this story wasn't about the clerk. It was about a rebellious little girl who was destined to test her curiosity. Or was it fate? I could never figure the difference between the two.

I remembered Mother holding my hand at the funeral home where Sammy Watson's father lay in his casket. I stared at his chest that did not rise and fall, and I wondered at the adult conversation about his "fate." He was hit by a bolt of lightning on a golf course. "It was his time," people said. I thought he had been stupid to be outside during a thunderstorm. At least that's what we learned in health class. I decided at the time that Sammy's father had been absent the day his teacher talked about lightning.

The mother signaled me to take her back up to the third floor.

The thought "this could be rich material" occurred at the same time as a rumble in my lower abdomen. Criminy. Not now.

"Mrs. Bolls," I asked of the notions clerk, "Could you cover me while I go to the restroom?"

"Sorry," she said, "Mr. Graham doesn't want us to leave our counters."

"Where is he?" I asked.

"I saw him go to the bank. He should be back in thirty minutes or so."

The next thirty minutes dragged by as though the clock had lead hands and stripped gears. The rumbles in my belly bubbled and threatened. When John finally appeared, I asked him for a break.

"We just opened, you know."

I adopted the universal face of "I have a feminine need," which was less embarrassing than revealing my digestive problems. I had learned like many other women that the "monthly visitor" was a useful, if not always truthful, way to avoid unpleasant situations. Gym, chores, sex. His expression changed to an embarrassed "Oh, I get it." He took over the elevator without another word.

The employees' lounge had been an apartment long ago in the building's history. The furniture was pretty tacky, obviously old stuff that didn't sell in the furniture department years ago, but the bones of the room were remarkable. The dark oak carving on the fireplace and the wooden arch between the lounge area and the little kitchen was intricate and bold. Green tile surrounded the impotent gas fireplace. The lounge offered light and windows to the outside world. The two tall windows had wavy glass, a sign of their age, but they let in marvelous light that Ohio had too little of. I appreciated the old-fashioned ambiance of the place. The room evoked the contentment that I always felt at my grandmother's century-old house.

I locked myself in the toilet stall next to the kitchenette. I had to put down the toilet seat—it was a bathroom for everyone. I turned on the water in the sink, just in case.

I sat. Nothing, only rumbles. I didn't have a crossword puzzle either. I saw a paper napkin and a couple of pencils on the little "necessity stand" by the toilet. Maybe I could write down some ideas. What a fine state of affairs, sitting on a toilet with a napkin and a pencil. Wouldn't my mother have been proud? Words and titles emerged and the rumbles became productive, drowned out by the running water. I managed to jot down "territorial clerks," "despot managers," and of course the title "Momma's Devil Child." The pencil wasn't writing well on the napkin, however, and every comma I wrote tore a hole in the paper. The torn napkin was a pathetic reflection of my muse. "At least I tried," I said aloud.

"Excuse me, did you say something?" asked a male voice in the lounge.

I froze. I hadn't heard Mr. Concord come into the lounge, and any chance for my muse to continue its inspiration evaporated.

Finished, I flushed, washed my hands, and pulled on the linen towel so the cranking would signal my attention to good hygiene. I pulled again so that the wrinkled linen swooped past and up into the dispenser. I still felt like the queen of idiots, and I sheepishly left the bathroom.

Mr. Concord glanced at me over the *Life* magazine he was reading. "Have a good day, Margaret," he said. "Stay out of trouble now—don't want you to mess up that pearly reputation of yours."

I stopped at the door and spun on my heel.

"What do you mean by that?"

Mr. Concord glanced up. "A little defensive, are we? What did Shakespeare say, 'thou dost protest too much?'" He had the beginnings of a smirk on his face.

"A woman doesn't like to be teased about her reputation. It's not gentlemanly."

"I stand corrected." He waved his magazine at me. "Speaking of Shakespeare, did you read this article about Faulkner? There is so much bad stuff out there. It's refreshing to have a real writer getting his reward." He pointed to Faulkner's visage on the page. "Now there's someone who can write."

I didn't know what to say. Faulkner? Mr. Concord went back to his reading. I had been dismissed.

I went downstairs to the cloakroom and put my literary napkin in my purse. Did Faulkner ever write ideas down while in the toilet?

Back at the elevator I rang the buzzer. John opened the doors and regarded me with some exasperation. "Good grief, woman, did you write a book or something on your break?" He bolted out of the elevator and hurried to his office.

"I hate this job," I said to the Monster. "I really hate this job." Monster 1, Mr. Concord 1.

9

The evening hostess was a tall and well-dressed middle-aged woman with the requisite hostess jewelry, makeup, draped chiffon dress and shoulder corsage that signaled "I'm important."

"How many, dear?" she asked, standing at a station that looked like an oaken conductor's stand. A little light illuminated the reservation and table list.

"Just one."

"Oh." She hesitated. "Of course. It will be about five minutes."

I needed a friend to talk to, a friend to share dinner with. I had asked several women at work but no one was available, and my mood declined with each person who said "no." In Pittsburgh I would have had many friends to call upon.

There I was at the Main Street Restaurant anyway, the place for elegant or casual dining, depending on how you wanted to dress. I had a running account at Main Street, thanks to one of my mother's generous moments, so I decided on a self-indulgent evening of prime rib and a drink.

The maroon carpet of the lobby gave the place an elegant air. I saw the tables covered with clean white tablecloths like brides expecting their grooms. I had no groom, no bridesmaid, nothing to look forward to that evening, and I certainly didn't deserve to wear white.

As I waited for a table, I watched the bustle of the restaurant. Waitresses in pastel uniforms and sensible shoes wrote orders on little carbon paper pads. They appeared more like nurses than waitresses except nurses didn't have little fan-folded hankies in their breast pockets.

The lobby walls were covered with black and white photos of celebrities who had eaten there. Well—celebrities by Liberty's standards. One photo showed the white teeth and dark features of the Cisco Kid, who had graced Liberty for a Red Cross charity event. He sat on a bench in the town square with a child on his lap. Both he and the little girl beamed at the camera. I studied Cisco's face to see if I could detect any disdain he might have for the small town denizens that fawned over him. No, he seemed fairly accepting of his lot.

Seeing the memorabilia of Liberty's history caused my brain and heart to send conflicting messages. I used to feel a connection to my community and its activities, all which served as glue to bind its fair citizens into a collage of Midwest lives. But my move from Liberty resulted in experiences that ate away the connections between me and my town, sort of like the rubber cement that bonded my school papers tightly to my mother's scrapbooks but eventually lost its grip over time. Just as the rogue papers eventually sat askew in my high school scrapbooks, my own life was also out of place.

I spotted a photograph of my parents and studied their beaming faces as they watched a hometown parade. I traced the lines on their young and happy faces, and my finger lingered on Father's cheek.

Meanwhile a steady stream of people, mostly parents of my high school classmates, came into the lobby—women with their Donna Reed hairdos and men with their fedora hats, which they took off immediately as they stepped inside. Some recognized me, some didn't, but everyone still smiled and said hello.

They paraded as happily married people who talked about their children. I wanted to shout out "I have a son!" But I had no photos to share, no stories to tell—only a secret son that sat beneath the surface of my consciousness, wanting to get out and be recognized. Some days I fought the urge to run to the Public Square, stand under the Civil War statue and shout "I'm a mother, too," all the while being protected by the bronze soldier, bayonet at his side.

After ten minutes or so, a hand fell on my shoulder. There was Pete, the traveling salesman I had first seen at the movie theater. I saw him talking to Mr. Concord earlier today on the third floor, and he seemed a little crude, but polite in a country way. Not my type but I wasn't getting those cautionary flags I experienced when I encountered him at the theater.

"Hey, young lady, are you by yourself?" He continued, "Ol' Pete here could sure use some company." He stepped into line beside me and looked at me beseechingly. I could smell his Old Spice Cologne. If I closed my eyes, I could be with my father, who had used the same aftershave.

I took a deep breath that I immediately regretted. Pete's smoky aroma overcame his cologne and invaded my nostrils. Still, I thought it might be interesting to learn about "Ol' Pete," and I would have company for dinner. I hesitated—there would be many witnesses to my dinner with a traveling salesman. Mother would be horrified. In a moment of rebellion I said, "Sure." Relief spread over his face.

Pete took my coat and his and hung them both in the open closet next to the hostess station. This he did with surprising grace.

"Oh, now I see you have company," said the hostess. She gave Pete a once-over.

"A booth for the little lady and me," he said.

I may as well have heard fingernails scratching on a chalk board, but I held it together as the hostess led Pete and his "little lady" to a booth in the far corner. Pete took a cowboy lookout seat—back to the walls, eyes to the entrance, which meant I was able to sit incognito with my back to the restaurant's occupants.

"I have to apologize," Pete said.

"I beg your pardon?"

"I saw you flinch when I said 'little lady.' I forgot that women of your breeding don't like that kind of talk."

I was surprised and charmed by his apology. An uncomfortable mixture of superiority and sympathy swirled through me.

I tried not to stare at the comma of hair that had slipped from his slicked-back head, and I shuddered a little. Great, I was having dinner with Elvis.

"I'm surprised you agreed to eat with me," he said. He looked at me with eyes that begged truthfulness, not pity.

"I don't know why you would say that," I lied. "Everybody, except some, has a heart."

"Huh?"

"Sorry," I backtracked. "It's just a line from a favorite movie."

"That's right. I sat behind you at the movie about the washed-up actress dame. You were totally into her."

I tried not to act offended, but Pete had hit at my soft under-belly. "That 'washed-up actress dame' has a lot of class, if you ask me. She's smart. A lot of times when I'm confused about what to do I'll ask myself, 'What would Bette Davis do?'"

"Wow, I don't think anyone would ask that about me. We travel-ing salesmen don't have such great reputations, you know."

"You're making an honest living just like anyone else," I said. His candor and his need for acceptance were an intoxicating blend of strength and weakness for me. He was a refreshing change from the overconfident Pittsburgh guys and so different from the coun-try club fellows in town—though none of them were single anymore. All of them were married to women who already displayed boredom in their "yes, of course I'm happy" eyes.

"Why did you decide to be a road salesman?"

Pete gave a fake laugh. "I can thank my mother for that."

"Oh, she was your inspiration?"

He looked up in surprise. "Um, no. The opposite."

I could tell by his frozen posture and his searching eyes that he was trying to decide whether or not he could trust me. I wanted to hear his story so I gave him my sincere, sympathetic posture that I gave police officers whenever I got pulled over for a traffic violation. It always worked with the law, and maybe it would work with Pete.

A waitress brought our drinks—Scotch and water for Pete and a gin and tonic for me—but Pete continued to study me. I gazed at him with trust-me eyes.

He broke the stare between us and locked his attention on the flamingo swizzle stick that he twirled between his right thumb and forefinger. He took the stick out, gripped his highball and took a long swig. He put the glass down and played with the swizzle stick again. Finally he pushed it aside. He leaned forward on his elbows, cupping the glass of courage with both hands.

"I didn't have such a great childhood." He lowered his eyes as if he needed one more moment to trust me. Then he straightened his gaze. "When I was seventeen, I ran away from home and got a job as a carpet installer in Akron. I lived in a YMCA, did my job well, listened to everything my boss said about the carpet business. I talked him into lettin' me try sales."

Pete laughed. "My boss said that talking him into lettin' me hit the road with a borrowed suit and a trunk full of samples was my first f—, excuse my French, my first real sales job."

He smiled and took another drink. "Been doin' this for twenty-five years." He leaned back and put his arm over the back of the banquette, drink still in hand.

"Sounds like you're a hard worker, Pete."

"Not everybody agrees. There's this guy in town who cheated me outa a good chunk of change. Wouldn't pay me as much as I asked for when I laid some carpet for him."

"That's awful. Did you ever get it?"

"I'm working on it. How 'bout you? I heard you lived in Pittsburgh and came home to help out your sick mother." He reacted to my flinch. "Um, word gets around in a little town, especially 'bout important people like the Landings."

"Yeah, right."

"Anyway, that's downright depressin' to give everything up to come back here."

I sighed. "Not really. Pittsburgh was OK, and I liked my job, but my mother needed me."

"Wouldn't have done that for my ma. Her and I didn't get along so well. Haven't seen her since I left in 1930."

"Oh my," I said. "Why haven't you kept in touch?"

"Keep in touch?" Pete laughed. "What touch? My ma never wanted me, never hugged me as far as I can remember." He drained his glass and motioned to the waitress to bring him another drink.

I did the same. I enjoyed the feel of gin once again warming my insides and loosening my brain. Our drinks refreshed, I urged him to continue. I wanted to hear Pete's tale. "I don't understand."

"Let's just say I was the result of my mother's encounter with a counselor at a church camp. And since her attacker was a God-fearing, trusted chap, no one believed it was, you know…" Pete couldn't say the word. "They all said my mother was Eve, tempting the poor counselor Adam with the apple that I bet she tried to keep from him. After I was born, lookin' at me was a constant reminder of that summer. I got a couple of scars and broken bones as proof." He drank nearly half of his highball in one chug.

My jaw dropped, and I was powerless to close it.

Doubt crossed his face. "I can't believe I told you that. You must think I'm white trash or somethin'."

I was vulnerable to those words "I can't believe I told you that." That phrase called to me faster than a chocolate caramel. "I have the power to bring out men's vulnerability" is what those words meant. I resisted the temptation for a second or two then dove for its seductive effect.

"You've certainly had a different life than mine, Pete." I hesitated. "But I've had my own pain."

Surprise registered on his face. "Your mother hated you too?"

Amused at Pete's conclusion, I continued. "No. But before I tell you more, do you mind if I have another drink?"

Pete was quick to respond. He ordered us another round of drinks, and while we waited, I gulped what was left of my second gin and tonic. I enjoyed the openness of improper company.

The waitress placed the drinks in front of us and Pete asked, "What were you going to tell me?"

I took a deep drink of the gin-laced support.

"I partied a lot in my freshman year in college. I flunked out, not dropped out. My parents were so ashamed of me."

I waited for his reaction.

He sat back in the booth and waved his hand toward the sky. "That's it? That's your big secret—disappointing your parents?"

I didn't know how to respond.

"Where didja go to college?" He took another swig of his drink.

"Grant City College."

"One of my territories in the forties. So you went to the Bible thumpers school. I heard o' that one, those kids were pretty caged up, guys in the area could count on some pretty good action with the girls. They say the birth rate was higher than the graduation rate." Pete laughed at himself.

I swallowed hard.

He did a double take. "Holy sh…, I never would have figured that from you. You were one of 'em?"

His expression showed his branding of me, not as a bad person, but as one in his league, a league I didn't want to belong to.

"I wasn't one of *them*," I lied. "So don't jump to any conclusions, and please don't share our conversation. People don't know I flunked out of college."

"Oh, hey, my lips are sealed." Pete did that zipping-his-lips thing.

He jumped out of his side of the booth and slid in beside me, pressing me against the wall. He put his arm over the back of the booth, uncomfortably close to my shoulders. "Pete, promise me you won't share what we've talked about. I don't want talk around town. You can trust me, can I trust you?"

"Darlin', your secret is my secret, although I suspect you're hiding more than bad grades." He winked with a smile. "I never met a woman like you, ya know…smart, trustin', and understandin' of what I went through. You can trust ol' Pete here."

I whispered, "Thank you." I tried not to cry but I was losing my battle for composure. He took my hand, and I actually welcomed the comfort. I looked up to find Pete's face in mine, looming with puckered lips. I dodged those smoky smelling lips as surely as the Cisco Kid dodged bullets from cattle rustlers. I pushed him to get some space between us.

Pete's reaction was immediate. He withdrew his arm from the back of the bench and frowned. "Hey, what turned you into a cold fish? Don't trust deserve a kiss?" His eyes were big question marks. "You were tellin' me your life story a minute ago."

"Oh, Pete….we hardly know each other."

"Let's get a motel room so we can get to know each other. You know, Grant City College girl and me." He winked without a smile that time and took a big gulp of his drink.

"Pete, really."

"Drink some of your gin and tonic, you might get friendlier." His voice had developed an edge to it as though I had touched some ugly part of his soul.

"That's not fair." My pulse raced. "Don't take this personally. I don't kiss anybody unless I know him really, really well."

He jutted his jaw toward me. "How well did you know those college boys?"

My eyes stung.

"Oh now the little lady gets weepy. Just like my ma when she felt guilty about hitting me. You may as well have hit me too. I thought you liked me." He moved back to his side of the booth and signaled to the waitress.

"I—"

"I get the message. You don't have to say anything. I can see I'm not good enough for you. You're like all the other women who tease men, acting all nice and then freezing up." He gave the waitress a ten-dollar bill and said, "Keep the change."

"See," he said, "I tip big. Ain't that what a gentleman does?" Before I could respond he said, "See ya, Miss Landings. If you ever want to get out of that spinster mode you're in, you better warm up a little."

I sat frozen in the booth. What had I done? Why does the truth about me always make men angry?

I sipped the rest of my gin and tonic, now watery from melted ice. I sat for a few minutes and pushed as many feelings as I could down into that deep hole of unwanted thoughts.

I slid out of the booth and staggered a little upon standing up. Facing the exit I locked eyes with Mrs. Walters sitting with her husband in the booth behind. I gasped to see her startled face. She was a friend of my mother's. How much did she and her husband hear?

I headed for the exit as quickly as my gin-influenced body would go. I bumped into only one table. When I reached the cloakroom I saw that Pete's coat was gone, and mine was on the floor. I picked up my coat and had a hard time coordinating my left arm with the left sleeve. I had only wanted company for dinner but ended up revealing too much to a man whom I barely knew.

10

The next morning I sat on my wooden stool alone, behind the closed doors of the elevator. I was hung over and reliving the accidental revelation of my past. I kept replaying the moment when Pete changed from a vulnerable sympathetic ear to an assailant. I rubbed my throbbing temples. Thank goodness store traffic was slow.

I considered writing an autobiography named *Margaret's Big Mouth. Love Is a Many Splendid Lie* was a possibility. *Big Mouth, Small Brain?*

"Margaret, are you talking to someone?"

It was my friend Lena, manager of men's wear. She was a spinster in her fifties, yet we had made a connection my first week at Graham's. Her department was straight across from the elevator, and we would steal minutes to chat between my buzzer and her customers. In the employees' lounge we gossiped with utter trust that our observations and critiques would go no further. We talked easily. Maybe Lena thought she saw her younger self in me. Maybe I saw a ready audience in her.

"I'm taking a break," I said in a low voice.

"Ooh, let me in," she pleaded through the door.

I opened the doors and feigned a "what floor, please?" I closed the door on our soft giggling.

"You sit on the stool, Lena, and I'll sit on the floor. It's pretty clean."

"This is so fun, do you think anyone will hear us?"

"I'll move the elevator between floors."

Settled in our sanctuary, Lena asked, "Were you talking to yourself?"

"I was trying out different book titles."

"Anything I should read?"

"Depends on what you like."

Lena arranged herself on the stool so that her black skirt covered her chunky knees.

"How do you sit on this hard thing?" she asked. She straightened the seam of her hose. It made a straight line down the back of her legs to her wide-heeled shoes with laces. Her blouse was a cotton cap-sleeve number with appliqued bodice lace that hid any suggestion of cleavage, and a star-burst brooch sat at her neck.

"The worst part is getting a splinter from the wooden seat."

She reddened as though she didn't think about people's bottoms. She was prim and kind of dowdy. Dowdy worried me. Dowdy came with being single in Liberty. Her salt and pepper hair was frizzed with a Toni perm most likely, but she had smooth Mamie Eisenhower bangs. Her grey eyes blended with her hair.

We made quite a pair—Lena in her 1940s spinster deportment and me in my more fashionable 1950s Lucille Ball shirtwaist.

"What was life like in Pittsburgh?" she asked.

I sat Indian style on the floor, trying to follow Lena's example of using my dress to cover my legs. "A cousin led me to a job with a publishing house, and I had an efficiency apartment near the Pittsburgh Zoo."

"That sounds wonderful, but noisy."

"At least I was free and not caged. I was okay—I had goals and a future, some friends, a few dates." I shrugged.

"So here you are."

"Yes, here I am. You know, Mother had complained to me about feeling sluggish, but she always complained about how she felt. It was for real, I guess."

"Will you stay in Liberty when your mother, you know…"

"I don't know." I picked some lint off my dress. "You've lived here all your life, what's your advice?" I really wanted to ask her why she never married but I didn't.

"Well," Lena's eyes took on a faraway look. "Liberty's a nice town. People are friendly." She focused back at me. "My lot in life is pretty set, I think. What about you?"

"I don't know. My life feels like a game of tug-of-war."

"Really? How?"

"I like the friendly hellos here, the reassurance of familiar sights. And there's an advantage to being a big fish in a small pond."

"But, there's another side."

"I liked being anonymous in a city, too. I can say 'Margaret Landings' without being connected to my parents and all those complicated expectations. I could do things without being reported."

"That's just the town you're talking about. What about what you want to *accomplish*?"

"I certainly don't want to spend my life being an elevator operator."

"Don't you want a family?"

Of course I wanted a family, but instead I said, "That's what we're supposed to want. What about you? You think it's too late for you?"

Lena drew in a large breath. "You must think I've settled for too little, and sometimes I think so, but I'm very good at what I do. Women come to me for their husbands' clothes because I know what they like and wear, and what size. Men come to my department because they know I'll be honest with them about what looks good." She paused and smiled at me. "You know, most nights I go home content. I've made a lot of men happy, and they make no demands of me. Life could be worse."

"But, but you live in an apartment above the appliance store."

"What more do I need? Coffins don't have pockets, you know."

"Hmmm." I considered what I would put in my coffin. The pockets would be long and narrow running alongside my still and shriveled body, so Mother's silver wouldn't fit. The drawer full of stories I've written could slip into a satin sleeve, but who would want to spend eternity with spicy stories with titles like "Momma's Devil Child?" If I had a photo of my son, I would certainly include that, but he would be in my hands over my still, cold bosom, not in a pocket beside me.

"Yoo-hoo, are you still there?" Lena put her face closer to mine.

"Oh, I was thinking about pockets in the casket. So…if you're not taking anything with you, what will you be leaving behind?"

She pulled on her skirt hem, which had inched above her knee. "I would hope I'd be leaving the world a little better and not damaged much by my having been in it."

"That's pretty deep." I regarded her with new curiosity. Here was someone who had settled, using Lena's own words. In my family, her life would be considered honorable but not a success. I wouldn't want to be Lena, but I would like to have her peace.

The buzz of an elevator call from the first floor interrupted our clandestine conversation. Lena hopped from the stool, and I sprang up and dusted off my dress. Navy, I found, was not the best color for sitting on elevator floors.

I opened the elevator doors to see a couple of middle-aged women and behind them, a man I loathed to set eyes on—Pete.

I wanted to be any place but in the same room or universe with him.

Lena was oblivious to my plight, and with a cheery wave to me she headed straight to her station in men's soft goods.

Pete entered without making eye contact, and as he entered the elevator, he lost the momentum of his pseudo-Hollywood swagger. It was delicious to see him trip over the brass threshold. Two women followed him in.

"Second floor please," one of the women commanded, in between bits of news and fashion ideas the two were tossing to each other.

Pete stood to the back. His presence stirred up a lesson I learned the previous night—when he exposed his vulnerability, it wasn't my doe-eyed empathy he wanted. He had used an effective weapon in the war against resistant women.

"Second floor," I announced with a shaky voice. I cleared my throat, opened the doors, and let the still chatting women out.

Pete said from the back, "Third floor, please. Carpeting." I closed the doors, started the car, and I sensed him take a step forward. He put his hand on mine to stop the forward movement of the handle. A sickening volt from his touch traveled my spine.

The air was thick with animosity as though he had sucked in all the oxygen. I took a deep breath but regretted it as soon as his smoky odor hit my nostrils.

His presence had changed the elevator into a jail cell. The sides pressed in on me like the walls of a padded room, only these walls weren't padded—they were wood-patterned steel. I was imprisoned with a man who knew too much, at least about me.

"Aren't you glad to see your new confidante?"

"I don't want to talk to you."

He leaned into me. "Really, don't our little secrets connect us somehow, you and me?"

I saw his rough hands, calloused and strong from hauling carpet samples. He experienced hard work, I'd give him that.

"I have a job to do, and I would appreciate it if you would take your hand off—"

"You were a little friendlier last night, at least in the beginning."

"That was a mistake. Now, please take your hand off."

The buzzer coming from the first floor made me jump, but Pete did not remove his hand. His grip tightened, and my stomach felt like there were a hundred ping pong balls inside, all going in different directions.

"So, where is the little bastard anyway?"

"That is so cruel. I never told you such a thing." I could hear the desperation rise in my voice. Maybe he was bluffing. "Don't you care that you're upsetting me?"

"Oh, the poor innocent babe thinks men will take care of her. That's what got you in trouble ten years ago, Missy."

I was totally vulnerable to my past, and if Pete told anyone his suspicions, people would be pounding on doors to the hidden rooms of my life. The child I gave up so long ago, who had gradually slid into a daily routine of prayer for his well-being, would re-emerge as a shameful reminder of reckless passion. How could I face my mother, tell her that I had leaked classified information to such an unworthy recipient? I craved the comfort of her arms to know everything would be okay, but all that I imagined was her disappointment.

I locked my eyes onto his, but I didn't feel at all like the tough woman I wanted to be. I felt like a bug caught in a blade on Pete's windshield and he had turned on the wipers. Flop, flop, my emotions swung from one bad position to another.

The buzzer rang a couple times more. Someone on the third floor needed a ride. An escape.

"Please," I begged. I wanted to smack him, but fainting into oblivion would have been an acceptable alternative.

Pete retreated, and my hand was red from his tight grip.

"You'll be seeing more of me."

When I opened the doors to the third floor, I watched Pete exit and imagined him running from one receptive ear to another, handing out the breaking news about my slutty college behavior.

"Margaret?"

Pete turned back and studied me with a sardonic smile.

"Your slip is showing." He walked away.

I burned with anger and embarrassment. I checked my hemline. He was right. A jerk's double punch.

The passenger on the third floor was a clerk who could run the elevator.

"You look awful, are you okay? Do you need a break?"

"Yes, please."

I made it to the safety of the toilet stall and considered ripping off my slip, but the specter of a rayon skirt clinging to my thighs stopped me from that short-term solution. My thoughts bounced to Pete's smug sneer. Why had I let this man enter my life? Back in Pittsburgh, a poor choice of a date and its consequences would have been swallowed up in the anonymity of the city. How could I have forgotten that a small town is like a glass house, everything open for viewing and hearing?

Closing my eyes, I summoned Margo. I imagined myself at a bar in Chinatown, having drinks with Miss Channing, each of us dressed to the nines, holding our drinks in manicured hands. I could feel my blood pressure ease and my pulse slow. "Why do I have such a penchant for chaos?" I asked my invisible friend.

You want peace and quiet?

"What could be simpler than being an elevator operator? I thought elevators were simple, like sex. You go up and down a lot."

Hmmm, a possibly pregnant situation. Go on, dear.

"I didn't realize that the operator could be a victim of the passengers."

Psychotics are so much fun!

I opened my eyes. Margo was with me, like a guardian angel.

11

B ack at my station, with the doors open and me on display, I stared at the brass control handle, the only thing I seemed to have some command over. It was command that was tenuous at best. Taking an ax to it, leaving it dented and inoperable was one solution. Of course the customers would have to huff and puff their way up the stairs.

"Margaret?"

I jumped to my feet and instinctively took hold of the elevator control.

"You seem a million miles away," said Lena. "Could you take me to the third floor again?"

I closed the doors but didn't start up. "How many elevator operators does Graham's go through in a year?"

"You may have elevator tedium," Lena giggled at her own cleverness, "but look on the bright side, you get to see a lot of people and get the news on everyone. The handsome guys are a bonus. What actually happens when those elevator doors close?"

Her question startled me. What did she know?

"How about getting me to the third floor?"

I pulled the control backward just right and guided my prison to Lena's destination. She chattered away, but reverberating in my ears were the words "What actually happens when those elevator doors close?" Before I took the job, I made an assumption that elevators were only conduits to other floors. And I had had absolutely no comprehension that the operators who took me from floor to floor in multi-story buildings were human beings with hopes, plans, ears, brains, and heart. How little thought I had given to any person behind the bar, the counter, the gas tank. The world had existed on my side, the customer's side.

I traveled back to the first floor, picked up another load, and saw the third floor button light up. Up, down, up, down. I could have screamed.

I swallowed hard to distract myself from the encounter with Pete. I shook my shoulders to unload Pete's hex and focused on the activity that would get me through the day—watching customers, waiting for entertainment from their comings and goings. But I had a gnawing feeling that we were all watching each other, like a circular zoo. We think we're on the outside looking in when we are all really being watched by each other. I never realized until then the value of an office—a place to do one's work, a place to hide when necessary. In the elevator, I belonged to the world—to them. I had no privacy, no purpose other than to serve those who crossed over the threshold into my car.

I pulled the ironwork door to the right, and the exterior doors opened to several people ready for their rides. One of the passengers was John Graham. I studied him as he came into the elevator. His green eyes had a tad bit of weariness, though I could not understand how his life could have any sadness: beautiful wife, two well-behaved kids, community stature. His nearness made me crazy.

I pushed the handle forward ever so gently. In spite of my best efforts, the car jerked to a stop at the third floor. That hadn't happened in a while, not to the "Queen of Smooth Landings," a moniker I hoped to earn.

"Sorry 'bout the bounce," I said to the passengers.

"That bounce was the only excitement we've had today, Margaret," John said. "It was kind of fun." He stepped off.

My eyes followed his exit, his trolling among the aisles, casting about for problems that needed fixing, and clerks that required coaxing. All of which he did with great class, comfortable smile, and nodding to reassure beleaguered sales ladies. I fantasized about the strong shoulders that filled out his suit.

"Howdy do."

A gentleman wearing an Eisenhower "Peace and Prosperity" button brought me back from my thoughts. I wouldn't have seen many of those in Pittsburgh. Liberty was the epitome of peace and prosperity instead of labor strikes and civil rights. I had to admit I liked the give and take of political talk with my Pittsburgh friends. So far I had only encountered people, my mother included, who felt America was doing fine and we didn't need change.

At the next stop my high school friend Susan stepped in and gave a wan smile. No smoothing eyebrows today, and there was awkwardness about her, and heavy pancake makeup.

I asked, "Are you all right?" She didn't look at me. As soon as I closed the doors, she burst into tears. Not sure what to do, I put the elevator between floors. Consoling a close friend was one thing, but it was more difficult to comfort someone who always had a superior attitude. After some hesitation, I patted her shoulder. She lowered her head into her hands enough to reveal an ugly purple mark on her neck.

There was a moment of connection between us, a sharing of the heartaches of loving someone. Then it was gone. The wall between us reasserted itself.

She took a deep breath and blew her nose into a hankie embroidered with purple pansies. "I'm so embarrassed, but thank you. Just don't tell anyone about this, OK?" She dabbed her eyes, put away the hankie, and took out a compact to powder away her red nose.

A much more composed Susan left the elevator on the second floor, and a story title appeared like the word of the day: "He Beat the Love Right Out of Me."

At noon I went to the third floor employees' lounge. I sat on the overstuffed sofa and sunk my head into padded comfort to loosen the muscles in my neck.

I grabbed a Coca Cola from the machine and sat again so that a ray of light shone on me. Its warmth drove back the talons of another headache. I closed my eyes and tried to empty my mind, but Susan's domestic battle scar stayed with me. We were compatriots of sorts—carrying secrets, fearing exposure. After the last gulp of Coke, I put the bottle in the wooden crate, and I remembered my grandfather's favorite saying: "I owe, I owe, so off to work I go."

I rang the buzzer (it was justice that I could be the ringer for once) and stood outside the elevator. The elevator stopped between floors and muffled sounds could be heard inside. One voice caused me to lean in closer to the door. It was the slurred voice of a woman.

"What are you doing here?" I heard John ask in a not too friendly voice. "You've been drinking again." The motor didn't kick in.

"You're ashamed of me, aren't you," the female voice whined. "I can never please you, even when I'm not drinking."

"I'm going to the first floor and let you out to go directly home." John's voice had a steel edge to it and a coating of fear. "Elaine, I mean it."

Elaine—it was John's wife. Even between floors the elevator shaft was serving as a radio transmitter. The chat Lena and I had earlier didn't seem so safe anymore.

So, the Monster transmitted sound for ears to capture. How many knew this? I had been thinking of the elevator as a movie set. Hearing John and Elaine made me realize the movie set was complete with a sound stage—a great way to find out about the goings-on in the store. For the ones that figured it out, that is. The others were the unknowing victims of the elevator radio station and the doors that didn't quell conversation.

"Afraid that someone will find out our little secret?" John's wife continued. Her strident mocking was a shocking contrast to the beautiful, refined woman I had seen before. John mumbled something, and then I heard a customer buzzing for the elevator.

"That's the second buzz. I have to get customers. Now please, go home," John said.

The elevator motors roared to life and I jumped back from my listening post. The doors opened and closed, and John issued an audible sigh that shuddered up through the shaft. He delivered the Monster back to me on the third floor and avoided eye contact as he left the elevator. He took the stairs down.

By the end of the day, the emotional corrosion on my ego had taken its toll. The visceral reaction to Pete's encounter had left a mild ache in my gut. As for my slip, I checked it a million times. And I thought about poor John, who deserved a more compatible wife.

I was on the first floor, sitting on the stool in the idle elevator when John approached the buzzer encased in the center column. His captain-of-the-team smile was back. The buzzer sounded and relief washed over the faces of the clerks. Jarring in the morning and welcoming in the evening, that buzzer brought the dead back to life at closing time.

I wondered if I were the only one who knew about John and Elaine. Being the spy was much better than being the spied upon.

12

When I arrived home, I saw tire tracks on the edge of the lawn. There were a couple of cigarette butts too—Pall Malls. I had seen the mailman smoke those, but two?

"Yoo-hoo." Elderly Mrs. Eisling from across the street held her mail with one hand and waved with the other.

"Hello, Mrs. Eisling." I kept walking to head off a tiresome conversation with her. She always managed to take chunks of my time when I didn't have any to relinquish. I hadn't yet developed the patience for small talk that Liberty citizens enjoyed, though I envied that ability to let time pause with mundane details of life.

"How's your mother doing, dear?" she shouted.

"The same. She said to say hello," I lied.

"When are you going to invite me in to see all the changes in your mother's house? She always kept such a fashionable home."

"Not this evening, but sometime," I called back.

Walking up the short sidewalk, I tried to push away the image of Pete's surly face. Were those his tire tracks? Was he stalking me?

I threw my coat and purse on the sofa and headed for the kitchen. I thought about the calloused hand in the elevator and shuddered. I made a gin and tonic and the first sip surrounded me with a protective veil. Hiding my past was so exhausting—my pregnancy, my son. I didn't want to think of my son as a badge of shame, but in Liberty, a nineteen-year-old who gave birth out of wedlock had a scarlet "T" on her shirtwaist. The "T" stood for the "tsk-tsk" that gossipy tongues waggled.

The *Post* magazine I had been reading at breakfast—the issue with Bette Davis' photo on the cover—sat on the kitchen table, and I held up my drink for a toast. "Here's to spunk," I said to Bette.

My parents had a nightly cocktail hour—a ritual allowing them to share a highball and the news of the day. I would drink a Shirley Temple, and they would ask about my day as well. With each drink their interest in me dwindled, my mother became more strident, and my father retreated into blurry silence. When my father died, Mother never had another drink. "Not the same," she said.

I opened the freezer to choose from the array of pot pies and Swanson TV dinners—gelatinous beef pie or fried chicken with questionable mashed potatoes and rubbery green beans all sequestered in their little aluminum cubbies. Television ads declared they were the modern, convenient meal for busy women who could offer a presentable dish—especially if taken out of its aluminum shell and placed on the plate like a real entree. I chose the beef pot pie and turned on the oven.

I carried my drink into the den, really a guest bedroom, which didn't have a bed and never had any guests. It did have, however, my father's mahogany desk and my mother's favorite reading chair, covered in pink-flowered chintz.

One foot of the chair was missing a caster, but a copy of my mother's *The Good Wife's Guide* placed under the shortened leg held the chair in perfect balance. The desk was as solid as I had wanted my father to be. Bette Davis in the *All About Eve* poster stared at me from the opposite wall, her eyes sulking and lips saying everything but nothing. How would she have handled Pete, and Mr. Comb-Over, and Howard?

Margaret, dahling, they are only men.

I saluted Bette with my glass of gin and headed for the chintz. Next to the chair a pile of books begged to be read. I ran my fingers across the cover of *Marjorie Morningstar*. Marjorie had the fortitude to try out a dream. Had I tried out my dream and failed or had it been postponed?

Instead of yielding to the chair, I stood in front of my desk, drawn to the black and boxy Royal typewriter. I fingered the keys, and a parade of people traversed my mind as stories—Mr. Graham, Pete, Mr. Concord, Mrs. Gibbons, Lena.

Pete and the tire tracks sat on the edge of my world, beckoning with a crooked finger for me to do something, but my imagination and skills were dry as a desert. I felt impotent, unable to make any authorial contribution to the planet I inhabited.

My eye landed on a matchbook cover. On a lark once, I had responded to an ad that invited "Can You Draw Wimpy?" I took on the challenge, one of many attempts to find my destiny, but never heard back about my Wimpy drawing ability. Even earlier in my life I decided that I would be a nurse. Illusions of grandeur led me to read all the Sue Barton books I could find, and I joined Future Nurses of America. I pictured myself in a white starched hat with patients beaming at me with gratitude and affection, but my candy striper trauma put a stop to any medical career. My mother wanted me to be an interpreter at the United Nations but the earphones were a problem. In my skewed adolescent mind, earphones and a pageboy were not compatible.

A knock on the back door made me jump, and I went back into the kitchen. Peeking through the curtain I saw my neighbor Kathy peering back at me with her eyes crossed and her tongue sticking out. She was a longtime friend who fate arranged to be a neighbor. We went to high school together and shared many experiences, including the boy we later discovered had taken both our virginities. I never did tell her about my baby, though. There was something about Kathy that prevented me from exposing parts of me that I didn't want judged.

"It's the cross-eyed, long-tongued Irish menace," I said to her through the door.

Kathy was short and chubby, compared to my tall and thin, her hair flame red and mine dark brown. Our differences cemented the friendship that grew from the interesting and disparate observations we made. She came to America with her parents and still had some Irish walk and talk about her. Not only was I envious of her colorful way of speaking, I was jealous she had gone to college and came home with an MRS. I went to college and came home with nothing.

"Having your gin and tonic I see," Kathy said when she came in. She spied the Swanson box on the counter. "With beef pot pie.

Yum. That would give me the scutters fer sure."

"That's easy for you to say, Mrs. Homemaker. And what is the 'scutters?'"

"It be the trots, as you call them." She ogled the updated kitchen.

"This is beautiful. Your ma has great taste. Good thing she redid all this before she handed the house over to ya." She stroked the yellow Formica countertop with the boomerang pattern.

"I tried to add splashes of red with the rooster decorations, but sometimes I feel like I'm in a barn! Do you have the urge to moo?"

Kathy laughed. "I saw an article in *Good Housekeeping* today that roosters are the latest craze."

"It's six. Aren't you having dinner with your husband?"

"He's at a dinner meeting. The reason I'm here is that I saw something odd today. There was a man parked in a green and white car outside your house. He drove away when I went outside to check the mailbox."

I glanced in the direction of the street. "That explains the tire tracks and the cigarette butts, but I don't know who it could be."

"It's probably nothing."

"Well, then, how 'bout a drink since your husband isn't coming home for his Betty Crocker dinner?"

"Wonderful. I'll have what you're having."

I fixed a strong gin and tonic for Kathy—she needed a little catching up. The mixture of gin and the proximity of a friend were beginning to add life to my evening.

"Hmmm, this is really good," she said after she took a sip. "Can you hear me purr?"

"I bet your husband would like to hear you purr. Has he recovered from dodging that pan you threw at him last week?"

"He knows now that a man should never tell his Irish wife that she's gained a few pounds," Kathy said.

"Amen."

"But I digress. Back to the tire tracks—I don't know how long he was there."

"He had to be there long enough to smoke two cigarettes. That takes about twenty minutes—I should know—my father smoked, and our house was a museum of every possible ashtray design."

Kathy took a long drink. Her manicured fingernails cast a red reflection on the ice and gin. "Remember the ones that were molded t' resemble sombreros, and the cigarette lay in the hat's crease?" She pantomimed laying a cigarette onto a sombrero ashtray.

She studied me. "Are y'all right? You looked worried even before I told ya about the car."

"I had an awful encounter with …" I stopped, considering how I could change the story. I wasn't ready to tell her about my son.

"I agreed to have dinner with someone I didn't know very well, and it went badly. He came onto the elevator today and threatened to tell people I got drunk and that we ended up petting in his car, which isn't true."

"The drunk part or the petting part?"

"Both."

"And who might this be?" My friend sat forward.

"Some guy who sells carpet to Graham's."

"His name not be Pete, is it?"

"You've heard of him?"

"Oh, Margaret...you didn't. I thought ya had more sense than that." She shook her head.

"Not so fast with the judging. I haven't had a date since I left Pittsburgh. The first time I saw him, he was a little, I dunno, a little scary. But I've seen him around town a couple of times and he seemed kind of harmless."

"Fell for that, didja?"

"But I found out that a couple of drinks changed him into a nasty, vengeful person when I wouldn't make out with him."

"I'd heard about him doing things like that. You're not the only Pete victim. Just don't go 'n be the mother o' his children. There are a couple of little Petes in town already, I hear. You'd think those girls would have known better. Do you think that was his car outside?"

I glanced in the direction of the street as though the tire tracks and cigarette butts might yield clues to their owner. "I don't know what color his car is."

Kathy held her glass and made the ice tinkle against the sides. "He has to move on t' his next customer, somewhere away from here. I'll keep an eye out. In any case, keep your doors locked, and use the dead bolt."

She pointed to the mangled napkin with scribbled notes from the spittle incident. I had brought it into the kitchen so I could ponder it during cocktail time. "What's that?"

"Oh, I have fantasies about writing again. I wrote some notes on this napkin, the only thing I could get my hands on. Maybe I can use the ideas."

"I'd get a notebook or something to fit in your purse. I think you'd have lots of material from customers and clerks at Graham's."

"That's the same conclusion I came to."

"Remember how we used to compare our English assignments and see who got the most comments? Our papers were all gloriously stamped with As."

"Whatever happened to your dreams of being a journalist?" I asked.

Kathy shrugged. "My husband, I guess."

"You know, you have what a lot of women wish they had," I said to her.

Her face brightened. "Let's drink to that."

We raised our glasses, which were mostly ice and no liquid. I filled our glasses with more fun-maker, and we raised them again and fulfilled the toast.

"I hope ya' write something fun and interesting, not that boring stuff you see in *Woman's Day*."

She piqued my interest. "Like what?"

"Let's think up some titles for stories."

The oven dinged its readiness, but I ignored it.

I told her about "Momma's Devil Child" and "The Comb-Over Companion."

"Clever but not up to ya' standards, if I remember." I saw a little Irish devil dancing on her shoulder. "How about 'He Went Up the Elevator and Down on Me.'"

"Let's drink to that." We took another gulp.

I added, "How 'bout 'He Had a Little Heart, But Big Feet'?"

We shrieked, tears rolling down our faces.

A litany of naughty titles rolled off our tongues: "He's Hard Up for Her and Soft on Me," "She Kicked His Can Down the Road," "He Hangs Better Than an Andersen Window." Our cheeks hurt from laughing so hard, and we both held our sides to try to catch our breath.

"My," Kathy said, finally able to breathe normally. "We can surprise ourselves, can't we? Let's drink to surprises."

"To surprises." I raised my glass to another toast.

"What about this Pete? How're ya' going to get rid of him?"

"I don't know. Any ideas?"

"Hmmm." Kathy traced one of the boomerangs in the table's Formica. "Never let him see you sweat. Bullies get their biggest kicks from seeing their victims fearful. And don't antagonize the man, or he'll get more aggressive, if ya' know what I mean."

"What do you mean?"

"Rejected men spill the beans."

"Criminy. I think you're right there."

"Enough philosho, philsoph, oh, you know what I mean." She gave me a crooked grin and stood up with some effort. "I'm envious, ya' know. I don't do anything but cook, clean, and go to society meetings. Dan, king of our cashel…" She giggled. "He's very strict about how our home looks. Got ta' go and make sure I'm ready to receive royalty. Mind yourself." Successfully on both feet she left, and the door slammed shut.

Alone with my thoughts, I was unnerved by the news of a strange car sitting outside my house, even in a small town where nothing more exciting happens than having a chicken stolen off a grill. That it might be Pete spying on me made my hair tingle. I got up to bolt the door as Kathy suggested, but only after a couple of tries was I able to turn the bolt in the right direction. I turned the oven off and put the pot pie back in the freezer.

I went to the den and yielded to the comfort of the chintz chair, but closing my eyes didn't stop the tumble of images and other scenes from the day—a green and white car, Pete's rough hand, the scent of Old Spice.

At dawn, I woke up in the same place where I fell asleep—the chair.

The dry acrid taste in my mouth was a reminder of the previous night's gin-a-thon. My first attempt to rise was unsuccessful, so I stretched my head right then left and flexed my ankles to loosen my stiff limbs. I had an hour to get ready for a day of Saturday shoppers.

13

Magically I had no hangover from last night's party with Kathy, and a hot shower counteracted the effects of sleeping all night in a chair.

The shower did not wash away my anxiety about Pete. My instincts told me to avoid him at all costs. I couldn't stand having Pete hovering over me like a radiation cloud—not knowing when he would appear or how exposure to him would affect me.

I parked my car a couple of blocks away from Graham's and walked along the tree-lined street. Old tree roots caused the sidewalk to heave in places. I commiserated with the concrete. Like Mrs. Gibbons and Pete, the roots had found openings for their invasion.

"Stop it," I said aloud. "Think positive so good things will happen."

In the distance I could see the bricked alley that bordered the back door of the store. For an alley it was very clean—not like the alleys in Pittsburgh—and the street sign at the corner announced its history as "Strawberry Alley." Farmers used to sell their fruit there when it was a street and not a narrow passage between buildings. I kicked a stone out of my way and watched it clatter and roll in uneven circles.

From behind I heard, "Hello, Margaret, beautiful day, isn't it?" It was Mr. Beals, leaving me to wave to his back as he strolled past me with a brisk and healthy stride. He still hadn't retired, and his vitality made me hate the elevator even more.

Underneath an octogenarian oak tree, whose humongous branches created a tent of leaves, a hunched-over figure in a rusted Chevy coupe caught my eye. A man's head was down and his hands were gripping the steering wheel. When his head rose, I could see his contorted face. It was—Pete. Crying? His emotional display countered the distaste I had for him. *Careful, Margaret, you're entering man-care mode again.*

I positioned myself behind a closer tree to watch—my curiosity at a peak. I saw sunlight bounce off the metallic outline of a gun he had picked up with his right hand. Was he pointing to his head?

"Pete!" I ran from my cover to his car and grabbed the passenger side door. I gripped the open window to support my adrenalin rush. "What are you doing?" Pete's tear-stained face looked up at me, his eyes wide with surprise.

"Margaret. Oh my god." His reddened eyes followed the path of my stare, straight to the gun, now at his side, still gripped by white knuckles that matched the pallor of his face. He shoved the gun under his thigh, and his jaw tightened. "Leave me alone."

"What's wrong? What are you doing?" I glanced at the gun's hiding place.

"I said to leave me alone," he muttered with clenched teeth. He put his head down on the steering wheel again.

"Pete, whatever is wrong, it's not worth shooting yourself."

His head popped up. His eyes searched my face—his mouth hanging open.

"Shoot myself, you think that's what this is about?" His gunless hand reached to the passenger seat and grabbed a dog collar.

I was really confused. "What are you doing with a dog collar? Are you going to hang yourself?"

Pete's face morphed from anguish to surprise, then dissolved into laughter. New tears came down his face, but they weren't from sadness.

"Would you mind telling me what is going on? Are you killing yourself or what?" I wanted to slap him with the dog collar and crack his head with the butt of the gun.

Pete's laughter subsided, and a sad demeanor washed over him.

"You're unreal, you know that? It's my dog. I don't suppose you'd understand." He directed his red-rimmed eyes back to me.

"Your dog? What about your dog? Why do you have a gun?"

"He, he was old, and sick."

I waited, still confused. Pete stared off into that unknown place again.

"I put him out of his misery." He sighed and took hold of the wheel again with his hands, the collar still part of his grip.

"Oh, Pete, I'm so sorry. I saw the gun and thought, you know."

Pete shook his head. "That dog was my best friend, he came everywhere with me. All the cheap bastards I deal with trying to sell some lousy carpet…I'd come back to the motel at the end of the day and there'd he be, wagging his ol' tail."

Pete stopped. His shoulders loosened, his face softened with the vulnerability I saw early in our encounter at The Main Street Restaurant. He raised his head. "You know, for a high falutin' gal, you can be very gullible, but now that I think about it, it was awful nice a' you to try to rescue me from hanging myself with a dog collar." Pete gave a weak smile and paused. I sympathized, but the memory of his threatening hand on mine in the elevator wagged its finger of caution.

"I didn't treat you very well the other night," he said, talking to the steering wheel.

"Or the other day, either, on the elevator," I said.

"Yeah. I just…I don't know, don't do well with women."

"Is that an apology?"

Pete didn't answer.

"What did you do with your dog?"

"Buried him out by the gravel pit." Pete's face hardened, and the hair on my arms stood at attention.

"Git now. Enough. Leave me alone."

"Pete, I—"

"So you caught me in a moment of weakness—a man missing his fuckin' dog. You've had your mothering moment, go away," Pete said through clenched teeth, and I stumbled back a couple of steps. He stared straight ahead and started the car. "Be seein' you, girlie."

I stood in the street and stared as he drove off. His car was blue.

14

After my first traumatic week, the next month went more smoothly—no Pete, the doctor pronounced Mother "improving somewhat" and said she could go to a nursing home, Adele and I talked on the phone a couple of times. On the minus side, Mr. Beals still showed no signs of retiring.

Amid the normalcy I learned that through the doors of my elevator came regular citizens, entertainers or devils. Mrs. Gibbons was an entertaining devil, and I looked forward to her appearances. She was a regular shopper and she delivered gossip as regularly as the mailman brings bills.

Mrs. Gibbons was also a distant relative of mine—so distant that the paternal connection was multiple branches over and across the genealogy tree. That slight connection was enough for her to regularly give me advice—more to coax out gossip than out of concern for her third niece once removed. I assumed she was as trustworthy as a rattlesnake.

Mrs. Gibbons stepped into the elevator one day dressed in a modest shirtwaist befitting the minister's wife she was, but she also wore bright red lipstick and too much rouge. Her persona reflected both a spouse of a cleric and the girlfriend of a mobster. The delicate gold cross that hung at her neck and her heavy ornate earrings added to the visual confusion.

She proceeded to ask me if a red-haired woman had been going up to the third floor.

"Why do you ask?"

"Well…" She leaned in more closely. "The Bridge Club is worried about Mrs. Concord. She's afraid her husband is having an affair." She peered at me over her glasses. "She found red hairs on his suit coat. Poor thing. I volunteered to investigate."

So, the copper-coiffed lady and Mr. Concord's brightened smile had meaning. I tucked away that tidbit to write down later, on a napkin perhaps. "No, doesn't ring a bell."

*   *   *

I saw Mrs. Gibbons a few days later. I had told Mother about the investigation Mrs. Gibbons was conducting, and she said, "Be sure to stay off her wanted list, but let me know if you find out anything."

"Good morning, Mrs. Gibbons. How are you?"

"I'm fine, dear."

"Third floor? Still searching for that perfect sofa?"

"Heavens, yes. I had picked one out," she sighed, "but that awful Constance Oppenheimer bought it before I could. She knew I wanted it." Mrs. Gibbons put her hand to her mouth. "Oh my, the things that come out of my mouth…that wasn't very charitable of me, was it?"

When the exterior doors closed, I used a gossip-baiting technique learned in the halls of high school.

"What's happening these days?"

"Well…"

Here it comes, and I couldn't wait.

"I heard something about you that couldn't possibly be true. I can't imagine it being true, you being so sweet and all."

Was that a reptilian hiss I heard from her overly red mouth?

"Some people are saying you, uh, are hanging around with an unsavory sort of man. I mean a traveling salesman, a ladies' man, I hear, with greasy hair. You could do much better, dear."

I willed my body, eyes, and hands not to give any reaction that would confirm Mrs. Gibbons' suspicion. I stood there, hoping the floor would give way.

"I don't know what you mean."

"Dear, we all look after each other, don't we? Why, your mother and I have been in the same bridge club for twenty years. We are related, you know." The snake winked her mascara-heavy eye at me.

We reached the third floor, but Mrs. Gibbons didn't get off. She scanned the immediate vicinity to make sure no one was close enough to overhear.

"You know, people talk. You're too nice to lower yourself to the likes of Pete Jordan." She patted my arm. "I'm doing you a favor."

I lifted my chin a bit. "And how do you know about this alleged situation?"

"A few weeks ago…" She leaned into me, her tongue unsuccessfully licking lipstick off her teeth, "…some friends were having dinner at the Main Street Restaurant," she said in a low voice. "They were in a booth in back of you, and they said you were arguing with some guy, that Pete guy." She did another scan for possible observers. "They heard him say, 'So how 'bout it? Shall we go to a motel?'" Her eyebrows rose in expectant arches. "Is that true?"

"They must've misheard or mistook someone else for me." I hoped the viper didn't see the fire in my face or the pulse throbbing in my temples. Weren't snakes heat-seeking predators?

"Oh." Her face twisted with disappointment. "I told my friends the Landings would not have a daughter who would have a, um, you know, a tawdry relationship. You are a good Christian girl—I mean, you came home to take care of your poor dying mother."

She patted my arm again, and I recoiled at her touch. "I'm glad to know it wasn't true."

My breathing thinned, and I could hardly get out the words "I don't think this is an appropriate topic of conversation, Mrs. Gibbons."

"Oh, I don't want to get anyone in trouble. I thought you should know what people think they saw. Remember what happened to the Smith girl."

The Smith girl. Whenever parents were afraid that their child might do something wild and unsavory, they always brought up the wanton teenager who smoked, hung out with the wrong type, and was found dead in the woods east of town. I was too old for my behavior to evoke "the Smith girl." Mrs. Gibbons was making me feel childish and weak. My sweating hands were cold on the brass elevator control.

"I'll keep it to myself. But mind me, stay away from that Pete. Your mother would be so disappointed."

She was almost out of the elevator, stepping over the thin gap between the threshold and the floor when she looked at me over her shoulder. "Your slip is showing, dear."

I had been bitten by the snake herself. The heat climbed up my face again and spread its venom through my body. I had forgotten that small towns provide friends during good times and bad, but people with insatiable curiosity came out of nowhere during the bad times. I may have learned to control the Monster, but it was the human creatures that were licking at my heels.

* * *

That night I promised myself I would find a way to fight the effects of Mrs. Gibbons' evil news. She was an apt candidate for my list of possible story subjects, which I planned to record on an old notebook—the one with a leather cover and three-ring clip.

I scooped and shoveled papers, newspaper ads, and bills until I had several semi-neat stacks of mail, but I could not find it. There was the paper napkin with the notes about Mrs. Remington and the spitter. That I put on top of the bills pile. Digging deeper into the mess on my desk I also found a lone church bulletin from the first Sunday I was in Liberty, plus birthday cards purchased for occasions and people long ignored. In the bottom drawer, the last place I tried, lay the notebook that I wanted to use as a record of grand story ideas.

I took it and tore out the used pages.

Confronted with empty paper, I paused. I tapped my pencil on the desk. I wrote: *Titles*.

Where was my muse? How do titles pop into my head uninvited only to disappear when the invitation is official? I put pencil to paper, hoping the pencil would start moving like a Ouija Board. I wrote:

"Elevator Madness"

"Revenge of the Clerk"

"The Gossip"

"Momma's Devil Child

"Short on Brains, Long on …"

A teenager's diary, that's how my list read. I begged the *All About Eve* poster for inspiration. *We're like bees, you know,* I heard Margo say. I was a dead bee lying on the window sill, not like a live bee pollinating story ideas. I threw the notebook on the floor, and it landed with a thump, tented on the floral carpet. Whom was I trying to fool?

Once in bed, I flipped back and forth, fluffed my pillow multiple times, turned to my back again and stared at the ceiling. Ghoulish images of Pete and Mrs. Gibbons flitted through my head, and I kept hearing them say, singularly and sometimes in a duet, "Your slip is showing, your slip is showing." I dreamed that Mrs. Gibbons was a bee, buzzing about the nectar-sweetened trap I had set for her. Her legs, stuffed with notes about all the people in town, split open and spilled their gossipy contents onto my desk.

Perhaps harvesting story ideas from Mrs. Gibbons was not a bad idea. Maybe feeding her some false rumor could show me how she spreads gossip—research for my writing, I told myself—an innocent story to feed Mrs. Gibbons' hungry ears.

* * *

Mrs. Gibbons came in a couple of days later. When we reached the third floor, I didn't open the doors right away.

"Anything new happening?"

"Heavens no, dear. I'm looking for a new chair so I can seat all the ladies for the prayer group."

"Really…what are some of the things you pray for?" I asked.

"Oh, whatever people need. It's confidential, of course."

"Of course." I couldn't believe my good fortune. "I know someone your group can pray for."

Mrs. Gibbons' head whipped back to me. "Oh?"

She sidled up to me. Her eyes were wide and her lips were parted in anticipation of the gossipy snack she was going to get. I got a curious buzz from the attention. The story I concocted during my fitful sleep emerged from my mouth.

"A friend of mine has an uncle who got caught embezzling at the plant. The family is really distraught. He lost his job and everything." I felt a momentary pang for gossiping, but it was a tap, not a slam, on my conscience.

"Really. Who would that be, dear?"

"I don't know if I should say."

"To pray for him we need a name, you see—to make the prayer personal and worthy." She looked at me with an evil posture and a saintly eye.

I thought back to the previous night's news about Russian spies and quickly said, "Boris Karlosi. I don't know him. Quiet kind of family, I hear. He immigrated sometime after the war, I think."

"Is he Russian? How much did he embezzle?" she asked.

"I don't know."

"Tell your friend that we will be praying for Mr. Karlosi and his family. The Lord heals, you know."

I opened the doors, and Mrs. Gibbons exited with a bounce in her step. She headed straight for a friend at the perfume counter. The friend's eyes grew big, and her hand covered her mouth. My insides did a somersault. Mrs. Gibbons didn't wait for the prayer group. I had become a co-conspirator with the town's gossip. So, that was how it was done, and none of it had any speck of truth.

15

Mother's condition improved, and the doctor had her moved to Rose Garden Rest Home, aptly named for the rose bushes at the entrance and flowered wallpaper throughout. It was the best one I could find as long as one wasn't allergic to roses, and I guess, didn't hate the sound of school children.

"What's so restful about a rest home? School started and the kids coming and going across the street are so loud, not to speak of the recess bell."

"They said you weren't needing hospital care, Mother. The doctor said you were stable." I sat in a chair next to hers.

"I liked it better in the hospital. People here are dying right and left. And no one has teeth. The nurses wheel me into the dining room, sit me at a table with some old coot with missing dentures, and I want to throw up."

"Mother, try to have some fun. Make some friends."

"I'm supposed to be fun, huh?" She shrugged her shoulders. "One minute I'm playing bridge and the next minute I'm tethered to tubes and sitting on a bed pan. That's fun?"

Images of Mother cajoling me out of a pre-teen funk reminded me that we had traded places. I'd heard about role reversal between adult children and their aging parents. This was more than a reversal—it was an all-out battle of wills. Why couldn't we have the sweet mother/daughter rapport I'd seen in my friends' families?

"Well, you're not tethered or sitting on a bed pan. You have a bright, modern room, private, I should say, on the other side of the house from the school. And it's decorated in your favorite colors—pink and cream. Look at the lovely view out the window. A rose garden, you love flowers." Mother glanced out the window.

"I pictured roses at your wedding, you know. Now I'll probably die before you ever settle down."

I saw a metal lunch tray on the nightstand and considered it as a possible weapon for murdering her.

"Let's talk about something else," I said.

Mother's face became pinched, and her eyes became wet.

"I'm scared. In the hospital I thought I was going to die and be done. Here I see people waste away. And what happens when we don't have someone or something to leave behind?"

"What in the world are you talking about, Mother? You have me."

"But what do *you* have? You're an elevator operator, not the famous writer your father and I thought you would be. We were so proud of you, and we dreamed of being grandparents, you know."

"Oh please, remind me again." I sat down and put my face in my hands.

"We'll never know if your son has children. We'll never know how the links of our family continue." She studied her fingernails. "The Landings will disappear."

I turned from her and caught my breath. Facing her again I said, "I don't know what to say. You convinced me to put the baby up for adoption. You insisted that he be kept a secret." I clenched and unclenched my hands. "You know I can't have any more children. Wasn't the guilt ten years ago enough? Do I have to take on responsibility now for breaking the Landings legacy?"

"Darling, humor an old person's fears. You'll understand when you get older."

"What, understand ways to make your child feel rotten? I won't have *that* opportunity."

Mother's eyes filled. "I'm sorry. I don't know what I'm saying. Things just kind of spilled out. Forgive me?" She held out her arms.

I held her reluctantly then caved into her embrace. She cried, but I didn't. I couldn't. The tears wouldn't come. Instead, my mind raced with the question, "What *would* I leave behind?" Maybe a son. I didn't even know if he were alive or what he was becoming. I provided an egg but no influence. Maybe a notebook full of stupid story titles. That would make Mother proud.

I pulled away. "Mother, are you that disappointed in me?"

She studied me from behind her tears. "Mothers are a mixture, you know, of selfish needs and loving wants. I want you to be happy. I guess I get confused as to how I can help you find that. Now if you were still with that nice minister fellow, he would have the right words to sort this out."

"Mother!"

"What do you want in a husband, dear?" She sat back in the chair and folded her hands. I looked down at my own and saw that I had mimicked her posture. I put my hands on the arms of the chair.

"I'm not sure. I don't want to be a preacher's wife."

"Why not?"

"You have to share him with so many people and you have to pretend to like everyone, potlucks, and God Blesses."

"How did you get so cynical?"

"From my mother, maybe? What do *you* think I should want in a husband?"

"Here's some motherly advice. If a man picks up after himself, he respects you and the home. The rest will fall into place." She punctuated her opinion with a firm head shake.

"Was Father like that?"

"Yes, dear, he was. I never had to pick up after him. And he took good care of us."

We sat in silence and I could hear the ticking of my watch. Each tick separated me more and more from what I didn't know about the purpose of my life.

16

Lena's forward posture and crazy-for-information look told me that she would do anything to be brought into the sisterhood of secrecy.

"Do you promise, under penalty of death, that you will not tell a soul about this?"

"My dear, you know you can trust me. Whom would I tell, anyway? I'm a spinster who lives with her three-legged cat and has only one real friend—you."

It was mid-September, and the air was so clear that the orange and red maple leaves sparkled. Lena and I were eating our lunches in the city park. She had been asking about the notebook that she had seen me pull out from time to time. I needed to extract total and irrevocable loyalty from her.

"You are my friend," I said.

The breeze played with strands of Lena's hair that had escaped from the rest of her frizz. She watched me earnestly, and the hint of sadness in her eyes conveyed that her lonely life would indeed guarantee that she didn't have an audience for any secret she might hear.

"I'm trying to do some writing."

Lena gave an exasperated fling of her arms. "That's it?"

"It's more than that. I'm writing stories for magazines like *Forbidden Love*."

Her eyes opened wide. "Tell me more. Are the stories true? Do you have a life you're hiding from me?" Lena gave me a shy grin. She opened a package of potato chips and pushed them toward me. I reciprocated by pushing a remaining Twinkie to her.

"The stories are all imaginary, but I get ideas from people I watch. I see human drama every time I open the elevator doors."

"Oh dear, what will people think when they know you are writing romance stories, and about them?" Lena tucked a wisp of hair behind her ear. "And why romance stories?"

"I know," I said. "Isn't it odd? I know what I write is too racy for our little town, so I am writing under a pen name. What do you think of 'Lydia Bailey?'"

Lena blushed. "Are you writing from experience?" The woman who had confessed to me she was a maiden cast her eyes downward as if my answer might titillate her too much.

"Lena, you are so funny. We women don't need experience, we only need imagination. I can create the perfect man and craft the wittiest and wisest conversations that a modern woman would ever want to voice. If the man is too controlling, I can rip him out of the typewriter and throw him into the wastebasket. If my female character is getting a little too emotional, I can erase her anxiety and write in power and confidence."

"How many have you written?"

I cleared my throat. "I have lots of ideas."

"You get all this from watching people?"

"Not always." I leaned forward on my elbows. "Just the other day there weren't many customers, so I had time to think about my character, a gossip. For the life of me, I couldn't think of a way to describe gossiping, but fortunately Mrs. Gibbons came along."

Lena shook her head. "A seed of gossip would find fertile soil in her. She's always so well dressed, but I swear her mind is a garbage dump. The stuff that comes out of her mouth is so contrary to her appearance." She sat back.

"I have to admit that I took advantage of her and 'greased the wheel.'"

Lena shifted toward me again. "How did you do that?"

"I made up a tale about a make-believe person, Boris Karlosi."

"Isn't that the Russian spy that's been in the news?"

"That's what makes it so fun. She didn't get it. Nothing I told her was real. But you should have seen her eyes when I told about this man in town who lost his job for embezzlement. Mrs. Gibbons ate it up. Her neck straightened, her eyes widened, even her color deepened as though gossip makes her breathe harder. It was priceless."

"Are you sure there is no one in town by that name you made up?" She frowned.

"Boris Karlosi, are you kidding? In Liberty?"

Lena was still worried. "You, uh, don't write about me, do you?"

"You're so funny. Your life is too quiet for *Forbidden Love*." Lena flinched. "Everybody's life is too quiet. A writer gets to kick it up a notch, or two or three."

"I suppose." She picked at her sandwich.

"This is where you come in."

"I'm listening."

"You see so much happening, especially in the men's department. How 'bout being my eyes and ears on the first floor? I bet you're witness to lots of happenings that I could use in my stories. What do you say?" I patted her hand as an invitation to join me in my harvest of human drama on the stage of Graham's Department Store.

She frowned. "I couldn't do that, Margaret. It feels a little like betraying my customers."

"I wouldn't use anyone's name in my stories. I'd let you read them, to be sure."

I fought off the doubt I saw in her eyes. "Think of the examples of human behavior you see. It doesn't have to be personal about anyone."

"I don't know. It doesn't sound right to me. Have you published anything yet?" she asked.

"You'll have to ask Lydia Bailey," I said, but Lena didn't smile.

She stood up and gathered our lunch items. "It sounds dishonest to me. Let's get back to work," she said without making eye contact.

"Oh, Lena, I've made you upset. Can't we have a little fun? I'll change names and places. Please?"

"It doesn't seem right, I tell you."

"Loosen up a little."

She jerked her head up. "Who are you to tell me how to live? I'd rather be a proper woman than someone getting fun out of other people's troubles." Lena's scalp reddened under her thin, gray hair. "Why are these stories so important to you anyway? It's not like you're a real author or anything." Lena jutted out her jaw and bore her steel gray eyes into mine. Her folded arms posed a barrier between us.

She gathered up her sandwich wrappings and stuffed them haphazardly into her lunch bag. "I've got to get back to work." She stood up from the picnic bench. "I won't spy for you."

Lena slapped me with her words, and I stood dazed as she stomped away.

"I'm sorry," I called, but she kept walking.

*　*　*

"How's your spy writing going?" Lena asked, taking her time to insert the card into the time clock. A palpable wall of distrust stood between us even though a couple of weeks had passed since the ill-fated lunch in the park.

"Okay," I said. It was Friday night, and the store had just closed. I punched my time card, and I could have been a free woman except that I had an unfortunate urge to make things right with Lena. I cornered her before she was able to get out of the store.

"Can't we talk about this?"

She stood aside for one of the clerks to pass. "I don't understand what you're doing. It seems voyeuristic to me."

"It's kind of like being a reporter, don't you think? Gathering information? Like an eagle, hovering with a keen eye to observe and record?"

"Uh-huh, and how about those sharp talons that grab their victim so their razor beaks can rip open their hearts?" She pushed by me.

Nearby Mrs. Remington stared at me with an unsmiling face. Had Lena said something to her?

Mining my surroundings for story ideas still did not strike me as bad. Mother had been hounding me to start writing "to get my mind off things," but I was certain she was still thinking about continuing the Landings name in some form. Like any proud mother she would refer to my senior literature prize as proof I had talent. "I am writing, Mother," but I didn't confess I was writing under a pseudo-name—authorship in *Forbidden Love* magazine wouldn't have promoted the Landings legacy.

*   *   *

I parked Bella in the usual place in front of my house. There were no cigarette butts.

I pulled my collar tightly around my neck insulating me from the October air, and I hurried past the dried-up mums, lonely in their forgotten state. Their browned stems and shriveled flower heads begged to be put out of their misery.

Once inside, I flung my coat and purse on the sofa, went into the kitchen, and poured myself a drink. I headed toward the den but the doorbell rang. I peered through the peep-hole in the door—a safety device that was rarely needed in a small town like Liberty. Staring back at me, slightly distorted through the tiny hole, was John Graham.

17

I surveyed the street and didn't see John's car. "How did you get here?"

He looked from me to the road. "I need a ride home." He stood on the front porch and shifted his feet on the concrete and kept his eyes on the porch light. "This is so embarrassing." He didn't make a move to come in. The skin under his eyes was dark, and he was dressed in a plaid flannel shirt and blue jeans—clothing that I had never seen him wear.

"I really need help. I know this is strange…but I thought you'd understand." He took a deep breath. "I know I'm rambling, but, this was a mistake…I should go." He started back down the steps.

I opened the door wider and stepped forward to take his arm and a thousand un-interpretable emotions exploded as my hand felt the angles of his elbow through the flannel shirt. *Down, Margaret.* "Come in. It's cold out there. I'll make some coffee."

"Okay." He looked behind him, then came through the door, and followed me into the kitchen. He sat with a thud in the first chair he encountered. I turned my back on him while I fixed the coffee. John Graham was in *my* kitchen.

I put two cups and saucers on the table and sat, waiting for the coffee to percolate. John traced the metal edges of the table with his fingers. The silence was loud.

"How did you know where I lived?" I asked.

"I've made many deliveries to your mother. Small town, you know." He kept fingering the table edge.

"Yeah, I know. And, where's your wife?"

He took a deep breath, and his shoulders dropped with his sigh. "We had a huge argument at the Country Club Autumn Dance."

"I wondered why you weren't working tonight."

I welcomed the sound of the percolating coffee and jumped up to bring the pot to the table. Relieved to have something to do, I poured the aromatic brew into the two cups. "Sugar, cream?"

"No, thank you."

I sat back down, blew into my cup to cool the coffee and to give John opportunity to continue his story.

"She took the car and left me there. I was too embarrassed to ask anyone for a ride so I pretended to leave too." He fingered his coffee cup. "This is as far as I could walk. I'm glad you live on the west side of town instead of the east."

He glanced up at me, but I continued to blow on the hot coffee.

"So," he said, examining the kitchen, "this is where you live. I've never been inside. It's very nice and inviting."

"Thanks." I put my cup back in its saucer. "I'm glad you didn't try to walk all the way. It must be five miles from the club to your home." I took a tentative sip from my cup.

John held on to his coffee cup as though his soul, instead of his body, needed warming. "You must think I'm crazy."

"I do crazy very well myself," I said. "Let me take you home." I got up to get my coat and purse, but I was aware of him watching me.

At the front door, we collided as both of us tried to get through at the same time. We each backed off but not enough to entirely separate. Our clothes barely touched.

"As long as I'm acting crazy…" John said in a whisper.

I could feel the warmth of his breath, and his lips were inches away. "We need to go," I said, and I stepped ahead of him and walked toward the car. He shut the door and followed me.

We were both silent on the ride to his house. As for John, he sat like one of the presidents carved into Mount Rushmore, stone-faced, staring straight ahead. His body on the car seat beside me pulled like a magnet.

I drove onto his street, one of those all-American side streets that are lined with old elm trees whose leaves and branches cradle the houses in its shadows. It was a neighborhood of families with husbands and wives and children.

"Let me off on this corner, please," he said.

John hesitated when he exited the car. "This is between you and me, all right?"

"I'm pretty good at keeping secrets. Please don't worry."

At the discreet distance from which I sat, I watched him walk up to the darkened and unwelcoming house. I drove away and wondered what story John would give to explain his ride home, or if his wife was even in a condition to hear an explanation.

Back home, I didn't know what to do. I paced between the kitchen and the living room, first sitting on the sofa and from there to the kitchen table. I stared at John's nearly full cup that sat on the table. I was tempted to take a sip to put my lips where his had been, but I caught myself and took both cups and saucers to the sink and squirted some dish soap on them to wash away his presence.

Once in my bedroom I sat at the dressing table and opened my Bette Davis drawer. Fingering the lipstick tubes and the makeup brushes, I expected to feel the pull of escape. I didn't, and I closed the drawer.

Second choice. I went into the den, sat in the chintz chair and pulled my writing notebook onto my lap. What was the argument about between John and Elaine—her drinking? I wrote down a possible title, "I Left Him on the Dance Floor, and She Waltzed into His Life."

18

Christmas carolers and harried shoppers provided a holiday backdrop as I waited at the elevator doors for my lunchtime relief to appear. I watched Lena straighten the men's shirts on an oaken display table. I missed her and our chats. I still didn't understand why she took such offense at the invitation to be my co-conspirator. I thought I was giving her something fun to do.

Grey wisps of hair escaped her chignon, and her tailored toile dress came well below her knees. The black-tie leather shoes were old but polished, and a barely perceptible sweat glistened on her forehead below her bangs. She was in command of her merchandising domain, but when she opened her mouth, her high pitched voice startled customers.

She had a practiced eye for measuring men's dimensions—she swore to me once that her eyes never lingered on a man's bulge, or lack of it. I smiled at the thought—that would be worth catching.

Behind her were shelves and more shelves of shirts, underwear, pajamas, and other men's clothing all stacked neatly in the wooden slots according to color and size—Lena's work, of course. I watched as she pulled an errant white shirt from a pile. She hated disorder, and I admired her for that. I thought of my den, organized with good intentions but disorganized with my bad habits.

"Ma'am?" A middle-aged man signaled for Lena's attention.

"I need some jockey shorts," he said, shifting on his feet a little.

I came to attention.

Lena faced her customer, and in her squeaky voice asked, "And what size do you need, sir?"

The man replied a size 34. Lena looked him over with an appraising eye and asked, "Could you please turn around?"

The man smiled a little but did as she asked. He gave one awkward revolution. "I think, sir, that a size 36 would be more comfortable for you."

A size lie—I have witnessed them many times in Lena's department.

"Uh, yes, you are probably right."

The man purchased four pairs. She wrote up the sale in a little tablet with carbon paper and sent it up to the office through the pneumatic tubes. The metal cylinder with his change and a receipt swooshed through the tubes overhead and clunked into a mesh basket at the cashier's side in the office mezzanine. Visible to everyone on the first floor, the cashier made change and waved to Lena, who responded with a business-like bob of her head. I hated those pneumatic tubes and the superiority of the cashier. Whenever I had to fill in for a sales clerk, I would always forget to carry this number or that for the total, and the cylinder would come zipping back, containing the sales slip with the corrections penciled in red.

"Ho! Ho! Ho!" I heard the town Santa approach the front doors of the store. His loud and deep signature call could be heard from half a block away.

"This is going to be good," I said to a customer standing near me. "Don't go away. I've heard about these Santa encounters."

I watched Lena jerk to attention when she heard Santa's bells. A blush crept up her face to her thin-haired scalp. It was Jess Barry, the town Santa, and as far as most people were concerned, he was the real Santa. Every Christmas, he chased Lena for a kiss. She was fair game for his mischief.

Jess really was merry and had red cheeks and a big belly. I had yet to encounter a Santa, even in Pittsburgh, who sweetened Christmas as much as he did. Part of me wished I had never been told who was underneath the costume that he rented from Graham's each year. It was too much reality when on one day after Christmas I saw a man with a white beard and a familiar face hand a large box to the elder Mr. Graham, a box that had red velvet and white faux fur peeking from under the lid.

Perhaps I would have time to harvest a Santa adventure before the elevator returned. I took my notebook and pen out of the purse I hadn't yet put in the employee's coatroom. I heard the sound of the elevator car being yanked up, down, down, up as my less experienced relief tried to get the car level with the third floor landing.

"Where is my Miss Lena?" Santa bellowed, all the while shaking his bells and continuing his ho-ho-ho's as he came through the front door of the department store.

"Excuse me," she said to a waiting customer. "I need to check an item in the stockroom."

She was too late. Santa came down the aisle and made tracks for her. He was bigger, faster, and determined to plant his yearly kiss on her spinster cheek. As she made her way around the large display table, Santa came from the other direction and blocked her escape to the stairwell. She was the only person I have ever seen glare at Santa Claus.

"Now, Santa, I have work to do," she said with no smile and an eye for a way past him.

By this time the customers on the first floor caught onto what was happening and were enjoying the fun. Both clerks and customers gathered to watch the show. Second and third floor customers leaned over the rail of the atrium to check out the commotion. The customer I had alerted said to me, "I see what you mean."

Santa was a loud cat taunting the frenzied mouse. I scribbled "cat/mouse" in my notebook. Santa and Lena made one more circle around the shirt table when a little girl caught his eye.

"Ho, ho, ho! I see someone special wants to talk to Santa."

He spun to face an excited little girl, young enough to relish a visit with Santa and old enough to seize an opportunity. Her face lit up with anticipation, and she let go of her mother's hand and held out her arms to be picked up.

Lena saw her chance to escape. She scurried toward the shoe department that hid a back stairwell to the basement. I tried to hide my amusement, unsuccessfully, and Lena gave me a withering look.

The customers and clerks began talking again, and the people who were leaning over the second and third floor railings went back to their shopping. Everyone was happy, having been entertained by the Jolly Man himself.

The Monster was still growling its protest over the mishandling of his engine, so I took the opportunity to check on Lena. I put my notebook away and went down to the basement storeroom. I stayed off to the side of the stairs and watched her fuss with the pajama tops and men's shirts on the inventory shelves. She stopped and listened for Santa noises on the floor above. Then she spotted me.

"Leave me alone! You think this is funny." Lena re-stacked the men's shirts on the shelf, placing the left ones on the right and right ones on the left. The cellophane wrapping on the shirts crackled in time with her anger.

"Lena, if you didn't run from him, it wouldn't be such a game."

"I don't want to be kissed by the likes of Jess Barry." She waved a finger at me.

"It's just Christmas fun," I said.

"It's humiliating. He's married. Now, again, leave me alone." She turned back to the shelves, repeating her sorting.

I stood there, not knowing what to do. I could hear Santa's bells fading out the store and up the sidewalk, and only then did Lena's posture soften. She smoothed the skirt of her dress, patted her hair for strays, and headed back to the men's department. As she passed me, she gave me another evil look.

"Thanks a lot for your help."

I felt chastened, my attempt to check on Lena misunderstood, and I followed her upstairs. My elevator substitute was still jerking passengers somewhere between the second and third floors, so I retrieved my notebook from my purse. I wrote down *Lena, Santa, attraction, denial.* Hmmm. Maybe I could write a scene like Shakespeare's woman who "doth protest too much." Could my protagonist have the hots for Santa?

I felt someone's eyes, and I glanced up to find Lena staring at the notebook in my hand. She spun on her heel and focused on re-tidying the men's pajamas on the shelves behind her.

* * *

That evening I sat in my chair with my notebook. Notes from the napkin I wrote in the lavatory were on the first page. The words waited to be used, but I couldn't come up with a story based on a spitting little girl. Hardly romance magazine material. Writer indeed.

I picked up the copy of *Forbidden Love* that was on my lamp table, and I opened to a notice for Christmas in July stories.

In my mind I saw Santa chasing Lena around the table full of men's shirts. I leaned back and closed my eyes, letting the projector in my head play out the movie. I watched Jolly Old Man's eyes gleaming as he concentrated on his prey. He licked his cherry red lips in anticipation of catching up with her. Lena darted around the underwear table out of Santa's reach. My mental camera did a close-up to her face, and I saw it—she had the tiniest bit of upturn to her mouth, a suppressed smile that didn't match her behavior. I kept the camera close in, and I saw them lock eyes. Then it was gone. That was the story. Lena and Santa had a thing going, and their annual chase for the kiss was a charade. Not only did Lena have the hots for Santa—he had the hots for her.

I moved over to the typewriter and sat down. The typewriter buzzed as I inserted paper and twirled the platen. My hands anticipated the words that were going to land on the paper.

Seduced by Santa, by Lydia Bailey

There on a park bench, half hidden by a curtain of willow leaves were Louise Hawk and Bob Royce. Louise was the men's dry goods manager at the town's only department store, and Bob worked at the Post Office but moonlighted in December as Santa.

I giggled to myself as I altered identifying facts. I changed the names and Jess' job—he really works at a local factory. But, I thought, I had to keep Louise in the men's department, underwear was key to the plot. It occurred to me that she would be identifiable, but I'd deal with that later. Nobody would know who the real author was anyway.

Louise, grey-haired and a tad chubby, was pressing herself into the equally chubby arms of the town Santa. She could feel the longing begin to stir in her, and it felt strangely welcome and knowingly sinful.

Bob, who grew his white beard year round, brushed his long whiskers away from her face and said to her, "After all these years of not letting me kiss you at Christmas, why are you giving yourself to me this year, and in July?"

Louise giggled. "Are you pretending to forget those looks you give me every time I see you at the Post Office? You wore me down, Santa!"

Bob gave Louise a bear hug and sighed. "I never thought it would happen."

"Oh, Bob! I can't believe that a gentleman like you would be interested in a spinster like me."

Ignoring her comment, Bob put his hand at her neckline and undid a button of her ruffled blouse. "Speaking of gifts...do ya have some toys in there for ol' Santa?"

Louise playfully slapped him. "And I just called you a gentleman."

Bob sat back and turned his face to the sun. He held Louise's hand and closed his eyes. In a low voice he said, "Let's just enjoy the sun and breeze for a few moments."

Louise cuddled up to Bob, and they sat motionless in the summer afternoon. Eventually Bob gave a snort and woke up. "My...it's time for me to go to work."

"I'm going to stay here a little longer, you go on," Louise said.

Bob gave her a peck on the cheek and left. A piece of paper fell out of his pocket as he rose from the bench but by the time she picked it up, Bob was out of sight. When she opened it, the first line of unfamiliar handwriting caught her eye: Bobby Darling...

Later, lying in my bubble bath, I tried to think how naive I wanted Louise to be and how deceptive I wanted Bob to be. I even pictured the title emblazoned on the cover of *Forbidden Love*— "Seduced by Santa." I fluffed bubbles onto my head for the up-do I would need for the publicity photo, and with a soaked washcloth I dripped water onto my face in lieu of the champagne that I would be drinking when I received my royalty checks.

Doubt. My story could be published, and I could be uncovered as the author. Maybe friends of Lena and Jess actually read *Forbidden Love* and would recognize them. But, I told myself, it's a story begging to be told. What woman hasn't fantasized about a Santa in her life?

I dried off and put on my flannel pajamas—hardly *Forbidden Love* type of garb—but like I told Lena once, a person doesn't have to act the part to write the part.

* * *

While other people worked on their shopping lists and Christmas cards, I continued to write in the evening after a day of working in my vertical cell. My fingers were on fire while I typed, and I pushed aside any qualms I had about the topics. I was alive with words and imagination.

On visits to Mother, I would tell her that I was writing again. "Novels?"

"No, Mother, short stories."

"Our own F. Scott Fitzgerald in the family." She beamed.

* * *

I was scared silly to send my prose out to the world—it would be like standing nude in the town square—but Lydia Bailey, my alter ego, was my safety net. Even though I had told Lena about my pseudonym, I counted on her not being the type to read tawdry magazines. I doubted she had ever been kissed.

I re-wrote "Seduced by Santa" several times over the week. One evening I would like it, the next evening I would be up until the early morning hours fixing what I hated. Who should be the woman who wrote the note that Louise found? How should the story end? I would stare at a page and in the span of two hours I would have changed one word. Or, I would read a page and mark out whole paragraphs. I went through two typewriter ribbons.

Finally done. I carefully wrapped the renamed "Seduced by a Summer Santa" in butcher paper and addressed it to the Editor at Smith Publications in New York. I cradled it to my breast as I marched to the Post Office.

I waited until there was no one else in line.

"Smith Publications, eh?" asked Mr. Warner, standing on the other side of the postal counter. "We have an author in our midst."

"Seems so."

"But you have to let go of it so I can weigh it."

"Oh, of course." I released my grip on the package and watched him place it on the scale.

"We will take good care of it." He printed out the postage and slicked it over the gummed sponge and smoothed it onto the right corner of the package. He hesitated when the return address caught his eye. "Lydia Bailey, eh?"

"You're bound by some kind of postal-client secret keeping, aren't you?" I asked.

"Sure, don't you worry, Miss Landings. It's none of my business." He placed it in the mail bin on top of other packages of multiple sizes and colors. It was like watching your teacher take your prized science project and toss it among the other poster boards. The few other things I had sent to publishers were such piffle—"Seduced by a Summer Santa" came out of me rather than from me.

What happened to it after that I had no choice but to trust the U.S. Postal Service and the anonymous secretary at *Forbidden Love* magazine who would deliver it to the desk of an overworked editor. Would they notice the aura of excellence emanating from the package?

19

The store was bustling with Christmas shoppers and frenzied clerks, and the holiday music had switched from pleasant background noise to a maddening cacophony of lyrics about the Christ child and Santa Claus. A big sign sat next to the elevator. It was hand painted in gold and red and kept track of the number of shopping days left. A couple of customers stared at the day's numbers, seemingly not wanting to believe that the holiday was so close. I heard one mumble, "My God, Christmas is such a pain in the ass," and she walked away shaking her head.

Every December I imagined my son at Christmas with his adoptive family—his toddler delight in the Christmas tree lights, his first bike, his new train set. From the mouth of the elevator, I saw boys who might be ten years of age, the age my son would be, and each one I spotted brought on more sadness and futility. I had no womb—cut from my body like my son was torn from my arms—and I would never feel the kicking of life within me again.

As Christmas Eve approached, more fathers were bringing in their children to buy presents for the "lady of the house," as many badly informed men were apt to say. Most mothers had taken care of the father gift weeks ago. One father and son duo approached the elevator with deliberation. "Good morning. Could you take us to the third floor please?"

The boy smiled at me. He was about ten or eleven, and I instantly liked him. *Stop it, Margaret.*

"What a nice young man your son is," I said to the father.

"Why thank you. We're shopping for his mother's Christmas present, aren't we, Bobby?"

The boy said, "We're getting a new sofa and tables for Mother.

We're having them delivered on Christmas Eve."

The father laughed and put his arm around his son's slim shoulders. "We just moved here and heard that Graham's was the best place to buy furniture."

I closed the doors and pressed the lever forward to start the ascent to the third floor. "You are in the right place. What brought you to Liberty?"

"Transferred to the plant."

The father and son didn't say anything else, but while we headed upward I examined the newcomers. The father's scarf was cashmere—he must be one of the new plant executives. The son Bobby clutched a leather flier hat with ear flaps. His crew cut revealed a finely shaped head, and his blond hair and blue eyes foretold a handsome young man.

I stopped the elevator with my smoothest landing of the day and opened the doors for the father-son shopping team. "Good luck with your Christmas shopping, Bobby. I'm sure your mother will love what you choose."

Bobby turned back and waved. I smiled at him and waved back. I would like a son like that.

The buzzer rang from the second floor, and down I went. I opened the door and there stood Adele.

"Don't you love the holidays? Oh, and take me to the basement, please. And you'll never guess what? Dr. Adkins tells everyone I'm his girlfriend." She beamed like the star of Bethlehem.

"How nice," I said. Adele had been back for only two months longer than I, and she had already landed a cool fellow. Hospitals were full of doctors, all men. I encountered mostly women, the shoppers who traipsed in and out of my elevator.

Whenever I visited Mother at the nursing home, she pestered me to get back with Howard. She continued to believe my lie that I thought Howard was too religious, so her persuasive tactics revolved around that theme. "Being a minister's wife is so stable, you'd never get divorced, dear." Her worst was, "If you have any troubles in your family, you've got someone who knows how to pray and say the right thing." I tried to ignore her campaigning, but she would get exasperated and roll her eyes. To my shame, I wished her eyes would stick.

Adele did arrange a double date at Main Street Restaurant with a friend of her Dr. Adkins, also a doctor, but even at the young age of thirty-five he already had hair in his ears. I didn't bother to tell Mother about him. She would have told me to ignore the hairy ears and focus on assumed stability.

Other men in my life up to then still included Pete—a jerk, John—unavailable, and that was it. Yes, Adele was lucky—she worked in a hospital with marketable men, excepting of course "The Man with Whiskered Ears."

I transported Adele to the basement, but she stopped me from opening the doors.

"Are you all right?" she asked.

"Sometimes the holidays put me in a bad mood."

"You're not alone…that happens to a lot of people. Tell you what. Tom and I will make sure you're not alone over the holidays." She patted my hand.

She waved as she left the elevator, but I couldn't shake my discontent. Adele, Kathy, Mother—they didn't comprehend who I really was. I customized each Margaret Landings puzzle so that the information people had wouldn't affect their acceptance of the woman I wanted them to know.

One important piece was missing from all the Margarets I presented—there was no one I could talk to about the holidays and my absent son. At the Crittendon home, we mothers, on the verge of giving up our babies, commiserated about the losses we would be facing in our futures, but once we left the protective walls of Florence Crittendon, we grieved alone.

I also couldn't talk about my nascent writing—the obsession with the right words, the victory of a well-written passage, even if it was a passage about heaving breasts. Proper women denied any interest in reading romance magazines, but those were the most worn and dog-eared at beauty shops. The air from the hair dryers wasn't the only thing that was hot under those hoods.

The buzzer rang from the third floor. Up I went, and when I opened the doors, there was the father and son team—both grinning ear to ear.

"We were successful," said the father, "weren't we, Bobby?"

"Mother will be so happy. And I saw a bed that I want for my room."

The father responded to his son. "We'll have to wait and see if Santa has time to build it."

"Oh, I know you're Santa, Father. I'm ten," Bobby said with a little indignation in his voice. "I'm too old for reindeer and all that."

"I hate to give up the Santa thing," the father said to me. "It's hard to remember that Bobby is past that stage."

I looked at the boy and felt another tug of a distant memory. He didn't resemble his father, either. Maybe he was adopted. Enough with the imagination, I told myself.

"What else do you want for Christmas?" I asked him.

"A train! A Lionel set with 027 gauge. It has a headlight and magne-traction."

"I had a Lionel American Flyer 0 gauge when I was your age," I said.

"You did? You're a girl." He looked at me wide-eyed.

"My father gave it to me. I guess he figured that if he didn't have a son, he could still play trains with his daughter."

"Cool," he said.

I dropped them off at the first floor, and Bobby repeated his goodbye wave. "Merry Christmas," he called. The two walked off hand in hand.

I took a last look at them just as Bobby took his nimble forefinger and dug for nose gold. The Landings never picked their noses.

* * *

Sometime during the night I entered the abyss of dreams. All I could see was the boy on the elevator, Bobby, who kept waving to me. I saw him on the street next to the shoe store. He waved as he passed. My weightless body flew through the night of dreams, and he floated by me, waving again and again. The sky was filled with giant crows, and Bobby hopped onto one and flew into the distance.

The last scene I remembered took place in The Main Street Restaurant. A crow with a saddle sat at the front door like Cisco Kid's horse Diablo. I went inside and walked toward the hostess station and endured a gauntlet of stares from the town's citizenry—Mrs. Gibbons, Pete, John, Mother, Adele, Kathy, and Mr. Cordon. I scanned the reservation list and saw my name—and Bobby's. I peered into the dining room and there he was, beckoning me to join him at the only table in a room decorated with English floral wallpaper peppered with images of still crows.

I alighted softly beside him and took a chair.

"Hello, Bobby."

"Hello, Mother." He smiled at me.

I managed to say, "I'm not your mother."

He continued to smile the beatific smile of a wizened old man. "Oh yes, you are. I knew it right away." Bobby looked into my eyes for recognition. Not seeing any, he frowned. "Why don't you know me?"

I covered my mouth as I studied him for any clue as to how he could be my son. The newborn I held briefly in my arms had no resemblance to the boy in front of me. "I expected I would know you immediately, and I didn't."

Bobby continued to frown, and disappointment registered in his young eyes.

I continued, "But you know me, so you must be my son."

I could feel his rising pain at my lack of recognition. Suddenly he burst into that giggly laugh of young children who have played a joke on someone. "April Fool!" The crows popped off the wallpaper, circled around us with grating caws, and flew out the room.

I woke and felt the cruelty of the dream in my chest. The small hand on the nightstand clock pointed to the "6." Three hours until work. I gave myself two hours to grieve my son.

20

A murmur of good news traveled around the cluster of employees. John had just passed out the Christmas bonuses—for the clerks it was a crisp Benjamin Franklin secured in a white money envelope emblazoned with a handwritten *Merry Christmas* on the front. The bonus helped to compensate for our woefully low weekly wages. Most of the managers peered inside their envelopes and quickly closed them. I found out why. Mr. Concord, unlike the others, flashed the *two* Bens he received. He and Mr. Beals tapped their envelopes together in a congratulatory salute.

"Store opens in ten minutes," John said, and everyone scattered. He hung back, waiting for the others to move away from the elevator.

"I need some Christmas shopping advice for my wife. Why don't you take me to the third floor and help me pick out some furniture?"

"I haven't clocked in yet," I said.

"This won't take long," and he motioned me to get in. I started to close the doors, but I could see Mr. Concord waving the "hold it" signal. John took a deep breath and let it out slowly.

"Did I hear 'furniture,' John? Let me help you." The wind had blown his comb-over open, exposing his hairless scalp. What hair he had made an upright tower of gray wisps. I swallowed a giggle and saw the same effort in John's face. The three of us rode up in silence. John stood with his hands crossed in front of him military style, and one thumb was tapping furiously on the other wrist.

I opened the doors, and Mr. Concord stepped out, but John hesitated. "I'll talk with you later," he said to me, and he followed Mr. Comb-Over.

Down on first again, I went to the time clock. I stuck the card in and pulled it out quickly—too quickly. The machine clunked and whirred when I withdrew it, so the time stamp on the card came out smudged and crooked. Embarrassed, I placed the mangled card back in the rack. That's my life—mangled, printed sideways, and difficult to read.

Back on duty, I waited for John to approach me again, but everybody wanted to ride the elevator. I wasn't sure I wanted to hear what he had to say. The shoulds and shouldn'ts swung back and forth in my mind. *He's married, Margaret. You're wanted, Margaret.*

Mrs. Gibbons came in and said her group was praying for Mr. Karlosi, Adele took a ride to the second floor, and Mr. Concord must have ridden up and down at least three times. Kathy came in and headed to the bargain basement.

John approached me several times but backed off when customers came to the elevator. When I was finally idle, he appeared from nowhere.

"How about a ride to the third floor?" he asked. He tugged at his tie, and his eyes scanned the store.

I had been around enough men to know that when they are exhibiting nervousness, like tie tugging and no eye contact, there's an issue at hand, and I didn't want any part of it. "Actually I need to make a phone call. Could you take the elevator for me?" I bolted out and made my way to the office.

"May I use the telephone, please?" I asked the office manager. She handed me the phone without pausing.

"Punch '1' for an outside line," and she continued to organize time cards.

I pretended to dial Adele's number. "Are you still interested in going to the movie?" I asked no one. "Swell. I'll see you there at 7:00." Though tempted to see what John was doing, I kept my back to the first floor. "Bye." I handed the phone back. I braved a look, there were several people waiting for the elevator.

I joined the small group, and when John returned in the elevator, I said, "Thank you." I took my post at the controls, gently shoving John out of the way, all the while greeting the customers. From the corner of my eye, I caught him staring at me in a dumbfounded way.

Finally, five-thirty. I brought the elevator to a rest on the first floor and let the last customer out just as John sounded the closing bell. "Don't go anywhere," he commanded—not quite gruffly but with a surety that I'd heard from men with authority, like my father, the principal, or the cop who pulled me over once for speeding.

The store cleared out within ten minutes

Lena was the last to leave, and she threw me a sneer of both distrust and curiosity.

John locked the doors and returned to the elevator. "Let's go to the third floor. I need your advice." He reached for the control before I did and took over. The urgency in his voice and posture had me confused. I stood obediently. He closed the doors and started the elevator upward. I watched him pull the control back to "stop" before we went more than half a floor. He turned, pulled me toward him and whispered, "Margaret." I was too surprised to react, but even in the split second before he held me I could have refused him. I didn't. I yielded to his kissing and sank into the strength of his arms. With my third invisible arm, I pushed his wife Elaine out of the scene.

Our embrace lasted less than a minute, John's apology took two minutes, and I was outside the darkened store in less than five minutes. My cheeks and neck were still vibrating from his kisses. He said he really did need some help with buying his wife a present, and he never intended to kiss me. He bid me a curt goodnight.

*   *   *

I'm not sure how I was able to drive home. The Christmas lights twinkling on people's lawns only heightened my excitement. Trying to hold the steering wheel, I relived wrapping my arms around John's strong neck.

I was barely in my house when I heard the knock. It was my octogenarian window-peeking neighbor, wrapped up in a mink coat and a woolen cap. Her breath made little clouds around her face, and she stamped her feet against the cold.

"Mrs. Eisling. What can I do for you?" I asked, half hidden

behind the door.

"I thought you should know that there was a car parked outside your house this afternoon for about twenty minutes. Pennsylvania plates. Never seen it before, but I was talking to my daughter-in-law on the phone, and she said Johnny was coming home from Korea in a month. He's been—"

"Was there a man or a woman in it?"

"Oh, it was a man, not too bad looking, maybe in his mid-thirties. It was a fairly new car, a Buick, I believe."

"Did you notice what color the car was? Did you get a license plate number?"

"It had a white roof and a pastel green body. Very handsome, I must say."

Was it the car Kathy saw a couple of months ago? "License plate?" I asked again.

"Just noticed that it was from Pennsylvania." She moved closer to the door. "Say, it's a little cold out here."

"Well you better get home. Let me know if you see it again. Call me down at Graham's, even."

"Oh I will, dear." Mrs. Eisling crooked her neck to make an unsuccessful peek beyond me into the house. "You've certainly been a stranger these days. Haven't seen you, are you okay?"

"I'm fine, Mrs. Eisling. I really need to go now. Take care." I forced a smile but closed the door just as she opened her mouth to ask another question.

I fixed myself a gin and tonic alternately thinking about Mrs. Eisling's intelligence report and John's kiss. John's kiss lost out to the second sighting of the green and white car. Who was watching me? I had seen Pete's car, and it was blue.

Pennsylvania? My only connection to Pennsylvania was Howard. Why would he come back and be sitting in his car at my house? His car was white. My insides became hot, then hollow. Was it Pete?

I headed for my chair in the den. The chintz was cool against my arms and I sank into its refuge. I tried to remember John's embrace, but it hid behind my worry over the mystery car—and other worries. Mother was getting crankier and more difficult to visit. Her pleas for my reconciliation with Howard ("I would die in peace knowing you had someone to take care of you") and her confused memory that had her talking to Father ("Now Adam, stop coddling Margaret") were driving me to the brink of death by gin. Mother always said that parents were never trained to be parents, they just did it. How circular life was. Children didn't train, either, for their parents' ebbing days.

My son wouldn't know to mourn me. The sweet baby smell came back to me, and I felt the gentle weight of his little body nestled in my arms. His breath was so soft and pure. That was the last time I experienced the nourishment of a perfect moment. I had insisted on holding him. The nurse broke the blissful spell by putting out her arms to take my baby to his new family.

I studied the Bette Davis poster and didn't see any sympathy for sentimentalism. I dried my eyes and thought about the mysterious car and its inhabitant. I picked up the phone and called a friend who is the manager at the Liberty Motel. Perhaps he could give me information about a possible guest from Pennsylvania— a risky move. A woman inquiring about a man was delicate.

"Dave, this is Margaret Landings." In the distance I could hear the soft rumbling of thunder, promising to bring a cold winter rain.

"Hey, Margaret, how are ya? How's life in the elevator?"

"Fine. Say…I was wondering if you had any guests from Pennsylvania?"

"Let's see. It's been pretty busy here."

I could hear his wheelchair squeak as he navigated closer to the guest register. I thought for sure I was on the right track.

"Yeah, I did. Checked out this morning. Why do you ask?"

"I have a friend in Pennsylvania who knew this, uh, person would be in town and she wanted me to meet him. Do you have a name?"

"Nope, he registered under the plant manager's name. He was here to check out some machines. Not a bad deal for me, company pays 'n all. Don't have to discount or nothing."

"How about the car? Did you see it?"

"You're asking a lot of questions about someone you don't

know. And no, I paid no attention to the car. Anything else, Detective Friday?"

"Very funny. Just wanted to make sure that I didn't miss him."

"Too bad you did. He was a good looking guy, but I don't think he's your man unless you're into something you shouldn't be."

"Why's that?"

"He had a wedding ring."

"Oh, he's a family friend. Thanks, Dave. Better luck next time, I guess."

"If you need some company, I'm available. A one-legged war veteran makes for a good time. Ha!"

"Oh Dave, stop it."

"Good luck finding your, what did you say, 'family friend?'"

I sat for a while, immobilized by failed efforts to find out anything about the owner of the green and white car. I hadn't eaten yet, so I went to the kitchen, and threw out the weakened gin and tonic. I poured myself some cereal and settled in front of the television for some distraction. I tuned to *The Honeymooners*, a show that I hoped would chase away my doldrums. I liked how Ralph would routinely threaten to send Alice to the moon in the middle of each episode but by the end he realized she was the greatest. I envied Alice. I would take a devoted bus driver, maybe minus the anger— just like the Gershwin song, "Someone to Watch Over Me," even a Ralph Kramden.

The doorbell rang. Oh, come on, Mrs. Eisling, leave me alone.

Through the peephole I saw a slightly shame-faced Howard who stood, or rather, fidgeted, in the glow of the porch light. He had no hat and was rubbing his hands against the cold. He glanced up when thunder rolled again.

Criminy jeez. I opened the door.

"Well, I'm not putrefying in a ditch anywhere yet, so I thought I'd come to apologize."

His self-effacing humor disarmed me. "You're awfully brave to confront a woman who wanted you dead."

Howard grimaced and shifted some more on his feet.

"Would you like to come in?"

Relief washed over his face, and he entered. We were both careful not to touch, although it took a little body maneuvering to avoid brushing against each other. I feared, and perhaps Howard did too, the slightest touch of even cloth against cloth would elicit a torrent of confusing and conflicting feelings. Was this really happening the second time today?

I led him to the sofa and offered him some coffee.

"Coffee? Sure."

I took a deep breath and asked, "I'm going to have a gin and tonic, do you mind?"

He frowned.

"Yes," I confessed. "The only time I didn't drink was when I was with you. You told me it was against your religion."

"Oh, it's not against my religion, it's against tradition and appearances." He hesitated. "I kind of wished I had known that you liked gin and tonics. That might have explained, or changed, some things."

I should have let his remark pass. Maybe Detective Friday was onto something. "Just the facts, ma'am" could have been a useful way to live.

"What do you mean 'that might have changed things?'"

"I'm only a public teetotaler. I thought you were the one who didn't drink. And by the way, I'll have a gin and tonic also."

"How can you live two lives like that?" I asked and went to the kitchen without waiting for a response.

When I came back to the living room, drinks in hand, I saw that he was reading the *Look* magazine with Bob Hope and Bette Davis on the cover.

"Still taken with Bette Davis, huh?" Howard thumbed through the magazine to the article about the movie *All About Eve*. He continued, "You kept this from four years ago? You're incurable."

I gave my best Bette Davis swoop. I almost forgot I was mad at him.

He sighed. "I did love sitting with you in the theater watching reruns of that movie. I think you got lost in the glamour of the theater. Do you think there's a part of you that wants to be an actress?"

I stared into a corner of the room, using the nothingness to consider what he asked. No one had ever asked me that before, and I had never thought of it myself. I had always envied actors and actresses and their facility with trying on different personalities, convincing an audience to see what the actors wanted them to see and feel. The closest I came to stardom was in my parents' living room, pretending to be at the Oscars. I turned my attention back to Howard.

"So, it's kind of late and kind of far from Pittsburgh. You're not in town praying with my mother again, are you?"

"Hardly, although she called me a couple of times."

"She has?" I wanted to drive to the nursing home and shake her.

"But that's not why I'm here."

"So tell me."

"I've been thinking a lot about our conversation in Pittsburgh, you know, in the restaurant. And when I received your letter, or rather your story, I..." He shook his head at me. "Talk about being stabbed. After I got over the shock, I kind of liked the story, but it was confusing. I'm not sure you know what you want."

"You're sounding like a pastor."

"Not fair. You caused me a lot of pain. You blindsided me and—"

"I caused *you* pain?" I shot him a look of utter disbelief.

"Yes, of course, it must have been upsetting that I took off like I did, and I'm truly sorry. Your news just came out of nowhere, and I reacted out of, well, I'm not sure."

"Your proposal came out of nowhere too. How about warning a lady?" I folded my arms.

"When all's said and done, we do, or did, have affection for each other, and I was not understanding of what must have been a very difficult time for you." Howard was fidgeting, looking at me, away from me, wringing his hands. His chest rose and fell heavily. I had never seen him so sad, so vulnerable. So unminister like.

I took a deep breath and exhaled.

He sat forward in his chair. "I drove around Liberty all afternoon. I was trying to decide whether to come here."

I walked to the window and saw a green and white car, lit by the street light.

"Did you get a new car?" I asked without turning.

"Yes. Do you like it?"

"Do you smoke?"

"Heavens no. At least not in public—"

"Like alcohol?"

"Come on. I try it once in a while just to prove to myself that I have the freedom of choice in spite of what my collar says I should do. And sometimes in a lot of stress when prayer doesn't help, nicotine does. Do I have to talk to your back and why are you looking at my car?"

Facing him I asked, "You were here this afternoon, weren't you?"

Howard hung his head. "Yes, until one of your neighbors stared out the window at me, then I got a little uncomfortable and drove away. It was part of my 'should I see Margaret or not' inner conversation." He tilted his head toward me. "Kind of junior high, huh? A neighbor must have told you."

"Did you park here a couple of months ago and drop cigarettes on the ground?"

"I may be smitten and juvenile, but I don't litter, Margaret."

It couldn't have been Howard. I had never known him to lie.

"Two cars looking the same, parked in my driveway sure is a coincidence."

"It wasn't me." Howard sat back in the sofa, took a long drink of his now iceless gin and tonic. "So, can we get back to why I am here?"

"Which is?"

"Can we start over? You've seen my bad side, a side I'm not proud of, and I've seen your struggle, which I didn't appreciate at first, so we'd be starting off with more truth than fantasy. I know you like me, maybe even have or had some affection for me. I don't want to let go."

John, now Howard. I couldn't believe it. The rain pelted against the windows, and for a moment I considered whether we would have an ice storm that night.

"You seemed to let go pretty well. I didn't hear from you

before or after I moved."

"I needed time to think about what really mattered and I decided it's not appearances. What really matters to me is courage, and a little fun," he added. "How does that song go about the great pretender? I was pretending to be a minister and a loving boyfriend, and I thought I knew what that meant. I figured out I wasn't pretending the right stuff."

I could hear my watch ticking. John's kisses merged with memories of Howard's kisses. John's were more recent, still palpable on my skin, but Howard was saying the right words.

"Howard, can we just be friends for a while? Life is so confusing now. I'm losing my mother, and I miss Pittsburgh. I feel I've compromised my ambitions, and I still wonder about my son." I felt my eyes sting and my nose drip, which I wiped with the back of my hand. Howard handed me his handkerchief.

"I was going to get defensive about the 'let's be friends' part. Listening to your grief about so many things, I'll be your friend, if you need it."

I put my hand on top of his and scanned his face for sincerity. "Yes, I need a friend."

Howard withdrew his hand and stood up. "I need to go. I have to drive back to Pittsburgh tonight, and the weather doesn't sound so good. Can't miss out on the Advent week activities."

He gave me a friend's peck on the cheek and let himself out the door. When he ran through the cold rain and got into his car, I turned off the porch light but stood watching him out the window. He sat there, not starting his car. The glass in the car began to fog, but I saw the glow of a lit cigarette. He rolled down the window and threw something out. He put his car in gear and noiselessly moved into the darkness. I saw a smoldering cigarette on the lawn.

21

The snow was ever present. The winter passed as only winters in Ohio do—slowly, chillingly, and with heavy gray skies. The boy and his father didn't come into the store after Christmas, and they gradually lessened in my consciousness. Mother was still hanging on, and *Mrs*. Beals died just after New Year's. I didn't have her anymore as an unwitting ally—hassling Mr. Beals to retire so I could have his job. In fact, Mr. Beals' cheeks grew rosier with each snowy day.

The green and white car hadn't made another appearance, but I was still cautious about going to the employees' lounge. That floor had the carpet department—Pete's territory—but I heard Mr. Concord tell a customer that the carpet salesman was over occupied with business in other towns.

Howard called about once a week. He would inquire about Mother's health and actually asked me about my writing. I kept the topics of my stories to myself. He had already demonstrated his inability to handle clandestine children, so tawdry romance stories would probably have silenced his calls forever. I wasn't ready to give them up.

Our short conversations would usually end with his "Gotta go. Just been thinking about you." I'd hang up feeling emptier than before he called.

In Pittsburgh, before my baby confession, he used to greet me with "How's my green-eyed beauty?" Arm-in-arm we entered theatres, restaurants, even church picnics, which I tolerated just to be with him.

I didn't mind the elderly ladies cooing over me, and I didn't balk at eating the greasy casseroles, all made in some fashion with Campbell's mushroom soup. It was the constant praying and praise-filled language that made me uncomfortable. "Pastor Howard is so fortunate to have met you. Praise be," said one elderly lady in a flowered chiffon shirtwaist, buttoned up to her neck. "We've been praying that Pastor Howard would find someone like you. If it's God's will, there'll be a wedding next year," said another woman who was bouncing a baby on her hip. "Then you'll have one of these." She kissed her child on its cherubic cheek whereupon he or she (no identifying dress) vomited, missing me by just a few inches, praise be.

As for John, we settled into a routine of stolen kisses in the elevator. They were just enough to "shake the vitals" as Mother used to say, enough to give us something to wink and giggle about. His marriage made him unavailable, and that was fine with me. We were innocent entertainment for each other.

*   *   *

I opened a post office box for any replies to Lydia Bailey, a.k.a. Margaret Landings, and checked its contents once a week. Each time I put the key into the brass keyhole, I hesitated. I tried to picture a letter sitting there, forming a hypotenuse to the right angles of the box. I walked away empty-handed each week.

In April, when nature was teasing us with chirping robins and warm sunshine, I checked the post office box every day the post office was open. On the seventh day (even God rested on the seventh day) I swung open the solid little door again and had to blink. There was a letter—positioned exactly as I had imagined.

I grabbed the envelope, and I thought I might faint. I ripped it open and out fell a check from between the folds of a letter. I picked up a remittance for $25, whose amount didn't excite me as much as its symbolism of my writing's worth. In the pay-to window was Margaret Landings a.k.a. Lydia Bailey. "Dear Miss Landings" the letter began. Oblivious to anything that was going on around me, I read the editor's acceptance of my Santa story, which would be published in June. Published!

I twirled and held the letter to my breast and caught the eye of the postmaster Mr. Warner.

"You seem pretty excited," he said, tilting his head. "Are you receiving love letters on the sly, *Lydia?*"

I came down from my mountain peak of headiness. "Oh, nothing like that. Just a response to a foreign pen pal I have."

"Must be some pen pal," he muttered, and he went back to work.

I wanted to run to the front steps of the post office and wave the letter to all who passed by. I couldn't tell my mother, she would want to read the story. I couldn't tell Lena, she was the subject. I couldn't include Adele or Kathy yet. I was trapped in my own private world of celebration.

I went home and celebrated alone with a congratulatory gin and tonic. I sat in my chintz chair, the scene of my writing revelations, and stewed about my dilemma. My drink was not enough company, and I realized that writing under a pseudonym had its drawbacks. I was just an elevator operator—the silent statue that bade the elevator to go where the customer needed, the sentinel that said little and heard much.

But the dramas I witnessed each day on the elevator were too rich not to use, and I learned to mine the gems of gossip. Ordinary worlds sat flat on paper, but the worlds of the complicated and coarse sprang from the pages I wrote—all fed from the mouths and actions of people I transported from floor to floor.

* * *

With check in hand, I walked into the bank the next day and scanned the barred windows for Lucy, the most unassuming and boring cashier in the establishment. Lucy was safe—business-like and so principled, she never let herself pay attention to the who or what of any transaction. I handed her the royalty check, and she proceeded to take, stamp, and drawer my deposit. I examined the receipt with a mixture of regret and joy. I was an anonymous author of a story about to be nationally published, albeit in a romance magazine.

There was just enough time to go to the Curl Up and Dye Salon to have my nails done.

"Bette Davis red, again?" asked the manicurist, popping and snapping her gum.

As she soaked my nails I heard several ladies dissecting the current issue of *Forbidden Love*. The salon was littered with that magazine and others of questionable repute, as my mother would say.

"What did you think of the story about the woman who had an affair with the local bank president?" asked one customer in the row of beauty chairs, each occupant in a different state of having her hair cut, styled, or permed.

"You mean the one about the community leader who was upright in matters of business but sneaky in affairs of the heart?" answered the lady with perm curlers. Several customers giggled.

"I swear that sounds like Mr. Hood, don't you?"

I jumped when I heard the voice of Harriet Gibbons.

"I mean…large bank, bald head, and a penchant for blonds?" she continued. The ladies nodded in the affirmative as well as they could, given their inhibited states under dryers or at the mercy of scissors.

"There are so many things in this story that sound like Liberty," Harriet continued. "And the affair is pretty darn close to, you know, what really happens here."

Another patron was under a dome of hot air, but her eagle hearing overcame the turbulence to catch the word "affair" in the string of muffled speech. She raised the bulbous dryer head, leaned forward to Harriet and added, "If you ask me, the blond has to be…" The commotion in the salon came to a standstill, and she faced the twenty eyeballs directed her way. Indecision crossed her face, and the gossiper disappeared under her dryer.

Careful not to move my hands that were under the polishing brush of my manicurist, I leaned in more closely to the group of women.

"It's almost like there's a spy in our town, watching us."

"Do you think?" asked one.

"Who would do that?" Harriet shook her head.

"Mrs. Gibbons, please be still," said the hairdresser. "I almost poked your ear with the pointed end of the comb."

"That's what I'd like to do to the hussy who's writing these stories," Donna said. "It's fun reading, but gosh, if it's at the expense of real people, I don't know."

The line of semi-coifed ladies murmured their agreement.

When my nails were dry, I mustered courage to take one of the magazines. "Let me see what you ladies are talking about," I managed to say with nonchalance. The story, "The Banker and the Blond," was about opening safes all right—the blond's. And the ladies under the hoods were right. There was a remarkable likeness to the town of Liberty and to Mr. Hood. The author was Kaye Langley, a name that didn't mean anything to me.

*   *   *

A few days later I received a proof copy of the June issue. There, on the cover, was the feature story, emblazoned in red: "Seduced by a Summer Santa, by Lydia Bailey." On the cover. I could scarcely breathe. If I could have wallpapered my living room with the magazine, I would have.

I took the magazine proof into my den and sat down to savor the moment. I caressed the paper as though it were my child. With my finger I traced the letters that spelled out "Lydia Bailey," and in my mind the letters changed into Margaret Landings. I opened the magazine and slowly turned the page to the table of contents. Page ten. My story has a home—page ten. Ignoring the other content, I opened the page and gasped. The illustration of Santa and Louise was dead on—there was no doubt that the main character of the story was Lena. I had described her too well, and the artist had followed my lead. My hands and feet turned to ice. "Oh, this is bad, really bad," I said to no one. One person who could identify Lydia Bailey was Lena, the woman who stared back at me from page ten.

*   *   *

My worry grew each day that the publication of my story came closer. Were people going to know the story was about Lena? April came and went with its rain. May dragged on in spite of the heady lilacs and the manic yellow daffodils that almost made me forget that I was about to expose Lena and her pretend lover to the world. The canaries, caged and singing on top of the displays as they were every spring, mocked me with their shrill cries: "We know-ee, we know-ee, we know-ee."

My anxiety wasn't enough to keep me from writing—my publishing success was a drug that compelled me to try again. I submitted another story to *Forbidden Love*. The idea for this one came from John's rejection at the country club dance— "I Left Him on the Dance Floor, and She Waltzed into His Life." With that story I took special care to describe the characters as opposite as I could from John and his wife Elaine. My protagonist didn't have John's football captain's grin but a Navy officer's firm jaw. Elaine wasn't an alcoholic but a shrewish accountant's wife. I felt a little guilty, given that John and I dove into each other's arms when the elevator afforded some privacy, but aren't writers supposed to write what they know?

On the last day of May, I went up to the employees' lounge to eat my lunch, and a flash of red caught my eye—there on the table was the June copy of *Forbidden Love*. Lydia Bailey's story screamed its presence on the cover. I was stunned—and confused. *Forbidden Love* had never been one of the magazines that people brought to the lounge. Never had I had such conflicting emotions—pride at seeing my magazine article on a coffee table and fear that people in Liberty would recognize Lena and trace the story back to me. I couldn't bear being judged as cruel to an innocent, well-known person like Lena. I would embarrass my mother. And Lena—I wouldn't want to be in her shoes.

Guilt thrust its accusing finger into me. "Do unto others" re-emerged from a long ago Sunday school lesson and bore into my Presbyterian conscience. An apparition of Mrs. Watkins, my church teacher, appeared to me, her finger pointing at us and asking if we liked being made fun of. We gave emphatic "no's" as only six-year-olds could do. We promised her we would never, ever make fun of our friends.

But I had an immediate problem—getting rid of the magazine. I didn't want Lena's countenance in the hands of Graham's employees. I looked around the room to see if there was a bag I could put it in so I could take it with me. There weren't any so I grabbed the magazine and hid it under a cushion of the sofa. I planned to come back for it later.

I returned to my elevator station and watched to see if anyone treated me differently. John smiled and winked at me as he left the elevator and headed toward the office. Beals walked by with a sign for the front window, and he gave me a little wink too. Mrs. Remington was whistling and dusting her glass cases, her flabby upper arms quivering with each swipe of her dust cloth. I looked from person to person but saw no evidence of anything out of the ordinary.

"Hi, Margaret." Lena smiled at me from the pile of men's shirts she was arranging. Strange, she was being nice to me.

I gave a weak smile and scrutinized her face for any sign of accusation or judgment. Nothing.

Someone on the second floor buzzed for a ride—it was Mrs. Gibbons.

"Hello, dear." Mrs. Gibbons was, I thought, being a little too friendly. Her smile was big and her gait a little too springy.

"How are you today?"

"I needed a dress for a wedding. Found one, but you wouldn't believe what I saw in one of the dressing rooms." Her eyebrows arched in anticipation of a query.

"And what was that, Mrs. Gibbons?" I pictured underwear or a torn dress put back on the hanger.

"Someone left one of those trashy magazines in there… *Forbidden Love*."

That hollow feeling struck my chest again. "Did you see which issue it was?"

"The issue doesn't matter…I would be too embarrassed to open its pages. I hate seeing those kinds of magazines at the beauty shop. Hope someone doesn't think I left it in there. I gave it to one of the clerks to throw away." With her gloved hand she mimicked tossing something disgusting into the trash.

"That was probably the right thing to do," I said.

I opened the doors on the first floor, and Mrs. Gibbons stepped out. She turned back and said, "I hope you don't read that kind of thing, dear." She walked away. She may as well have told me that my slip was showing again. But this time it was Margaret Landings making her literary debut as Lydia Bailey.

Ambling toward me was another nemesis of my life—Pete. He walked to the stairs, hesitated, and came onto the elevator.

"Margaret." He cleared his throat.

"Pete," I said, looking straight ahead. "Third floor?"

"Yes, thank you." Where was the usual sneering Pete?

When my break time came, I hurried to the employees' lounge to get rid of the magazine under the sofa cushion. I pretended to be fixing my hair until the notions clerk left, but Mrs. Remington came in.

"I hope I won't bother you. I'm going to do a little reading on my break." She waved her copy of *Marjorie Morningstar*. "I'm reading the best book., can't get enough of it. Dashed dreams, ambition." Mrs. Remington stopped. "I'm sorry, dear, I'm rambling. I'll just sit down here."

Mrs. Remington sat atop the cushion that was hiding *Forbidden Love*. Her bottom and my story would stay united until her break was over.

"I need to get back now," I said. "Enjoy your book."

Mrs. Remington's eyes were glued to the novel, and her brain had already locked onto Marjorie Morningstar's life. Ambition and dashed dreams, indeed.

It was two more hours before I could have another break. I glanced at the clock hanging between the two windows—1:15. At 3:15 I was able to get John to take the elevator for me.

He stopped between floors, grinned and put out his arms for his daily stolen kiss.

"Not now, John, I…I'm kind of in a hurry, if you get what I mean." He got it and started up again for the third floor.

"Tomorrow?" He pouted like a boy who expected a root beer and got a pat on the head instead.

Mrs. Remington was gone, and the lounge was empty. I dove

to the sofa. I reached under the cushion and expected to grab the edges of the magazine only to feel—nothing. I pulled up all the cushions. All I found were crumbs and a few coins. I was a mouse, being toyed with by a noxious cat.

I sank to the sofa and put my head in my hands as though holding my head would replace the reality I was living. My writing dream had become a nightmare.

"I'm helping empty the trash today," I later said to the dress saleslady. "Things are a little slow on the elevator." She expressed her relief since she had to leave work right at closing, and I made a fool of myself emptying trash in the dress department, including the restroom, to no avail.

The last two hours of work was a blur of elevator beeps, landings and take-offs from four different floors. I was an automaton, willing my body to do its job while my mind scoured any possible explanation for the missing magazine, or magazines. Time crawled by on clock hands that could barely tick off a second.

Closing time, finally. In the cloak room, I put on my coat and touched something large rolled up in my pocket. The message that traveled from my hand to my brain said, "magazine." I pulled it out and to my horror saw the June issue of *Forbidden Love*. Beads of sweat popped out on my forehead. I immediately rolled it back up and put it up in my left sleeve. I looked around at the people coming and going in the cloakroom, and no one's behavior was any different than before. The smiles, the goodbyes, the end-of-day chatter seemed normal.

With an arm splinted by *Forbidden Love*, I half walked, half scurried to the back door.

22

I parked in front of the hospital. Mother's condition had forced her return. I climbed each stone step, all fifteen of them. I had memorized them by now. They sagged in the middle from years of visitors' feet plodding their way to sick patients or newborn babies. The third step had a brown stain from iron ore leaching through the stone. Its shape always triggered a memory of that fateful party so many years ago—it had a lion configuration like the fraternity crest. If no one were coming down the steps, I would avoid the stain by walking up the left side of the stairs. The tenth step had a large chip on the edge that I learned to steer clear of on my way down. I had a near miss once when my heel caught on the rough edge. Now it was my life that had a chip in it and that chip was about to become a chunk.

I needed mother comfort. If I could withstand her initial blast of disappointment, I could count on Mother loving me in spite of anything I did. When I lost the seventh grade spelling bee that I obstinately didn't prepare for, Mother made me hot chocolate and we talked about how to get ready for next year's contest. When Roddy dumped me for an ugly, rude rich girl, Mother and I went to the downtown drugstore and shared a Belly Buster hot fudge sundae. But authoring a story that made fun of a well-known Liberty citizen put me beyond the loving arms of my mother. The Landings were proper. The Landings were prominent. The Landings were private (the three P's of small town stature). I would be the talk of the town for being the errant child of "good parents." And I was an adult, not a child doing childish things.

When I reached Mother's floor, I heard a child's soft crying before I reached her room. I leaned toward the sound and through a door saw a young boy with ice packs on his throat and a blood transfusion bag with a tube of red snaking to his arm. It was Bobby, the young boy in the elevator last Christmas. His father recognized me and waved me in. He motioned for me to stand next to his son's bed.

"Bobby, remember the nice lady in the elevator last Christmas?"

The boy raised pitiful brown eyes to mine and swallowed a small sob. "H-h-hi." He put his young hands on his throat and cried again. His eyes grew big with the pain and realization that talking as well as crying was going to make the soreness worse. His cheeks had a feverish red shine.

"Tonsils? I had my tonsils out too. You get lots of ice cream and Jell-O…that makes your throat feel so much better."

Still holding his throat, Bobby pointed to the empty Jell-O cup beside his bed.

"How have you been?" his father asked. "Our son talked about you for days after we were in Graham's. He was so impressed you knew so much about trains."

"How sweet," I said. "Trains are fun to talk about. And your name?"

"I'm sorry. I'm Trent Taylor, Bobby's father. We had just moved here from Pennsylvania when we met you on the elevator." He motioned toward the door. "Bobby's mother stepped out for a moment."

Pennsylvania? "What color car do you have?"

"Excuse me?" Mr. Taylor looked perplexed. "Oh wait, I forgot this is Ohio State country, and I hear everyone wears, drives, or thinks in scarlet and gray. I'm afraid I don't have a red car yet, it's blue." He leaned over and whispered, "For Penn State, you know."

"Of course." I gave Bobby a sympathetic smile and felt a momentary ache for the want of a child like him.

"I'm on my way to see my mother, she's down the hall. You'd think the hospital would have a separate area for children so they wouldn't have to listen to old people complain."

"It's probably the other way around, don't you think? Actually, Bobby had some complications after his tonsillectomy so he's in this extra-care wing of the hospital. Your mother's here too?"

"Yes, heart problems. Believe me, a young child is easier to deal with than an aging parent." I patted the bed beside Bobby's arm. "You'll feel much better in a couple of days."

I waved goodbye to Bobby. Something was familiar but not recognizable about him—maybe I just wanted it to be so.

I entered Mother's room to see Adele and my mother chuckling, as much as Mother could giggle in her weakened condition. Adele was reading something to her—from a magazine—it was the June issue of *Forbidden Love*. The sight punched me in the stomach.

Adele saw me and motioned for me to enter. "You've got to join us, Margaret. I'm reading this hysterical story to your mother about a woman's affair with Santa." She brandished the magazine toward me. "Who in the world thinks up these things?" She pulled the magazine back and read aloud. "'Do you have any toys for Santa in there?'" Adele giggled, and my mother grinned. "And get this…the illustrator drew someone who looks like the woman in Graham's menswear department—it sounds like a Liberty affair to me."

I couldn't breathe. "Why do you have a copy of that magazine?"

"I get them from the newsstand. It's great entertainment for my patients."

I looked at Adele, then Mother.

"Someone named 'Lydia Bailey' wrote it," Adele said. "Never heard of her. Not great writing, but it is a funny story. I guess that's what these magazines are all about."

All I heard was "Not great writing."

"I hope the lady at Graham's doesn't see this." Mother took in more air. "She would be so humiliated."

A thundercloud of emotion opened and dumped on me. The story I wrote with glee I then regretted with everything I had. I bolted out of the room, the image of a delighted Adele holding up the magazine searing my brain.

I went to the end of the hall where a small alcove gave me some cover, and the thunderbolts crashed. Like an overwrought actress, I put my face in my hands and cried. I squeezed my eyes shut, and I felt my mouth open and contort into a silent wail. Lena would hate me. Nobody would trust me. I was stupid, stupid, stupid.

I heard a soft step behind me.

"Margaret, what is wrong? You were white as chalk when you ran out of the room."

Adele put her hand on my shoulder.

I started crying for real this time, with real cry sounds and tears. My nose started running, and I had no tissues.

"Here."

I saw a manicured hand reach around me and give me a Kleenex. I turned and buried myself in Adele's arms, and I started blubbering onto her shoulder, the inadequate tissue between us.

"Adele, I'm so stupid. I thought I was being so clever. I can't believe what I've done. Someone is going to tell on me."

"Wait, hold on a sec. Slow down. What are you talking about, what do you mean 'tell on me?'"

She patted my back while my nose dripped onto her. I could smell her Lily of the Valley perfume, and I saw rings of wetness that my running nose made on her uniform.

I pulled myself away. "Adele, can you keep a secret? I need a friend. I need a real friend. I've made a real mess of things." I held onto her forearms so she could not get away or refuse.

"Of course, Margaret, you can count on me. I would be honored…really."

Her cheerleader smile was gone and all I saw was a compassionate and accepting person—someone who would not put me high on a pedestal or bury me with condescension.

I paused for courage. "I write these stories about the customers and clerks at Graham's to fill time." I took a deep breath. "I actually sold the story but I can't tell anyone… and the magazine is everywhere…what if people find out I'm the author… Lena will hate me, I didn't mean for the illustration to look like her… my mother will be so ashamed. How could such a fun idea become so ugly?"

Adele stood there in silence. A thousand seconds went by. Finally she said, "You wrote that story?"

"Y…yes."

She tried to hide her surprise. She opened her mouth, closed it. Opened her mouth again, "Goodness, you do need a friend. I mean, it's very entertaining, but…"

She smiled and squeezed my hands, and I appreciated her calm acceptance of my rambled craziness. She glanced at her watch and said, "I'm off duty in twenty minutes. Let's get a drink. Fate has brought you to the right person."

Adele laughed a little when she saw my puzzlement.

"I'll tell you over drinks at my house. I hope you like gin and tonic."

* * *

"I almost lost my previous job because of an employee newsletter that I helped write."

Adele went over to the bar, an array of carafes and liquor bottles on a silver tray. The ice bucket and an ice tapper sat ready. There were glasses for all sorts of drinks, arranged by height required of the cocktail—tall glasses for highballs, shorter glasses for Manhattans, tiny glasses for powerful liqueurs. I could see Adele had special glasses for gin and tonics—tall glasses with superimposed turquoise and gold triangles.

I sat still, waiting for both my drink and the rest of Adele's story.

"What my co-conspirator and I thought was humorous was highly offensive to many of the staff." She donned her apron, inscribed with "Hooray, one more job to do and it's gin and tonic time," and set out a lime on a little wooden cutting tray. "Most embarrassing was the column on hobbies people secretly had. One woman did not find the revelation of her pole dancing to be very funny. And worse, we had to make a public apology as well as a private one to the pole dancer."

"You're kidding."

"I mean, we all do things we regret later, I guess."

She proceeded to make our drinks. She took the ice prongs and put ice in her hand, then used the ice tapper to crack the ice into smaller pieces. The solid round head of the ice tapper whipped back and forth on its aluminum handle. Watching the destruction of the ice made me wish I could do the same to my story... crack it into bits and put it in a glass to melt away.

"So I'm not the only one to make a public fool of myself."

My chest loosened a bit.

Adele dropped the mangled ice into the gold and turquoise tumblers. I loved hearing the tinkle of ice falling into a glass—it was the sound of a promise, a promise of deadening the sharpness of reality.

Next she measured the gin in the shot glass, poured, hesitated then poured in an extra slurp.

"Careful, Adele, I have to see to drive home."

"It's just a little girlfriend adjustment."

We clinked our glasses together, and I took a sip. The gin began its magic loosening. Maybe there was life after doing stupid.

"What was it like working there after all that happened?" I asked.

"The timing was good. I never really did feel at home in Columbus. It was too big, and I missed Liberty."

"I'm the opposite. I loved Pittsburgh. It opened my eyes to, shall we say, the tapestry of life. There are people of different colors, nationalities, and interests. Gingham is about as exciting as Liberty gets."

"You bring up a good point. We all have our destinies."

"I've screwed mine up, that's for sure." I took another sip.

"Is it possible you are giving yourself too much credit?" Adele lit a cigarette, offered me one, which I refused. She blew a puff of smoke up toward the ceiling.

"I'm never going to write again."

"Are you giving up because you wrote a tawdry story that people may recognize as the local men's underwear saleslady?" She picked a piece of tobacco off her tongue. "So, what would your heroine Bette Davis do in this situation?"

"Maybe you're right. The town be damned."

"What's that line you quote all the time from your favorite movie? Something about peanuts and better days?" She handed me a dish of peanuts that was sitting on the bar. We clinked our cocktail glasses again.

"Let's come back to the word 'tawdry' to describe my story," I said.

"I didn't mean to insinuate that romance writing is bad." She crushed out her cigarette in a porcelain ashtray with painted roses and a wren. I watched the ash spread over the bird's beak. "It's not *Guideposts* or *Look* magazine, but it's entertaining to a lot of people. You just didn't cover your tracks very well."

"No kidding," I said.

"Your story was based on very real people and events. Changing the names wasn't enough." Adele took a non-too-gentle sip from her own drink. "You've made me wonder what it would be like to write medical stories, inspired by what I see. But, I'd have to be very careful about patient privacy. I'd have to take a disease, for instance, and give it to someone of another gender, description, place...I dunno." She waved her manicured hand in the air. "It would be hard. I wouldn't know where to draw the line. Certainly other authors base their stories on real life events. Wouldn't that make a great television show, 'Ripped From the Headlines?'"

"Doesn't sound like something people would watch, at least I wouldn't." Adele didn't even hear me. She had a faraway look as though she were already accepting her Emmy award.

"For instance, there is an interesting case at the hospital of a young boy who had his tonsils out. He needed a blood transfusion—the poor little guy started to hemorrhage—but the parents didn't match his blood. They were very embarrassed. Turns out he was adopted. They didn't want to tell us, and they didn't want the little boy to know either. Doesn't that make for a good story?"

The earth's rotation screeched to a halt. "He was adopted? Was his name Bobby?"

"Why do you ask?"

"He was in the room a couple of doors down from Mother's. I've seen him and his father in the store, and the father invited me in to see him. Aren't they from Pennsylvania?"

She grimaced. "I've already said too much. See how easy it is to get in trouble?"

I put down my drink and sat next to Adele on the sofa. "Please, you've got to tell me." I took her hands.

"What's this all about?"

"There's something else I need to share with you. I gave a baby up for adoption, ten years ago."

Adele stared at me as though I had gone crazy.

"You? Does anyone in Liberty know?"

"They shouldn't. My parents insisted I tell no one. They would have been mortified if it were to become Liberty news. And I actually met someone and was beginning to fall in love, but he backed off when he heard about the baby. I wasn't pure enough, I guess. He's come back in the picture, kind of, after thinking about what a jerk he was."

Adele's eyes widened and her jaw dropped with each detail I revealed. I got up from the sofa, circled the living room, and sat back down.

"Oh, you poor thing." She squeezed my hands. "Your parents put an incredible burden on you. Having an out-of-wedlock baby isn't so unusual. I have seen both sides of that giving and taking, and it's really, really hard for everyone."

"Especially for the Landings."

Adele shook her head. "Have you had any contact with the father?"

"No, it's so embarrassing. His name was Charles. I was so drunk, feeling so rebellious. I never tried to find him or tell him. I dropped out of school at the end of the quarter."

Adele sat back on the sofa.

"You've got to help me. What if Bobby is my son? He's the right age. I've seen him at Graham's and I felt a really strong connection. Can you find out his birthday? Where he was born? What if—"

Adele held up her hand. "Wait a minute. I understand your need to find out, but I think you're asking me to do something unprofessional. Remember, I've already been through that."

I stood up and paced in front of her. "Please, you have access to his chart, couldn't you please find out? It would mean so much to me."

Adele tapped her teeth with her pen. "I see his chart every day, but to divulge confidential information—"

"Please?"

"I could get fired." She gave me a warning look. "I don't want to risk that."

"No, I don't want you to risk your job." I sat back in the sofa.

"Not to change the subject, but you are carrying around some pretty heavy secrets. Maybe you should let your mother know about Howard's betrayal. You did the right thing to tell him. Tell your mother and get that guilt off you."

"When she's so sick?"

"Her body's sick, not her love. Just don't ask me to do something unprofessional. I've been down that road."

23

A few days later I stood at the door of Mother's hospital room. The bed was empty. The oxygen curtain stood like an accordion at the end of the bed, and smooth sheets graced the mattress.

"Hello, dear."

I turned to the left and saw Mother sitting in a chair upholstered in orange vinyl. Someone had combed her soft white hair into a semblance of a hairdo, and she had a dab of lipstick on her thin lips. The sunshine came through the window and illuminated her face like a Rembrandt painting. She wore a second hospital gown as a bathrobe, and pink fuzzy slippers covered her gnarled feet.

"I tried to die last night."

I sat in the chair next to hers. "You tried to die?"

"I've had enough of this rubbish. I told myself not to wake up…it's time to be with your father. I evidently don't have much influence—I woke up this morning feeling better. The doctor had ordered some new medicine for me, and those damn nuns keep praying for me." She paused, but her breathing wasn't as labored as usual. "That nice nurse Adele gave me a bath and helped me into the chair. So here I am."

I took my mother's hands, and they were warm and pink, not cool and bluish like they had been. "I'm glad you didn't have the power to make yourself die, and I'm glad the nuns *are* praying for you."

My mother's resurrection stunned me. What about my plan to tell her what really happened between Howard and me? Confessions are supposed to take place in the dark with whispers and tears, and I had pictured telling her about Howard's retracted proposal in the dimness of a hospital room. But the sun was streaming through the windows, and my mother was alert. I didn't think I could tell her while looking into her bright eyes and very alive face.

We sat there for a few moments without saying a word. Mother closed her eyes, and she smiled contentedly, her face tilted upwards to take in the warmth of the sun. Her kind grey eyes opened and gazed straight into mine.

"You know, dear. Someday the nuns may be remiss and forget to pray for me, and I'll get my wish. Is there anything we need to talk about? Every time you visit me, you act as though you want to say something and then you don't. What was it your father used to say, 'Make hay while the sun shines?' Well, the sun is shining." She stopped. "What have you been trying to tell me? It can't be that bad."

A deer in the headlights—that's how I must have appeared to her.

She patted my hand. "You can't shock me with anything," she said. "Remember, your father rescued me from that speakeasy on High Street. I'd have had a much different life if he hadn't seen the sweet Presbyterian underneath the flashy flapper costume."

I shook my head. "You tell me about those days, but I can't picture you in short beaded dresses doing the Charleston."

"We all have pasts that don't line up with what people see in us."

I saw an opening and took a deep breath. "Mother, I do have something to tell you."

"I know. You're the author of that steamy story everyone is reading." She sat there looking self-satisfied.

"How did you know?"

"How do you think? Who's the biggest gossip in town?"

"Mrs. Gibbons?"

"You better believe it. She beat a path to my hospital room under the pretense of bringing me some cookies—cookies for someone in an oxygen tent and barely able to eat? Good grief. That poor woman wants so much to be important."

The snake, Mrs. Gibbons, had coiled and struck again. "When did this happen?"

Mother shifted in the chair a little and settled back for the rest of the story. "Yesterday. She claims she saw the magazine at the beauty shop, but the one she showed me had an address label—addressed to her. Does she think I'm dumb? But anyway, it was the illustration of 'Louise' that gave it away, as well as the yearly Santa ritual that everyone knows about." Mother was getting visibly tired and short of breath again. Her color paled a little.

"But…how was the connection made to me?"

"Mrs. Gibbons took the magazine to Lena, who told her that you were writing under the name of Lydia Bailey."

I sat back to take it all in. So Pandora's Box had been opened by the snake herself. How many other people would know, and how soon?

"I feel really badly for Lena," I said. "I didn't mean for her to be so easily recognized in the story." I searched my mother's face for the emotional support I needed. "There's more."

Mother took my hand and patted it. "Poor Margaret. Life's lessons are hard, aren't they?"

I pulled my hand away and sat back. "What lesson do you think this is?"

"The lesson is more yours to know than mine." Mother took a deep breath. "That's enough for today, don't you think? What's done is done." She closed her eyes a few moments. "Could you get the nurse to put me back to bed, dear?"

"Can't we talk some more?"

"I'm tired, Margaret. It can wait."

"You don't mind that I write stories like that?"

"Just be more discreet, dear. Now please get me the nurse." She closed her eyes a moment. She opened them again and said, "You write a good story, it was very funny, but do watch those dangling participles. I'm surprised they got past the editor." She closed her eyes and was snoring in a few seconds.

Half of a confession—that's all I accomplished. But my mother said the magic words, "You write a good story." Those crumbs of praise may well have been a double chocolate cake. I ignored the grammar lesson about dangling participles. Buoyed by

Mother's words, I went to get the nurse on duty, who happened to be Adele.

We walked arm-in-arm, slowly, back to Mother's room.

"Did you tell her?" Adele asked, her eyes wide with anticipation.

"I only got as far as the Santa story."

"I'm afraid you're going to have to muster your courage again if you need to give the rest of your confession. I don't think it would affect her condition."

I watched Adele gently wake Mother to help her to bed. She pulled the plastic tent around her and turned the knob that began the hiss of renewing oxygen. Mother slipped off to sleep again, a little more color returning to her face. Adele and I retreated to the corner of the room and talked in conspiratorial whispers.

"She didn't seem at all upset about the story I wrote. I think she even liked it. She told me once that coming of age in the 1920s meant that she was no stranger to the seduction of booze and boys. Her luck was she was rescued instead of caught."

"You didn't tell me about Howard's visit."

I glanced over to be sure she was still asleep.

"He is having second thoughts. He thought he reacted too quickly about the baby. He'd like to start over, and I don't know what to do. I told him that for now I just want to be friends." I paused. "There's someone else now."

"Who?" she asked a little too loudly.

"John Graham and I are...how do you put it, having an elevator fling," I whispered. There, it was out. I waited for Adele's reaction.

She shook her head in disbelief. "But he's married."

"I know, but very unhappily. It's not an excuse but I don't let it go beyond stolen kisses in the elevator. It's innocent fun, I guess—just enough to keep us both from going crazy."

"Nothing is innocent. Think of his wife, if anything. Margaret," she continued, looking directly into my eyes, "as your friend, I beg you to stop. Isn't your life complicated enough?"

I didn't want to admit it, Adele was right. But how do you explain to anyone the pull of a little happiness in a sea of boredom, grief, and disappointment?

"Speaking of complications, are you sure you won't tell me Bobby's birthday, the boy who had his tonsils out?"

She pulled me closer as if there were Soviet microphones in the room. "I felt badly turning you down. I'll make note of his birthday, but you are to tell no one I've done this. And frankly, I'm only doing it because I think it's so unlikely he's your son. Maybe knowing that will put an end to your craziness."

I silently clapped my hands. "Let's meet as soon as you find out."

Adele studied my face. "What will you do if Bobby's birthday does match your son's?" Then she added, "Which it won't."

"I don't know, and at this point I don't care. I just want to know."

"I think that you should start caring, just in case."

I went to my mother's bed, pulled the oxygen curtain aside, and gave her a kiss on her forehead. "Oh, Mother," I said to her sleeping face, "I have so much to tell you." She grunted a little, but that was all, and I was free to go home and wait for word on Adele's detective work.

24

I fidgeted, causing little embarrassing squeaks on the leatherette booth seat, but Adele was all business. We agreed to meet for coffee at The Office, aptly named so men could tell their wives where they were going and not lie. "I'll be late at the office, honey." It was a friendly bar—no fights, tattooed patrons, or womanizing— and single women could meet there without scandal. It was the perfect setting for Adele to report on her investigation of Bobby Taylor's birth date.

We each ordered a cup of coffee, black.

Adele opened a little spiral notebook. "What day did you give birth to your son?"

"May 30, 1946, 6:50 a.m.," I told her, then holding my breath.

Adele, relishing the disclosure of such significant information, licked her forefinger and dragged it across the paper to reveal the second page. "What city?"

I held my coffee mug with both hands to keep from grabbing the damn notebook. "You know that. Pittsburgh. Come on, don't do this piece by piece. Tell me."

My friend inhaled deeply to foster momentum for her news. "I was able to find out a lot from Bobby's medical chart."

"That was the idea."

"I couldn't believe it, but he was born on May 30—" I held my breath, "1946, and it was in Pittsburgh at the Sisters of Charity Hospital, but I don't know about the time."

I let the news dive deep into my soul. The words roamed through my brain. Synapses fired and exploded.

"Oh my God, Bobby is my son." I clapped my hands on my face and waited for Adele to celebrate with me, but her face was solemn.

"Maybe." She hesitated. "It's a big hospital, and there are several delivery rooms—"

"It has to be him. Oh my God, what am I going to do?" I brushed my hands through my hair and looked upward toward the old tin ceiling. My eyes roamed the patterns of the ceiling tiles as though they might reveal some code that would lay out a plan of action for me.

"Good question. What are you going to do?"

"You don't look very happy for me."

"It's such a coincidence, and I'm concerned where this might lead you or what the impact on Bobby's family might be."

"It will lead me to getting to know my son." I stared off into nothing, smiling a bit. I wanted to savor every moment of the news, and I ignored my friend who continued to play devil's advocate with her uptight demeanor. "What a nice young man he is. I passed on good features, didn't I?"

"I hate to be a Debby Downer, but some of those features may belong to his father. *If* Bobby is yours. I do believe he is blond and you are a brunette. "

I stopped smiling. "Oh, that. I don't remember much about his father other than we were having a good time."

"Obviously."

"I don't remember much about that night, I'm afraid."

"That's probably good."

"I wonder if he still has the mustard seed."

"Huh?"

"The mustard seed pendant I put with his things before he was given to his new family."

"That was your remembrance token? I've seen that done. It would be another clue to his identity but I don't know how we could find out something like that."

We stared at our coffees, saying nothing, each deep into our own thoughts. I was tapping the coffee cup and smiling to myself. Domestic scenes with Bobby danced through my imagination—going to birthday parties, maybe. Doubt clawed into me. Would his parents let me be part of his life?

Adele nodded toward the door. "Don't turn around yet, but guess who walked in." She watched a figure approach us, and as he passed our table I saw that it was Pete. He walked past us and sat in a back booth.

A waitress came over to refill our coffees. "More?" she asked. Adele looked up. "Uh, sure." The waitress shrugged her shoulders and filled our cups.

Adele broke the silence. "You've got to be careful, Margaret. You can't go up to people and say 'Oh, I think you adopted my son, and may I take him out for ice cream?'"

"That's not such a bad idea—taking him out for ice cream. I wonder if he likes mint chocolate chip, like I do."

"Whoa. I said I would find out when he was born, but not for you to do something stupid. He doesn't belong to you."

"What do you mean he doesn't belong to me? He's my flesh and blood, my only chance at motherhood."

"You'll have other children. Don't you want to get married?"

"It's complicated."

"Tell me."

"I can't have any more children. The delivery was rough. My uterus ruptured." There, it was out. My barrenness was no longer kept in my house of secrets.

"I am so sorry." Adele put her hand on top of mine. "There's always adoption."

"That's ironic."

She leaned back. "Not very astute of me, huh? Did you tell Howard about that too?"

"I never made it to that bit of information. So you see why it's so important that I try to meet Bobby. He's the only child I'll ever have. He doesn't even have to know who I am."

Adele leaned forward and jutted her face toward me. "Are you crazy? You're going to keep a secret from your secret son?"

"I thought you were on my side."

"I am."

"Doesn't sound like it."

"If you can't count on me for truth, I'm not much of a friend."

She leaned back and examined her coffee. "I don't want this to come between us, but you need to think this through. If you do something selfish with this information, I'll be sorry I helped you."

"Selfish…you're calling me selfish because I want to know my son, and you're saying that I can't have any part of him?"

"You gave up all rights to him when he was born."

"If I knew what I know now, I never would have given him up." I paused to control the tears that were stinging my eyes. "The party line was that what I did was for love and for Bobby's best interest. And that's partially true, but at the time I really had no choice, or didn't think I did. My parents were in control, not me. I let everyone tell me what to do."

"If you had had the choice, would the outcome have been any different?" Adele asked, her face softening.

I didn't say anything. I played with my napkin and tore it into tiny little pieces of indecision.

"I assumed I would never see him again, now he's here, in Liberty."

"*Maybe* he's in Liberty."

When there were no more pieces large enough to tear, I said, "I need to go." I couldn't meet her eyes and I couldn't handle the doubt she slung at me. We paid our bills and got up to leave. Adele took my arm and faced me.

"I'm serious…you can't be 100 percent sure that Bobby is your son."

"Stop worrying. You've only confirmed what I suspected. I felt a connection to him the first time I saw him. At the hospital his father said that Bobby liked me a lot. Fate has brought us together again. Don't you believe in fate?"

"Don't assume that fate is the same as destiny. Fate gives us lessons and can lead us astray. Destiny is what we are meant to do."

"You're way too philosophical."

"Be careful. There are more people involved here than you."

I broke free of Adele. "What did you think would happen if you helped me identify Bobby?"

"I guess I didn't think that through either." She closed her eyes a moment. "Please, don't get carried away with what you want instead of what Bobby and his parents need."

"I just want to see where he lives." I lifted my chin toward Adele. "That's not so bad."

She walked away, and I was glad to get rid of her doubts. I turned to see Pete at the back of the restaurant staring at me. Did he make any sense of the drama between Adele and me?

* * *

I went back to Graham's and clocked in for another four hours of transporting customers. Idle in the Monster's mouth, I pictured my mother, lying in the hospital bed. If only I had someone to confide in, like a sibling. I remember begging for a brother or sister. I was sure that parents put in an order at the hospital—somewhat like calling the grocery to reserve a Thanksgiving turkey—and brought a baby home.

"A penny for your thoughts?"

I came out of my reverie to see John at the doors. I put Adele's caution out of my mind as easily as I did my mother's advice not to party too much when I went to college. Never mind how that turned out—a thought I pushed out even faster.

"Need a ride?" I asked.

"Please."

We paused between the second and third floors, and I let John put his strong arms around me. "Why is life so hard?" I asked him.

"I ask myself that all the time," he said. He nuzzled my neck. He put his hands on my cheeks, "I have a business trip to New York next month. Why don't you meet me there?"

My heart stopped, at least my brain did, or maybe both, for a second.

"I can see I've made you speechless. Just think about it."

"That would make us a very different situation," I managed to say. I put the elevator car in gear. John let go of me and stood to the side.

"I keep asking myself why we've come together now, when it's too late," he said to the door.

"I don't know." I stopped at the third floor and let him out. New York. I thought my next journey was going to be a few blocks away to see where Bobby lived. I fingered the address I had written down from the phone book at The Office and had put in my pocket. I saw Bobby and New York as tests, but I didn't know the answers.

25

A Fourth of July parade would have been faster than the way I drove Bella down Pike Street. I looked at the torn piece of paper I had written the Taylor address on—420. Squinting, I studied the numbers on the houses, barely visible in the dark, lit only by porch lights, and abuzz with summer insects. With each progressing number my hands grew clammier. Finally I reached 420 and pulled in front of a small white house with a green tin roof. Was everything green and white?

I surveyed the white picket fence, the swing set in the side yard, and the white geraniums in the orderly flower beds, illuminated by porch light. It didn't take long for my imagination to place me in the Taylor household—watching Bobby's excitement as he opened the birthday present I gave him, his adoptive mother mouthing "thank you" for being part of his life, Bobby running to give a big hug to "Mama Landings."

There had to be a way to spend some time with Bobby, to get to know him. Maybe I could volunteer at his school. Maybe I could join their church and teach in Bobby's Sunday school.

The sound of the front door opening interrupted my fantasizing. I froze and dared not breathe. I hoped that the porch light didn't reflect off the whites of my eyes that certainly had enlarged with the fear of discovery.

With relief I saw a cat coming out, and the door closed. I allowed myself to breathe again. The cat sat on the sidewalk and licked its paws, first one, and then another. Its black, white, and orange fur created a kaleidoscope of color as the cat tended to its grooming. I wondered what its name was, and whether Bobby named it. I hated cats—they were sneaky and they made me sneeze.

On the other hand, maybe there was something nice about them I didn't know. The cat sauntered to the tree next to my car and disappeared.

I gave myself a few more luxurious minutes of my imaginary life with Bobby. Certainly my destiny was to reunite with my son, but it was late, and I decided to head home. I started the engine, put the car in gear, and pulled out onto the street. I heard an unearthly howl and felt a slight bump under my tire. No, no, no. I stopped and exited the car only to discover I had run over Bobby's cat. I had squashed the poor thing right in the middle—its head was intact but the eyes were bulging—blood oozed from its ears. I looked up nervously at the house to see if anyone came to the door. Quiet. The other houses along the street were also silent.

The happy family scenario I had created moments ago evaporated. I considered my options. I had none. If I continued on home, I would run over the cat again with the back tires. I sat frozen with indecision.

The door opened again, and a woman leaned half way out and called, "Magoo, Mr. Magoo." She opened the door a little wider and stared at me standing beside the car. "Are you all right?" she called through her cupped hands.

I stood immobilized. "Achoo." I took out some Kleenex and blew my nose. "Achoo, aaaachooooo!" Oh, how I hated cats. Even a dead one made me sneeze.

"Do you need some help?" The woman waited a moment for an answer. Not getting one she closed the door.

The door opened again and out stepped Mr. Taylor, who was looking very concerned as he cautiously approached.

"Ma'am, my wife seems to think you need some help." He took another step closer and his face lit up with recognition. "Oh, it's you, Miss Landings. What are you doing here?" and without waiting for an answer he asked, "Are you having car trouble?"

I felt blood racing through my veins, trying to keep up with the pace of my pulse. "I'm afraid I ran over your cat."

"Oh no," Mr. Taylor said , his features losing their suspicion and taking on alarm. He dashed over to the car, and when he saw Mr. Magoo's smashed body behind the front left tire, he gagged. "Oh, this is bad, really bad."

"I'm so sorry, Mr. Taylor, I started pulling out and never thought to look underneath and—"

He took a step back from the feline corpse and brushed his hand over his hair. "Wow, I'm not sure what to do."

I started crying. "I'm so sorry, I—"

"It's not your fault. Please don't cry." He made a tentative move to comfort me but stopped short. "Magoo had a bad habit of lying under our car, and we always knew to look." He leaned in closer to examine the dead cat. He grimaced. "The bigger issue is Bobby. He adores Mr. Magoo. I thought he was a pain, always throwing up on the carpets." He stopped. "I guess it's not nice to talk about the dead that way, is it?" He studied me. I still hadn't moved from my hide-out behind the car door.

"Let me get a shovel and a box and we'll get Mr. Magoo out from under your car."

I stayed, unable to react. I watched him walk to the garage and open the heavy door. He talked to his wife who had come outside. She put her hand to her mouth. She looked toward me and said a few more words to her husband before she went back inside. They must hate me. He came back with a shovel, an old blanket, and a citrus box that once carried grapefruit from Florida. The shovel made a scraping sound as it slid under poor Mr. Magoo's lifeless body. He lifted the cat carefully onto the blanket and put Bobby's beloved pet in the box. The grisly deed done, he leaned the shovel against my car.

"What are you doing here anyway? Know someone in the neighborhood?"

"I was going home for dinner and decided to hunt for front yard ideas. I want to do a little landscaping." He looked expectantly at me for the rest. "I like your fence and the geraniums in front, but I didn't know you lived here, and I stopped for a minute to take a closer look and oh...I am so sorry about your cat." Tears threatened again, and Trent reacted like most men who see the probability of tears—he backpedaled.

"Oh, no, don't feel bad. It was an accident, Miss Landings. I'd invite you in for some coffee, but, well, my wife is upset too. That cat was our substitution for children until…until we had Bobby."

I wiped the wetness off my face and sneezed.

"I'd be glad to get another cat for your family, if that would help."

"Give us a few days. We'll talk about it. Next time we're in Graham's maybe I could let you know."

"Oh." I faltered. "Just give me a call. I need to be going."

I started the engine, and in the rear-view mirror I could see Mr. Taylor leaning on his shovel, watching me. He then walked into his house, and a little boy's voice wailed through the open door, "Mr. Magoo, what happened to Mr. Magoo?" I pulled into the street and drove away. My grip on the steering wheel was as tight as the hold I had on my horror that I had brought sadness into little Bobby's life. A mother is supposed to give happiness to her child.

*   *   *

I lay curled in a fetal position long after my normal rising time. I had the day off from work, but I wouldn't have a day off from the tormenting image of Mr. Magoo's bulging eyes. A grief-stricken Bobby would not stop playing in my head. I saw his face superimposed on the horrified visage painted in Edward Munch's *The Scream*, complete with swirling reds and oranges in the background, Bobby's hands pressed to his cheeks in horror as he realized what had happened to his precious Mr. Magoo.

I called Adele. Even though our last conversation was rocky, I needed her level head to help balance my teetering one.

"How awful for you." Adele clicked her tongue and uttered sympathetic "mmmm's" but she did not give me the dreaded "I told you so."

"I wanted to see where he lived, and I ended up killing his cat. Mothers aren't supposed to do that." My voice choking, I said, "It's probably good that I gave him up for adoption. I'd just make him miserable all the time, doing dumb stuff."

There was a moment of silence. "For starters, if the cat sneaked under cars, his fate was sealed. You happened to be the one who got him. Secondly, I'm not a parent, but it's not the mother's job to make her kids happy, it's to get them ready for living on their own. Parents who think otherwise are as unhappy as their kids."

"I suppose—"

"Why don't you wait a few days before offering to get Bobby a new cat? Then stay the heck away from them. You're the birth mother, maybe. You're not the mother. You did kill the cat, but you're not responsible for Bobby's happiness. Does that make sense?"

Adele's solution pierced my brain and startled me out of my wretchedness. I could get Bobby a new kitten. But that would mean I'd have to go look at the sneeze-inducing things. They scratched and jumped up on countertops. A mother thinks of her child first, though, doesn't she? I had to forgo my feline distaste for Bobby's sake.

Taking a kitten to Bobby was also a ticket to being with him, getting to talk with him and being in his house—as well as reclaiming my maternal reputation. I sprang into action. In twenty minutes I showered, dressed, and was at the kitchen table reading the pet section in the classifieds. I circled the addresses where new kittens were being given away and tucked the paper in my purse. Within moments I was in my beloved Chevy and driving to my first destination.

I turned left on Vine Street. Trash lined the lower edges of chain-link fences, and worn-out sofas sat abandoned on some of the porches. I stopped in front of a yellow brick ranch where a hand-drawn sign in the grassless front yard announced "Free Kitens." In nervous anticipation, I walked up the cracked sidewalk, and my hand shook a little as I knocked on the weathered screen.

A gray-haired woman in a dirty housecoat opened the door, and after an exchange of pleasantries, she led me into a kitchen that had a decidedly feline odor. I pinched my nose to keep from sneezing, but my eyes started watering. In a large box set on the yellowed linoleum floor was a mama cat with three suckling kittens. Another larger cat walked by and rubbed its chin on the legs of a kitchen chair. Cat hair danced in the sun beams and on the upholstered seat. I had to let go of my nose so I could breathe better. A sneeze immediately formed in my burning nostrils and I lost control. I sneezed so hard that I almost wet my pants.

"They don't look old enough to be taken from their mother," I said, trying to talk without breathing.

"Dearie, I want to get rid of these things as soon as I can. I took in the poor mama cat a couple of weeks ago when I saw her on my porch in the pouring rain. The thing was soaking wet. The next morning there were three more cats in my kitchen." The woman looked at me. "You wan' 'em?"

The smell of cat urine was burning my nostrils and the sight of gooey stuff in the cats' eyes elicited a gag reflex. I started a retreat, backing up, then turning and scurrying out the door. "No thank you, but good luck," I called over my shoulder. I heard the screen door slam shut. Back in fresh air, a couple of deep breaths cleared my lungs of the odors in the woman's house, and I emitted one loud, long, and expectorant sneeze.

The next address circled on the paper was on Pine Street. As I got into my car, an automobile sped by—a little fast for the narrow road—and with a squeal, turned the corner. I did a double-take and caught the flash of green and white

I put my head on the steering wheel. Please, green and white, get out of my life.

Back on the road, I drove about five minutes to Pine Street, an all-American street in a quaint residential area of Liberty. Mani-cured yards and tidy houses. Good. I arrived at the house listed in the next ad, perused the property for signs of cleanliness and an interest in sanitary living. Passed. Neatly printed on a wooden sign was "Free kittens to good home." The house was small but well taken care of.

I rang the doorbell and was led in by a well-groomed middle-aged woman who introduced herself as Karen.

My eyes watered a little, but no super sneeze threatened.

"Looking for a kitten, are you?"

I sneezed.

"I have two tiger kittens left, a male and a female. Is it for you, dear?"

Karen was likable and the tidiness of the house was reassuring, but I still took a cautionary sniff, which the woman caught.

"It's all right. You're trying to decide if I take good care of the cats. Is this for you?"

"No, I'm getting a kitten for a young boy who had a cat that met an untimely end." Seeing alarm on the woman's face, I quickly continued, "In an accident, hit by a car."

"Oh dear. The boy must be traumatized. Of course, these days you should use that new Kitty Litter so you don't have to put a cat outside."

"I'll get some," I said.

"The kittens are this way."

One kitten looked like a gray and brown striped feather duster with short little legs, droopy ears, and a pink nose. I sat on the floor, and the kitten toddled over to me. Too irresistible, and I took the fluffy animal into my lap. The kitten yawned and fell asleep. I sneezed. I didn't even bother with the other kittens. This was the one for Bobby.

Safely ensconced in a lidded and blanket-lined basket in the back seat of my car, the kitten slept through the drive to the pet store for the lifesaving Kitty Litter. Windows down gave me plenty of fresh air and minimal cat hair. I was beside myself with joy. I was going to help Bobby get over the death of Mr. Magoo, and I gave myself an imaginary pat on the back. My mother never let me have a dog, which I desperately wanted. Instead I got a goldfish that I named Goldie, which I fed to death, literally. That was proof to my parents that I couldn't be trusted with pets.

I pulled up to the house, and Bobby was practicing croquet on the manicured green lawn. His blond hair had whitened in the summer sun, and he carefully studied the right angle for smacking the ball. I sneezed, and he looked up and eyed me with suspicion. I gave my best maternal smile, and Bobby yelled, "Mom, that elevator lady's here." He stood, croquet mallet at his side.

Not sure what to do, I stayed at the side of my car.

Mrs. Taylor came out and pulled Bobby to her. "Miss Landings, what are you doing here?"

That was my cue. I opened the passenger side door and pulled out the basket that was making mewing sounds. Bobby pulled away from his mother and inched toward the basket.

"Is that a kitten?" He looked up at me. "My cat got killed last night."

"I know. I'm so sorry." I turned my head to sneeze so the explosion from my nostrils avoided either of the Taylors.

"This is a little soon—" said Bobby's mother.

"I know, but I couldn't resist. It's the least I can do after Mr. Magoo, you, know." I stopped, unsure how much to say.

Bobby wrinkled his face. "How'ja know about Mr. Magoo?"

I ignored his question and asked Mrs. Taylor, "If it's OK, I thought a kitten might cheer him up."

Bobby turned his brightened face to his mother. "For me? Can I, Mom? Please?"

His mother frowned. "This is a little unusual. Is it a boy or a girl?"

"A girl."

"I'll name her Maggie," said Bobby.

Did he know my name was Margaret?

He pulled Maggie out of the basket, and she screeched and clawed him. Big tears welled up in his eyes, but Bobby was not deterred. He licked the bloody streak off his hand and held Maggie close to him. The kitten calmed down, but Mrs. Taylor didn't.

"Is this a feral cat? We can't have a wild cat in the house."

"It's from a very good litter, I promise."

Bobby let go of the kitten, and she jumped back into the basket, peering out suspiciously.

"She just needs to get used to her surroundings," I said. "I got her from a very clean and loving home. And I brought some Kitty Litter so you don't have to let her outside where she might get hurt."

"Mom, can Miss Landings play with me and Maggie?"

"I suppose so," she said but without much energy. Bobby ran over to me and gave me a hug—a hug!

"I'm glad you like the kitten, Bobby."

"How d'ja know my other cat died? Someone ran over him. Squish." He flattened his palms together. "We had a funeral for him."

"Well—"

The kitten mewed, and Bobby didn't wait for my answer. He ran to the basket, sat beside it, and said "meow."

* * *

The sun was extra bright, and the birds were singing songs just for me as I pulled away from the Taylors'. I had spent an hour inside Bobby's house, talking to him, playing with him and his new kitten. If only I had been able to ask about the mustard seed charm that I had put with his clothes so many years ago.

Several blocks away, a green and white car on my left caught my attention. Startled, I drove straight into the path of a turning car. The squeal of brakes did not stop it from hitting my doomed Aqua Bella. The useless braking was simultaneous with the sickening crunch of metal and breaking glass. The jolt threw me against the steering wheel and then sideways against the side window. Quiet descended as quickly as the mayhem had started. Something warm dripped into my eyes. I lifted a hand to wipe away the wetness from my face only to see that it was blood. I saw the driver of the other car get out. But someone else got to me first—the driver of the green and white car.

"Margaret...Margaret, are you all right?"

I saw a familiar face, then I sneezed and passed out.

26

When I woke up, the room and the furniture came into focus bit by bit. My head pounded, and when I raised a hand to identify the source of pain, I felt cotton batted gauze. I was in the hospital, not in good shape. The sensation of feeling trapped gave way to an odd sort of peace where no calamities could find me within the protection of a hospital room.

The antiseptic clean of the sheets hit my nostrils, and I opened my eyes upon a man who had concern painted on his face, a handsome face. He was tenderly holding my hand.

"Who are you?" I asked the stranger. Too weak to remove my hand from his, I waited for his response.

"Don't you remember me?" he asked.

There was a familiarity about him I couldn't quite place. He had a faint, stale cigarette aroma about him—but he was much more attractive than Pete. He had a patrician nose, blue eyes, and neatly trimmed hair. The slight wrinkles at the corners of his eyes told me this was a mature man, someone who took life and people seriously.

"You scared me when I saw you pull in front of that car."

The mist began to lift from my consciousness, and I blinked to clear my vision. His name jumped into my mind. "Charles? What are you doing here?" Exhaustion made my eyelids heavy. The fog and the night descended on me again.

* * *

When I woke up the next morning, last night's dream about my wild night with Charles a decade ago kept its hold on me. The charming young man who sat beside me in American Lit class asked me to go with him to a fraternity party. Talk came easily to us, as did the rum and Cokes. Each drink lowered our resistance to the attraction we were feeling and eventually lowered our pants in an upstairs bedroom.

My dream had more detail than what I actually remembered. I'm sure we fumbled with our clothes, but the pleasant floating from pain killers allowed me to replay the sexual abandonment of the past.

Charles. I bolted up in my bed, the sudden movement shot searing pain through my skull, overwhelming the impressions of him hovering over me with that look of complete control to which I willingly yielded. Bobby's father.

"Oh criminy," I said out loud as I collapsed back on the pillow. That was Charles who came to my rescue at the accident. That was Charles holding my hand yesterday. He was once again a part of the gigantic and disordered puzzle of my life.

As much as I tried to reassemble pieces of my past, the puzzle had its own life, insisting on completion so I would be forced to see the whole picture. The curvy, pointy, multifaceted sections of my history snapped back to their proper places no matter how many times I broke them up and scattered them around the edges of my being. I lay back down, and my eyelids were like garage doors on their downward march to the cement floor.

When I woke later in the morning, the room was empty—there were no hands holding my hands, no nurses fussing about my bed, and my head didn't hurt as much. The fog was gone. I thought about Charles at my bedside. After all these years, why now? And why did my heart beat a little faster when I thought of him? Guilt played at the edges of my reminiscing as I recalled the pregnancy that my fun with him caused and had never shared with him.

Adele knocked on the door jamb. Thank God I had a friend I could tell about Charles.

"Woman, you lead an exciting life."

"Almost getting killed, you mean." I tried to roll my eyes but little muscles that controlled ocular movement complained too much. "Owww."

"No, I mean the men in your life. The floor nurse told me a

parade of handsome men came to see you this morning—all shooed away because you were sleeping."

"Really?" I rubbed my temples. "Did you see any of them?"

"No, but a nurse recognized John Graham as one of them." She waited to see if I had any reaction. I didn't. "And there was a tall, good looking man that no one had seen before," she continued. "You were the envy of the nurses."

I motioned Adele to come nearer. "The tall, good looking one?"

"Yes."

"That is Bobby's father." I folded my arms in triumph.

"Mr. Taylor?"

"No," I said. "Bobby's natural father, the one I—"

"Impossible." She pulled up a visitor's chair and sat close to my bed.

"Maybe he's the one that's been following me. I saw that green and white car again, just before the crash."

"That's kind of creepy."

"You're right about that. What this all means is another man and another complication."

"And why is he back in your life now?"

"Strange, isn't it?" I glanced toward the sunshine coming through the window of my first floor room and noticed a green and white car in the parking lot. I grabbed Adele's hand and pointed. "You'll never guess what's out there."

Interrupted by a soft knock, Adele and I both looked to the door where a tall presence stood. It was Charles. Speechless, we both stared at him. I noticed that Adele gave him a once-over. Was that sexual melting I saw in her face?

"Is this a bad time?" He shifted slightly from one foot to another and looked at the floor, holding his fedora in his hands, twirling it by the rim. He had a sort of James Stewart air about him. Piercing blue eyes, sharp nose, strong jaw. Careful, I thought.

Adele finally broke the silence. "Are you the famous Charles?"

"Uh, yes, but I don't know how famous. Infamous, maybe." He cleared his throat and twirled his hat again. "Maybe I should come back."

"I think I'll leave you two alone," Adele said. She blew me a kiss and left.

"It's good to see you awake and alert," Charles said.

"Do you have a green and white car?" I fixed my eyes on him.

"Huh?"

"A green and white car seems to appear wherever I am, and now where you are. Is it yours?"

I studied his face. Guilt? Deception? I wasn't sure. I saw a mixture of vulnerability and strength in him.

"I do have a car as you describe, but it can't be the only one in town."

"Have you been driving by my house and following me?"

"Occasionally." He dropped his gaze to the floor.

"Why?"

"Can I sit down for the inquisition?"

I pointed to the chair Adele had pulled up to my bed.

I glanced at the nurse call button to be sure it was close by. I both liked and distrusted Charles' closeness. All my man trouble alarms were clanging and flashing red in my already hurting head.

"How are you feeling? Gosh, you are as pretty as I remember, even with the bandages."

Charming, very charming. "Much better. I have more bruising than cuts so they'll take off the bandages tomorrow before I go home." I paused and compared his features to Bobby's. I couldn't tell if there was much resemblance—I would have to see them side by side. "Let's get back to why you are here."

He took a deep breath. "I found out a couple of years ago that you had a baby—mine, I'm sure—nine months after our…well, our date. I felt terrible. I was married when I learned all this and didn't feel there was anything I could do."

I sat a little straighter.

"Well, a divorce and all that, you know. I always thought you were a pretty special person, and it was stupid of us to do all that drinking that night…and when you wouldn't answer my calls, I kind of went on with things. But when I got divorced, I thought about what my friend said, and I wondered about you and the child, a lot."

"Wait a minute," I stopped him. "Who told you?"

"She didn't mean to tell me, I mean, she was talking about someone hypothetically, connected to an adoption case we had, and I put the pieces together. She had to be talking about you." He paused. "When I brought up your name, she got all defensive and embarrassed, and couldn't have known I was the guy—"

"Who?"

"Your cousin Penny Landings…she worked in my office in Pittsburgh."

A nurse came in to do something that nurses do, but when she saw me glaring at Charles, and Charles looking guilty, she made a quick exit.

"I don't know what to say." I stared at the crucifix on the wall. Part of me wanted to nail Charles right up there too, but another part of me wanted him to stay at my bedside, confessing, acting contrite and, I thought, maybe he could help me get to know Bobby.

"You're looking very tired. May I see you again?"

"Yeah, sure." Inside I was cheering, but I didn't know why. "I guess you don't have to ask about my address." I folded my arms, pretending to be punitive about his spying.

"Uh, no."

A candy striper appeared at the door with fresh water. "May I come in?"

"Of course," I said.

Charles moved out of the way, so the pink and white striped volunteer could replace the water canister. "I guess I should go. I have to go to Pittsburgh to meet some clients. I'll come back to check on you in a few days."

Pittsburgh. Of course he had a life somewhere. "What do you do?" I asked.

"I'm an attorney." He put on his hat and tipped it toward me. "At your service, ma'am." He smiled and left. A trail of unanswered questions followed him down the hall like shadowy footprints.

I turned my attention to the fresh-faced candy striper.

"I brought you some fresh water, Miss Landings."

"Thank you. You have a bit of an accent. Are you new here?"

"My parents and I came here from Russia after the war," she said as she straightened the bedside table. "But we will be leaving soon."

"What's your name, dear?"

"Katrina Karlosi."

Karlosi. Oh no. I crossed my fingers to wish away any connection to the last name I grabbed from the news and gave to the Russian embezzler I had created to test Mrs. Gibbons' gossip mill. "Liberty is such a nice place to live, why would you leave?"

Katrina's face hardened. "Not such a nice place when there are stories about you." She caught herself. "But I'm here to help you. Is there anything else you need?" Katrina regarded me with a warm smile underlying a cold countenance.

"What's your father's name, Katrina? Maybe we have met in Graham's Department Store. I run the elevator."

She hesitated. "Vladimir. Do you know him, or about him?" She held onto her friendly demeanor in spite of the suspicion in her eyes.

"No, I guess not." I sank into my pillow, the excitement about Charles overcome by a chance meeting with the daughter of a very real Karlosi.

I tried to pour some water into a cup but my hands were shaking. I sat back and closed my eyes to block out the poor girl's anger at a town that must have turned on her.

"Let me help you. Are you all right, Miss Landings?"

"I'm just tired of being stupid," I said, my eyes still closed. I listened to Katrina's soft-soled shoes making a barely audible scuff out the door.

I turned and faced the wall so I might prevent the world from complicating my life any further. I lay there, staring at the green painted walls in my hospital room. I escaped into my favorite scene from *All About Eve*. The party. The elegant clothes, the witty conversations, the maid with the black dress and white apron—all according to script, not like my life, unscripted and randomly plotted.

27

A dele stood in the doorway of my hospital room with a wheelchair in front of her. "Enough about the men in your life. Let's go see your mother," she said. "You need to focus on something other than yourself."

Feeling sorry for myself, I asked, "Why are you still my friend in spite of the calamity I cause?"

"'Cause' is the operative word, my dear. You're afflicted with great ideas but you don't understand the relationship between cause and effect."

"Guilty."

"Isn't that what Bette Davis said when her lover told her how annoying she was?"

"I'm impressed. But I wasn't thinking of Margo, I was thinking of me."

"That's another one of your problems, but I still love you."

I grunted an acknowledgment.

Adele found a wheelchair and moved me into it with the grace of someone who had practice in moving an awkward, sore body into a rolling steel vehicle.

"Won't Mother be worried to see me with bandages?"

"She'll just be glad to see you."

We wheeled into Mother's room and saw she was awake, staring at a soap opera through the plastic of her oxygen tent. When she noticed us, she gave a slight motion to Adele to turn off the TV. She smiled, and as soon as I saw it, I felt my face wad up into a sorry-for-myself cry.

"Come here, Sweetie." Her voice was weak, and she was barely able to lift her hand to pat the bed.

Adele rolled me over to the bed, and I lifted the plastic so I could give her a kiss. Her breathing sounded raspy, and the hand I took felt cool. I raised my head to wipe the wetness off my face, and I drank in her motherly smile.

Mother took a deep breath and looked at me quizzically. "Why is your head bandaged, and why are you in a wheelchair?"

"I was in a car accident, but I'm going to be fine."

"Oh, that's good, dear."

I patted her hand, and she closed her eyes briefly then looked at me. "What about your car?"

"It can be fixed," I said, thinking of the crumpled bumper where Bella took a beating from the other vehicle. The splintering and cracking windows replayed in my head.

"That's nice. Now I need to sleep…I am so tired."

"Mother, I—"

"I love you, and I've always been so proud of you," she said. She closed her eyes again and fell asleep, really asleep, judged by her soft snoring. Under the sheets a tiny "toot" sounded.

Adele and I giggled.

"I've never heard my mother do that before," I said.

"In our trade, we call it a butt burp."

We giggled again.

"You gotta love 'em."

"Amen," I said.

I put the plastic sheeting back. My mother's loosened face conveyed her peace with the world. I rolled back to where Adele was standing.

"Your mother loves you so much," she said. "Do you think you need to tell her?"

"What, that I heard her fart?" I laughed, and I put my finger to my lips. Adele grinned then took on a more somber tone.

"That Howard broke up with you because of the baby and that her grandson may be living in Liberty?" she whispered.

"Oh, that." I took a deep breath. I couldn't escape the family secret—unimportant in Pittsburgh, so like yeast in Liberty. It expanded and bubbled when added to receptive ears.

"Was it important to her to be a grandmother some day?"

"She doesn't like to talk about it. Neither do I." I paused. "A mistake keeps popping its ugly head up, doesn't it? Taking on different forms?"

"A poignant cliché."

The summer breeze was rustling the leaves of the giant elm outside, but I could not discern any guidance from the wizened limbs.

"I'm just tired of pretending to be something I'm not...a goody two shoes, as we used to say in grade school."

"So you think you're a bad person for giving birth to an illegitimate son? Do you think you are the only one?" Adele threw up her hands. "You think you dropped off some kind of pedestal when you got pregnant. There are no pedestals, Margaret, and having a child didn't push you off of one. Sometimes I think you take pride in having a shame. It makes you special."

"Ouch."

"Besides, you want to break free of that, or you wouldn't be telling people about him, testing your reactions against their responses."

A muffled sound came from the bed. Mother was saying something.

I rolled over and lifted the plastic. She gestured for my hand, and I stood up out of the chair so I could get my ear closer to her mouth. Once we made contact, and with her eyes still closed, she whispered something to me. When I heard what she said, I put my head on her shoulder and said, "I love you, Mother."

I waited until she was asleep again before Adele wheeled me out of the room. Neither of us said anything until we got to the elevator. Once inside and alone, Adele asked, "What did your mother say to you? Can you tell me?"

"She said, 'Howard is an idiot.'"

* * *

My neighbor Kathy took me home from the hospital. She made me tea and helped settle me on the sofa.

"You call me if you need something, I mean it."

"Yes, ma'am," and she left. I savored the quiet. No intercom, no visitors making loud talk, and no one appearing in my hospital room with a personal agenda.

The doorbell pulled me out of the calm. Who was it this time? John Graham—having another fight with his wife? Pete—telling me how he owns my reputation? Howard—looking for a purified wife? Or maybe it was Charles—trying to find purpose in life.

I looked through the porch window and there was Charles, twirling his fedora in his hands again like a baton twirler who can't get the courage to throw the darn thing up in the air. I opened the door.

"Hi." He might have been the father of my child but I didn't know him very well, so I stood at the half-open door.

"May I come in? I would like to talk." He cleared his throat and gave his hat another twirl. He had the air of the corporate busi-nessman right out of *Marjorie Morningstar*—gray flannel suit, white shirt, skinny tie, closely trimmed hair. His suit was cut narrower than most men in Liberty who were still stuck in the padded shoul-ders and looser pants of post wartime. I had to admit that I liked what I saw. Even a headache didn't keep me from admiring an attractive man.

"Sure. Come in." I pointed to a chair, and he entered but stood until I sat down on the sofa opposite his chair. He put his hat on the coffee table. "Can I get you something to drink, Charles?" The father of my son was in my living room. I couldn't believe it.

"Please, call me Charlie. No one calls me Charles."

"Okay. But stick to Margaret," I warned him.

"You must be surprised that I'm here, that I'm even in Liberty—"

"The drink?"

"Oh…" I saw him glance at my tea. "I'd have a rum and Coke, but that's close to what got us into, well, you know." He gave a self-conscious laugh at his attempt for humor.

"Good thinking, so how about some root beer?"

"I'll get it—you just got out of the hospital."

"Okay, I'll take one too," and I sat down, glad to be waited on.

I heard him open the refrigerator, retrieve the beverages, and fumble around in drawers for the bottle opener. The hiss of the soda and plunk of the bottle caps hitting the counter told me he had been successful.

Settled with our bottles of root beer, we looked awkwardly at each other for a few minutes. Did I really have sex with this man? Was he wondering the same thing?

"Margaret."

"Charlie." We almost synchronized our address to each other.

"How are you feeling?" he asked.

"Oh, I'm fine. Just a big knot on my head. There's a lot more damage to my car, however."

He cleared his throat again. "Do you need any help? I mean, could I run errands for you or something?"

"That's very kind, but I really want to know why you are here."

"This may not be a good time."

"Believe me, I need to know what's been happening. How long have you been following me?"

"A while. I couldn't get up the nerve to approach you. I'd come to town every so often. Funny…I'm an attorney who can battle in a courtroom, but I'm locked into this teenager mode of dogging the woman I'm curious about." He scratched his knee. "I have to admit that the episode with the kitten and the little boy was kind of intriguing. Who is he?"

Words jammed in my throat—the yearning, wondering, and regrets. There wasn't room for all those ghosts to make their way out of my mouth.

We sipped our drinks in silence.

"First, tell me about yourself."

He inhaled. "My divorce forced me to look at my life differently, you know." Holding the root beer with his hands, he tapped a worried rhythm on it with both forefingers. "In those few hours we had, and frankly I don't remember much of the last few," he looked down shamefaced, "I felt more connection with you than I ever have had, even with my wife. Oh, jeez. The idea that we were meant to be together took on a life of its own."

I waited for him to finish.

"I had to find you. It wasn't easy…you've moved around a little."

"Yes, you are right there." I took a swig of my soda.

"I'd take time off work and check out the town, see where you lived and such."

"Do you have any children?" I put down my soda.

"It never seemed to happen, and given the circumstances I'm glad we didn't." He stopped to take a drink, and he tilted his head back to catch the remaining liquid. His tongue played with the lip of the bottle and caught the last drop of root beer that lingered. It was a mesmerizing display of grace and dexterity. *Down, Margaret.*

He put the bottle down carefully on the table and with his thumb and forefinger wiped the last bit of moisture off his lips. He dropped his gaze to the floor, took a breath, and brought his head back up to fixate on my eyes. "I'm sorry about the car accident, but if that hadn't happened, I might still be spying, trying to get up the nerve to approach you."

"I'm glad you're not spying anymore either. Why didn't you call me when you found out?"

"I didn't want to make a fool of myself, I guess. I wasn't sure if what I heard was true. I couldn't just walk up to you and say, 'I heard you had my baby.' Speaking of which, why didn't you ever tell me?"

I took a moment to think about that. "I was so embarrassed, and I hardly knew you. I figured I was on my own. I was in shock, to say the least." I stared back at him. "Why did you get divorced?"

Fear swept over his face, for a second, and then disappeared.

"It's a long story. But I've learned from it, and now I'm ready to move on." He inhaled, for courage perhaps?

I burst open with one of my ghosts. "Charlie, I've found our son."

He sat straight up. "You what?"

"The young boy with the family—that's our son the Taylors adopted. I'm sure of it."

Charlie stood up, rubbing his hands through his hair. "How do you know?"

"He was born on the same day and at the same place as our son."

"Wow." Charlie rubbed his hands through his hair again. "Do his parents know who you are?"

"No, they don't know."

Charlie moved next to me on the sofa, took my hand and kissed it. His knightly kiss had more tenderness and sincerity than any of the stolen kisses John and I shared, and it repelled any caution signals my brain was sending.

"It's fate." He shook his head. "Can I meet him?"

Charlie's request hit me in the chest. Bobby was *my* son. A father had not been part of my maternal daydreaming for years. Charlie had never been in the imaginings of who my son was or where he was. "I don't know. Let me think about that." I played with the buckle on my dress, flipping the inch of leather that extended through the loop.

Charlie brightened with an idea. "We could be out on a date, and we could stop in to check how the cat is doing."

"You're not sounding much like a lawyer."

"I never thought I would be a father. I want to meet him."

He took my hand in his, warm and safe. We sat for a while, entwining our fingers.

"I'm barely getting used to the idea of finding my son," I finally said. "Can we postpone this talk?"

The rest of the evening we talked about everything but our son. Bobby hung between us like a jumping rope—back and forth, back and forth—could we hop into the swinging cable without tripping? Did we have the energy and rhythm to navigate its cadence together?

"It's getting late." He pulled me up from the chair and held me, there in my little house in Liberty, far away from the college where we once connected. His embrace had a gentleness, and I anticipated a shared adventure. When he left, he gave me a soft kiss. Finally, there was a gentleman in my life.

Adele's voice burst in my head, "Don't let fate lead you astray from your destiny."

Whistling, Charlie strode down the sidewalk to his car.

28

John nuzzled me in the elevator between the second and third floors. "You are a little distant today."

I was healed from the accident and back at work, but Aqua Bella was going to take more recovery time. Charlie went back to Pittsburgh but called me every day to make sure I was okay. John called once to see when I would be back to work.

Never did I think that within the same week I would have two embraces to compare. John's arms were strong and protective; Charlie's were nurturing and soft.

It was John's turn. "Aren't you glad to be back? It's been a long week without you here."

I didn't move away from him, and I blocked any reason for why I should. "I've got a lot on my mind with Mother and all."

"Have you thought more about going to New York with me?" John held my face with confident hands as though he didn't have much experience with rejection. His confidence didn't sit well with me. My man-trouble flag hoisted high above my confused head.

"What about Elaine? I couldn't do that to her." Saying her name aloud made John's wife a haunting presence in our elevator hideaway

He took his hands away. "What about Elaine? We're just having a little fun."

I had been telling myself the kissing was innocent. John's affection during our stolen moments filled that empty, dark place in me that hadn't been quenched in years. I thought of my father, so devoted to Mother. I overheard them laughing once about a woman who tried to flirt with him at a country club dance. "She couldn't hold a candle to you, my pet," and they kissed noisily. Father had been gone over eight years, and I wondered if my mother had her own empty, dark place that needed filling.

The buzzer rang, and we both jumped from the jarring noise.

"We'll talk later," he said. When I opened the door to the second floor customer, John walked out without another word. I watched him square his shoulders as he headed toward the second floor manager.

In the employees' lounge, I was alone with my root beer and my thoughts. I sat at the table, running my fingers across the rose bedecked oilcloth. Should I go to New York with John? Of course not, it would be wrong, but that dark place in me beckoned. I put my forefinger on each leaf surrounding an orange-red rose. Go, don't go, go. Hmmm…I needed more direction. I used the aqua blue checkers between the big rose and the smaller yellow rose. Go, don't go, go. I pictured Charlie's reaction if he found out about John and me, and I wondered if I even deserved a good man.

The door to the lounge opened, and Pete walked in. I knocked over the sugar container. Criminy. He hesitated but proceeded to the cola machine while I sat frozen, watching. I heard him deposit his coins, open the lid, and slide out his drink along the metal grooves. He turned toward me, and we stared at each other for a long moment. Gone was the bravado in his eyes and the cockiness of his posture. He stood like an ordinary man with the weight of the world on his shoulders. He opened his mouth to say something but didn't. He walked out without saying a word.

I looked down at the roses on the tablecloth, my oilcloth Ouija board. Charlie, John, interrupted by Pete. I examined the spilled sugar on the table, and I wrote *Mrs. John Graham* in the granular mess. In the recesses of whatever decency I had left, it didn't feel right. I quickly scattered the sugar into a nameless pile and thought of Charlie and his gentle nature. I wrote *Mrs. Charles Warner*. I pictured us curled up on the sofa, laughing at *The Honeymooners* or singing along with *The Hit Parade*. I imagined time with Bobby— Uncle Charlie and Aunt Margaret. Maybe his parents would invite us over for the prom photos. Would I be in the elite group of family wearing a corsage at his wedding?

I returned to my elevator duties.

It didn't take too many elevator ups and downs to draw John into our lair.

"People may notice the elevator stops between floors every time you get on," I said to him.

"Keep going to the third floor," he said. "You'll have time to say 'yes' to my invitation." He brushed a strand of my hair behind my ear. I loved how he did that.

I halted the elevator before reaching the floor. As was his habit, John moved closer to me and kissed the back of my neck.

"I would love to show you the Empire State Building."

With my hand on the Monster's control and my heart in my throat, I said, "I have to say no."

John stepped back, and I waited for disappointment in his face. He sighed and said, "Oh well, it was worth a try." On automatic, I resumed to the third floor and opened the door. He stepped out.

Criminy. I closed the doors and stood there immobile. For this I counted leaves on a damn rose? So much for dark places. I'm giving mine the boot and going for sunlight and Charlie.

*   *   *

Once home, I sat at the kitchen table and ate a pot pie for dinner. What was I missing by turning down John's invitation? I poked at the pie's crust, hoping a genie would pop out and grant me some wishes. What would they be? Know what would have happened had I gone to New York? Publish a bestselling novel? Rewind my life so I could keep Bobby?

Later, I sought solace at my Bette Davis dressing table. I skipped the makeup and went right to the wig. My coloring and the hair didn't mix well, and I looked like one of those tourists who stick their faces through the head in a standup cutout.

Since escaping as Margo Channing failed, I tried writing. I spent several hours that night crafting a story about a man named Jim who was seduced by the Elks Club vixen. His wife Irene stomped off the dance floor because he had been drinking too much. The vixen and Jim had a rendezvous in the parking lot that made me blush as I wrote it. Well, more than blush.

29

At four o'clock a few days later, I walked through the door of The Office and scanned the bar for a place to sit. Isn't it always corner booths where people hatch clandestine plans and reveal secrets? I signaled to the waitress that I would take the back booth. While I waited for coffee, I tried to imagine what in the world Howard had to tell me.

"Here you go, honey," the waitress said. "I'll watch for your friend."

The wall clock read 4:05. Where was Howard?

The day began so nicely, I thought, daydreaming about life with Charlie, and when the phone rang I anticipated his soothing voice. Stirring my coffee, I watched the brown liquid swirl like the conversation I replayed in my head.

"Margaret? Don't hang up, please, I have to talk to you."

Howard. Heaven and hell collided whenever I heard his voice. Charlie, John, Pete, now Howard. At least Charlie was dependable, a gentleman. And to think I almost gave that up for a cheating trip with John. Good riddance, Mr. Graham. Yes, dispense with Howard, and then I could focus on Charlie and our possible life together. Mother would approve—he was kind, handsome, and a lawyer. What more could a mother-in-law want? Mother might even agree to bring Bobby's existence into the open. Wounds heal better when they are exposed, Adele told me. I'm tired of keeping my wounds bandaged.

What was it Howard said? "I need to talk to you."

What was it this time? So many aspects of my life were open season for gossip or guilt. I was a train that never got to a destination—always circling on a track of calamities that had no stops.

I stirred my coffee faster. He probably wants to get back together. The jerk. He should take lessons from Charlie. If he thinks I can forgive him for that humiliating scene in the restaurant, he's crazy. I hoped my icy voice had chilled the phone line to his ear. Frostbite would have been a bonus.

So he wanted to meet at The Office—a public place with private booths, he said. At four. It's ten after four, Pastor Howard, where the hell are you?

As if on cue, Howard came up to me and said, "Thanks for meeting me."

A pensive Howard with a worried brow stood at the table. I'll make him beg and then I'll refuse him.

"May I sit down?" He gestured toward the opposite bench.

"That's why we're here, isn't it?"

He sat. "I know this must seem very strange to you." He flagged the waitress. "Refresh her coffee, please, and I'll have mine black." He turned his attention back to me. "This is hard. When I visited you in the hospital, I noticed that a man from Pittsburgh had come to see you."

He's jealous. "Now wait a minute, Howard. What business is it of yours who's interested in me? You broke things off, if I remember correctly." I flared my nostrils like I had seen Bette Davis do when she was really angry and in charge.

"I couldn't forgive myself if I didn't tell you what I found out."

Found out he wanted me after all, huh? Did he have the ring in his pocket again? Maybe he exchanged it for a bigger one.

"So what did you find out?" I accepted the coffee from the waitress, and I moved Howard's cup so the handle was accessible to him.

"I have to confess that I didn't like Charles within a few moments of meeting him—in the hall of the hospital—I introduced myself as a family friend. Something wasn't right. I worried you're getting involved with the wrong person."

"And I suppose you're the right one," I said, feeling smug.

Howard did a double take. "No, this isn't about me, it's about Charles."

I gulped. Maybe Charlie is not really divorced. Maybe he's dating other women. Maybe he's an Adlai Stevenson supporter or something equally abhorrent to a registered Republican like Howard. Maybe he's defending a mob boss. "So, this is about Charlie?"

"You're calling him Charlie now, are you?" Howard held his coffee with both hands. He stared into the cup.

"Get on with it, please."

He winced. "Hear me out. I took it on myself to find out more about him, so when I went back to Pittsburgh, I did some digging."

"You spied on him? How dare you…spying on a friend of mine." The next words rushed out of my soul and through my mouth. "He's the father of my son." Criminy. I said it.

Color drained from Howard's face, and he dropped his head into his hands. Behind that shield I heard him say, "This is even worse than I thought." He pulled up his head.

"Margaret, listen." He stared hard at me, insisting on my attention. "You're not going to like this." He hesitated and I waited, daring him to tell me something that meant anything. "I couldn't believe it, didn't want to believe it…and now knowing Charles' connection, maybe this was a bad idea."

"Believe what?"

Howard cleared his throat. "Charles is a homosexual."

At first I didn't comprehend what he was saying, and after a few seconds his words made their way to my brain. I started laughing.

"A what? Oh Howard, how typical." I caught my breath and tried to continue. "You can't stand that I would be interested in someone else, so you soothe your ego by framing the new man with the worst possible label. Charlie has been married, for heaven's sake. Has McCarthy gotten to you too?"

"I'm telling the truth."

"Sure, square with me. What is this really about—a minister spreading a vicious lie? I can't believe you dragged me down here for some male face-saving. Those are weird people you're talking about. Charlie is not one of those."

He narrowed his eyes. "Men know. It can't be hidden. And

ministers see this sort of thing all the time. I followed him. I followed him into one of those neighborhoods in Pittsburgh. The ones that people don't talk about."

My world careened to a stop. I couldn't believe it. Those kinds of people were perverted—I had read about them in *Time* magazine. Charles was kind. What was Howard saying? Not Charlie.

"He must have been lost, or visiting a client, or delivering papers."

"I saw him dancing, with another man."

His words were foreign to me. Men dancing with men. A censor's curtain blocked the image in my mind. "You went in a queer bar?"

"Yes." He didn't look happy about his answer.

I put my hand up to ward off any more information. "This is ridiculous, such trash coming from someone like you." I got up to leave, and Howard grabbed my arm.

"I'm only trying to protect you. Charles is not normal."

I jerked my arm from his grip and stumbled out onto the street.

A homosexual? A queasiness came over me as I recaptured a memory of our night together.

* * *

"It's possible." Adele sat in my living room, watching me fume over Howard's insinuation.

"What's possible?"

"That Charles is a homosexual." Sadness filled her face, and I could feel the fury in mine.

"How can you say that? You just don't want me to be happy," I accused her. "You've met him…he's such a gentle, kind person—"

"Gentle and kind has nothing to do with it. People are who they are. I'm trying to be honest with you. If your friends aren't truthful, who will be?"

My head pounded, and my palms broke into a sweat.

"Take a deep breath and hear me out."

I sat beside her but didn't sit back into the cushions—my stomach taut against the blows my insides were going to get. "Go on."

"Why would Howard make up such a story?" Adele asked.

"He's…he's jealous. He doesn't want me to be happy with anyone else."

"Do you really believe that?"

"This all seems so impossible. Why did you say he could be a homosexual?"

"I think he's a little bit effeminate."

"I don't see that. Charlie fathered a child, for heaven's sake."

"It's very difficult to be homosexual. Many of these men try marriage and live a lie. The alternative is so painful. They are ostracized, ridiculed, cast out from their families." Adele put her hand on mine. "Charlie may have suspected his condition early on and married to prove himself wrong. Besides, if he were found out, he might be fired from his job…or unable to get one."

I rose from my chair and paced, weighing Adele's words. I spun to face her. "And how do you know so much?"

"I'm a nurse. We encounter many kinds of people, people who confide in us," she said gently. "People like Charlie are in a lot of pain."

"Can't he be cured? I could help him."

"I'm not so sure that's possible, but there are doctors who claim to cure them. The homosexuals I've come across don't want to be that way, but they've always felt different, and sometimes they fall in love with another man. One patient I knew had been with his…well, lover for twenty years. It is kind of weird to think about, though."

I shuddered to recall Charlie's warm embrace that may have embraced a man in the same way.

"What can I do?"

"Talk to Charlie."

30

Charlie arrived a week later to have dinner at my house. He kissed me, the soft kiss of a gentleman, not like John Graham's hard, insistent buss. During dinner, his conversation was calm, oblivious to my internal torment.

I studied him. His wrists moved normally. I listened to his speech. His voice was deep, and his Adam's apple moved with his words. But what about the dancing Howard witnessed?

My words were fast and nervous, anxious to fill up any milliseconds of silence, avoiding *the question*. I mentally rehearsed broaching such a sensitive topic with Charlie. What terms would I use or should I have just brought it up like "Say, do you know any homosexuals?"

Stalling, I played with the leftover peas on my plate, pushing them from pork chop bone to the small pool of gravy beside the remnants of the mashed potatoes. I noticed that Charlie was making dents in his potatoes with the tines of his fork. He did have very manicured nails, like a woman, not like my father's with ragged cuticles. I put that observation in the "uh-oh" column.

"What've you been doing this past week?" In spite of my attempt to be casual, I heard a catch in my voice.

"Not much. Same thing I always do." He regarded me with casualness. "How about you? Any more repercussions from your Santa story?"

"I watch the buzzards circling overhead, waiting for me to succumb from paranoia."

"Good image." Charlie wiped his mouth with his napkin, leaned on the table with his elbows, and rested his chin on his folded hands. "You've been staring at me all evening. What is it?"

I put down my fork and sighed, resisting the urge to say "Oh, nothing." Instead, I said in one breath in double time, "A friend of mine thinks you're a homosexual."

Charlie dropped his hands, pushed back his chair and snarled, "That is the meanest thing I have ever heard. Do you believe that?" His beautiful blue eyes had darkened and narrowed.

"I don't think so, but—"

"But what?" His face paled, and he looked at me with disbelief.

I panicked, fearful I had chosen to believe a mean spirited ex-boyfriend. "Oh, Charlie, I'm sorry I brought it up, it's stupid, I—"

"You what? Are suspicious? I fathered a child, for heaven's sake."

I got out of my chair and knelt beside him. I took his hands, kissed them and rested my head on his knees. "I'm sorry, I believe you. You're such a good person, I never should have given that malicious lie any thought. Please forgive me."

Charlie first choked back soft, mournful barks and finally let go into sobs. He withdrew his hands and covered his face. There were no words, only the inconsolable sounds of a man crying his confession. My heart fell into the earth.

"Charlie, I—"

"Stop," he turned away, "I don't want your pity."

I needed a moment to myself to gather my wits and sanity. "Go sit in the living room and I'll bring us some tea." Yes, hot tea always made the unbearable bearable, my mother would say. I made a hasty exit into the kitchen and hoped he would follow my suggestion. Between getting the cups and saucers out of the cupboard and putting the teakettle on to boil, I heard Charlie's chair scuff back on the wooden dining room floor. I wanted to disappear through the kitchen wall back into my make believe world where Charlie and I had a future.

I took a tray in with the teapot, sugar, creamer, and cups. As best I could with shaking hands, I poured the tea and whispered "sugar?" as though a louder voice might crack the veneer of control. He nodded "yes" and held up two fingers for the number of sugar cubes he wanted. He waved away the cream. His eyes were vacant, and he stared at nothing.

We sat in utter silence for at least five minutes. An occasional sip of tea, and the clatter of a cup reuniting with its saucer were the only sounds. I didn't know what to say so I didn't say anything. I didn't even have the right words to think, so I didn't think. I sensed we both needed a respite from expression or judgment.

Charlie broke the silence. Still looking at nothing he asked, "Who told you?"

"Howard, the minister who wouldn't marry me because of my impurity. Figures, huh?"

"A minister. Saving the world from Satan." Charlie got up and walked to the window. He pulled the curtain back to peer outside. "How did he know?"

"He was suspicious and followed you in Pittsburgh. He—"

"He followed me into a bar." Charlie continued to look at nothing out the window.

"Charlie, I don't know anything about your condition, or your life—"

He glared at me, accusation written all over his face. "My condition?"

"It's a condition, isn't it, I mean, you can be treated, can't you?"

He threw up his hands. "Ask anyone in my situation. It's like the direction the river runs, the way the sun rises and sets, the—"

"But you and me and Bobby—how?" Questions throbbed in my head.

"I tried to be normal, as they say." He rubbed his forehead. "I got married, you know, but she eventually found out. I hated myself. And when I heard about you, I thought maybe I could try again, away from Pittsburgh. But I'm finding out that it's hard to run from the truth, my truth, at least." He looked down at his feet. "I'm sorry. I wasn't thinking of you."

"I'm so confused. I don't understand things like this." The honest glimpse into Charlie's life stirred something in me. "Help me understand."

Charlie took a seat and we sat in silent retreat. He finally spoke. "I guess this is it, isn't it?" His face registered with resignation and defeat. His eyes were moist. "I had such hope for a family and such fear that it was impossible. For you to find out about me was worse than death." He wiped his eyes. "Not very manly to cry, is it?" He looked away.

"It takes courage for a man to cry."

"You probably don't want anything to do with me, and I'll have no way to watch my son grow up." He put his head in his hands again and moaned.

"Charlie," I began, "I can't pretend to understand, but I'm willing to try. I still want you in my life. Can't we be friends?"

He looked at me with stunned gratefulness. "You're willing to do that?"

"Of course, we have a history together."

"Margaret, can you possibly understand what it means for me to have a son? I still want to meet him."

His words stuck in midair.

"You think I could be a bad influence on him, don't you? That's what people assume, and I can see it in your face." Charlie's face was glum, and he picked at some non-existent lint on his arm.

"I have a lot to learn about homosexuals, Charlie. Please be patient." I took his hands and caught his eyes. "Correct my thinking."

"First of all, drop the word 'homosexual.' It's too clinical."

I was confused. "Isn't 'queer' a bad word?"

Charlie shook his head. "No, Margaret, not 'queer.' More and more we are using the word 'gay,' at least in the cities."

"You're happy?" I felt stupid in addition to uncomfortable.

He blinked at me twice. "No, it doesn't mean happy. Forget it."

"Okay, 'gay.'"

"We don't recruit boys, you know—like missionaries recruit Christians."

"Mother wouldn't like that analogy."

"We are who we are and leave well enough alone. Do you believe me?"

"I'm trying."

Charlie stood up and walked from one end of the living room back to me. "Please, can I meet my son?"

The pleading in his eyes prevailed. "Let's see what I can do."

* * *

The following morning I stood in the elevator, hand on the control, wishing I could push the lever to "answer." Did it matter if Charlie was a homosexual? Did I want Charlie in Bobby's life?

I greeted customers as they ambled by, engaged in small talk about weather, but the movie playing in my mind was in the living room with Charlie. It still hurt to remember his plaintive crying, his confession about his homosexuality.

"Morning, Margaret, you seem awfully deep in thought."

Lena's voice brought me back to attention. "Oh, stuff," I said. "Nothing important."

Lena was cordial, but the closeness was gone forever. We rode in silence, and I accepted the stab of remorse as I remembered how her pitiful life was a backdrop for my Santa story. Watching her exit onto the third floor, I wondered what pains she had suffered that made her so fussy. And who was I to assume her life was pitiful?

The buzzer rang, and I went down to the second floor. I opened the door to Mrs. Gibbons. "Basement please," she said. I had been the victor in our last encounter when *her* slip was showing. But today there was no pleasure from that victory.

"How's your mother?" Mrs. Gibbons asked.

"The same."

"Did they ever find out who put that awful magazine in the dressing room?"

I shook my head "no" without making eye contact.

With Mrs. Gibbons gone, I closed the doors and sat on the stool, waiting for the next call.

It's all so difficult. Last night I committed to being Charlie's friend. I wasn't even sure what a friend did—I never gave it much thought before. Adele listened to me, laughed with me, and helped me identify Bobby. I remembered with some pain that she cautioned me about my connection to Bobby, even at the risk of our friendship. So honesty in the face of judgment was also a moniker of a friend. That was a tough one.

I fingered the bracelet Charlie gave me last night. He intended to give it to me, but my confrontation and his confession gave it even more meaning as a friendship bracelet.

But being a friend with Charlie was uncharted territory for me. What might help him would probably make life more difficult for me. I couldn't think of anyone except Adele who would understand why I would choose to be friends with a homosexual. And he had asked to see my...well, our son. What if the Taylors recognized who, and what, Charlie was? Did it matter?

What would Margo do? I searched the many scenes of the movie in my head and landed on the party scene. I imagined myself on the staircase, drink in hand, mocking the admonitions of my friends to be more gracious and more cautious with my words. My skirt rustled as I climbed the stairs and said something about a bumpy ride and seatbelts. Okay, Margo, you've told me this one before. I heard your call to throw caution aside.

I examined the elevator control and decided to trust fate. If my next call was *down* to the basement, I wouldn't take Charlie to meet Bobby. If my next call was *up* to the second or third floor, father and son would get to meet. I took a deep breath of relief.

The buzzer rang. I grabbed the control and pushed the black handle forward and started upward to the third floor.

31

Charlie and I stood outside the Taylors' home, and the door looked a hundred miles away. His hand was slippery in mine.

Mrs. Taylor had been cool but cordial when I called to ask if I could visit Bobby and the kitten. I had to wait four days, a lifetime, between that call and the moment on the doorstep.

"This is what I've been dreaming about recently, getting to know our son, together."

Charlie inhaled and let out his breath slowly. "They don't know our connection, do they?"

"No, and I don't want them to. I want to be a friendly lady who gets to be part of Bobby's life. Every minute with him subtracts a little bit of pain from the last ten years."

Charlie squeezed my hand, and we approached the front door. I knocked, and when the door opened, hope opened with it.

"Hello, Margaret." Mrs. Taylor's smile changed into a quizzical frown when she noticed Charlie. "I didn't know you were bringing a gentleman friend."

"I hope it's okay," I said. "Charlie is visiting from out of town, and he likes cats and all, and when I told him about the new kitten, he wanted to come along." Charlie stood there and gave a beatific smile to Mrs. Taylor. He was good. It must have been his lawyer training.

"I suppose so," she said with her head cocked. "Come on in." She motioned us to step inside. "Bobby, you have some company."

We saw Bobby clomping down the stairs in Roy Rogers cowboy boots holding Maggie, the kitten. He brightened to see me and turned shyly toward Charlie. "Who are you?"

"I'm a friend of Miss Landings. You must be Bobby."

Charlie put out his hand to shake. Bobby had an armful of cat, and he made an awkward move to return the gentlemanly greeting.

Bobby came closer to me. "Look, Miss Landings, I taught Maggie a game." He put the cat down and pulled out a string with a plastic fish tied on it. "Come on, Maggie. Let's go fishing." He dangled the toy in front of the kitten, and she batted at it with her paws, first one then the other. Bobby bounced the fish up and down, making Maggie jump, roll, and spin in an effort to get at the blue-green prey.

"May I try?" I took the string and waved it in front of the kitten, who stared at me instead of the fish. No amount of string waving and "go fishing" directives had any effect on Maggie. To make matters worse, a tingling sensation danced in my nostrils, and I pinched my nose to keep from sneezing.

"No, no," Bobby announced. "You have to bob it, like bait," which he did, and Maggie started jumping at the fish.

"Let me try it," said Charlie. He did as Bobby directed, and the three of us laughed as Charlie teased Maggie with the toy.

I couldn't believe I was watching my son, but I ached to be more than an onlooker. I was Bobby's protector when I was pregnant, nourishing him through his months of residence in my body. When he was born, his personality was a promise, hidden behind the dependent, sleepy softness of infancy that I wouldn't witness.

As I watched him playing fish with the cat, I thought of Bobby as an infant, snuggled in my arms before the social worker took him away. If there was ever a definition of bliss, it would be the weight of my newborn son in my arms. The meaning of hell is having that blessedness whisked away.

I glanced up to see Mrs. Taylor studying Charlie and me.

She broke her stare and said, "I'll be right back."

She turned on her heel, almost tripping over an ottoman. She came back with a bewildered Mr. Taylor in hand. The Taylors' stares filled the room. I watched as they surveyed the scene, first to Bobby—who was still engrossed in his fishing cat, to Charlie—who looked rapturous as he knelt beside his unknowing son, and back to me. Their eyes bounced between Charlie and Bobby, then to me, and then back to Charlie and Bobby, but most between me and Bobby.

"I think it's time for you to go," Mt. Taylor said to me.

Charlie frowned at the sudden dismissal. "I guess we should go." He got up off the floor. He helped Bobby get up and patted the boy's crew cut, but Mr. Taylor brushed Charlie's hand off his son's head.

"Please leave. Bobby has chores to do."

The atmosphere in the room chilled, and Bobby stopped playing. "But, Dad, we're having fun."

"Go to your room."

He did what he was told but not before scooping up Maggie and waving a goodbye. As soon as Bobby was out of the room, Mr. Taylor stepped toward me. "Who are you?"

Charlie took a protective step toward me, but I answered, "I don't know what you mean. I came to play with Bobby—"

"I don't know what you are up to, but we don't like you being here." He handed over my coat and purse. "And Miss Landings, we appreciate the kitten, but we need to get on with things, and so do you, so we would be grateful if you would not come here again."

Humiliation crawled over my skin. "I don't understand."

Mrs. Taylor opened the door. Charlie and I made it to the front stoop, but Mr. Taylor stopped me with a strong hand on my shoulder. "You have no right to disrupt our family like this. I trust this is the end of the matter." He hesitated. "You can't be part of our lives," he said with a catch in his voice. He let go, and I hurried to the car where Charlie was already waiting in the driver's seat. We pulled away as soon as I shut the car door.

"What the hell happened in there?" Charlie asked, his hands tightening on the steering wheel. He looked at me with confusion and became alarmed when he saw my face. My eyes were burning, and I was sure that my nose was crimson red. Charlie pulled the car over and turned off the engine. He put his back to the car door and said, "Let's talk."

"They looked as though they had seen a ghost. Do you think they realized we are Bobby's parents?" I rubbed my shoulder where Mr. Taylor's squeeze lingered. "I didn't think we could be identified. I just wanted us to spend some time with our son."

He shook his head. "I'm an attorney, I should have known better." He rubbed his temples with his thumbs. "It's their child. What were we thinking?"

"Can you blame me for wanting to be near my son?"

Charlie regarded me with pity. "Yes, I can. You gave up your parental rights ten years ago." He stopped and stared at the dashboard. "Bobby is theirs. That's all there is to it."

I put my head on Charlie's shoulder and cried. "All these years I've wondered who he was, what he was like. I don't want to lose him again." Charlie took my shoulders and pushed me away.

"Get a hold of yourself. The reason you gave Bobby up for adoption was so he could have a good upbringing with two loving parents, and he has that. You also needed to get on with your life, and you did that. You have to see things as they are. You can't turn back time."

He let go and grabbed the steering wheel like a podium. "It's time we both get on with our lives. I have a life in Pittsburgh that may not be the best in most people's eyes, but it's satisfying and sufficient."

Numb, I listened to him.

"I didn't realize how sufficient it was until I tried one last time to make it different. I'm taking you home, and I'm going back to Pittsburgh."

"Don't you want to see Bobby again?" I wiped my nose on my coat sleeve. Charlie handed me his handkerchief.

"It doesn't matter if I want to see Bobby again." His voice had a hard edge. "I don't know why I let you draw me into your fantasy." He looked away.

"Draw you into *my* fantasy?" I shouted. "You're the one who searched for me."

Charlie put his head on the steering wheel and spoke through the triangles of space. "We *are* a pair, aren't we? We messed up a second time. Bobby is a wonderful boy who wouldn't exist if we hadn't gotten together. But he's a gift to the Taylors, not to us."

I didn't know what to say. His words slammed me against the obvious.

His posture softened and he took my hand. "I'm sorry I blamed you for my misjudgment. You gave Bobby up in his best interest, and that took a lot of courage. I don't blame you at all for wanting a relationship with him. Maybe in the future birth parents will have contact with their children, but not in this day and age."

"That's easy for you to say. You've only thought of being a father for a few weeks. I've been a mother for ten years. I felt him grow in me, for heaven's sake." I glared at him.

"You gave up Bobby for adoption, but you really never did give him up, you know, and when you found him again, you were under the illusion that you could compensate for giving him up."

"And you never gave up hope of being normal." I saw the stricken look on Charlie's face. "I didn't mean to say that."

Charlie's gloom was written in his dulled eyes. "It's all right. We've both fantasized about being the American family, haven't we?"

We sat for another few minutes, letting words and thoughts tumble around and fall into some recognizable shape. Charlie broke the silence. "You've been a good friend. You accepted me as I am… well, maybe," he sighed, "after the initial shock."

I broke down again. "What if I never get to see Bobby again?"

"Let's take it a day at a time." Charlie patted my knee, and I moved back to the passenger side. He put the car in gear and drove, eventually reaching Vine Street, just off the main drag.

We waited for a traffic light to change, and Charlie looked over to the curbside newsstand. "What about the other crisis in your life, your stories?"

"You would have to bring that up." I blew my nose. "I'm excited to see the next one. I tried really hard to camouflage the characters. I don't need any more drama."

Charlie pointed to the magazines on the sidewalk stand. There in the front rack was *Forbidden Love* magazine, its cover emblazoned with a waltzing couple and a title "I Left Him on the Dance Floor, and She Waltzed into His Life."

I gasped. "Oh, criminy."

32

We sat on the sofa, Charlie and I, each with a cup of tea, and *Forbidden Love* magazine spread across our laps.

"I'm going from one calamity to another," I said. An hour ago I was chased out of the Taylors' house. Nothing but bad, it seemed, had happened since I came back to Liberty. All bad except Charlie, and he was, well, half bad. The good half was gentle, caring, and intelligent. The bad half, for me, was that he preferred men.

"Life is not boring with you, I'll say that."

I stared at the magazine, afraid to open it yet glad to have a distraction from the heartbreak of the visit to the Taylors. "At least that doesn't resemble John Graham on the cover. I can't believe I didn't get my copy before it came out on the newsstands." Charlie made no move. I took a deep breath and opened to page forty-eight—the home for my story.

I gave the magazine to Charlie and stood up. "I can't stand it. You read it while I straighten up the kitchen."

I wiped the counter top in furious circles while I waited for Charlie to finish reading. Each circular swipe evoked another fear. Would people know that the story was based on John and his wife? How would I be able to face him at work? Then I had a cringer—those thoughts that almost stall the heart. What if people thought I was a terrible writer? Both outcomes were abhorrent—John's anger toward me for telling a story that revealed his sham of a marriage, or worse, shame for bad writing. I rubbed away the imagined worries on the counter top.

"Margaret, let's talk," I heard from the living room.

Was Charlie's voice sympathetic? Neutral? Annoyed? Fearful?

I put the exhausted dishrag on the kitchen faucet and wiped my hands.

I sat down next to Charlie and waited for his judgment. I searched his eyes for any clue to his thoughts.

"Well," he said slowly. I held my breath. "Not bad." He looked at me with a professor's candor. "The first paragraph is a grabber, and I wanted to keep reading to see what happened."

I let out my breath. "How man-like of you. I don't want a technical review—I want to know how much trouble I'm in."

"And how would I know that?"

"Can you tell it's about John Graham and his wife?"

"I don't know them well, but does John have dark brown hair and blue eyes?"

"Yes."

"Is her name Ilene?"

"No…it's Elaine."

Charlie grimaced.

"Do they belong to the Elks Club?"

"No."

"Don't worry about it. People read themselves into any chronicle that resembles their lives. Either guilt or hubris does that." He patted her arm.

"Great. So everybody will think themselves the inspiration for the story." I put my head in my hands.

"I imagine there are a lot of people who think themselves as candidates for trashy stories."

I straightened. "Trashy stories?"

Charlie gulped. "I…I don't mean trashy in the sense of badly written." He studied my face to see if he were successful in retracting his gaffe. "It's just a story about trashy people."

He didn't redeem himself.

Charlie sat back and returned my stare. "Have you ever considered newspaper reporting?"

"What's that got to do with anything?" I looked at him, caught off guard by the change of subject.

"You describe setting and scene very well."

"Let me tell you about trying to get a newspaper job in Liberty. The Neanderthal news editor here told me to get a sales clerk job, something more suitable for a single woman."

"Ouch."

"He said he doesn't hire girls as reporters anyway, and he didn't have any secretary jobs. What a jerk." I folded my arms.

"You obviously like to write."

"I do. I cried when I had to resign my job in Pittsburgh. I liked helping people with their own writing. Obviously there are no magazine publishers in a small town like Liberty, but you'd think I'd find something. I thought that being a dutiful daughter would give me some favors, but no."

"And from whom did you expect these 'favors?'"

"Fate." I looked at him, defiant.

The phone rang, making us both jump.

"Maybe that's Fate calling," said Charlie.

I got up to answer. The blood froze in my veins when I heard John Graham's terse voice ask, "How could you?"

"What are you talking about?" I turned toward Charlie, gestured to the phone and shook my head in disbelief.

"My wife brought home a magazine with a very familiar story. Like the one I confided to you. It's us, isn't it?"

"What made you think it was about you?" I swallowed hard.

"The Elks Club *harvest* dance? The *alcoholic spouse*, maybe? Or, how about the *plaid shirt* I wore?"

"I—"

"This is going to be all over town. I defended you over that Santa story as a coincidence, but you promised me that was the end of your tattling stories."

"I—"

"Come in to work tomorrow, early. We have to talk." John hung up.

I scowled at the phone, the dial tone drilling holes into my head.

Charlie stood up. "What's wrong?"

"John knows."

33

I arrived at eight the next morning. Even the shininess of the new paint job on Aqua Bella didn't distract me from what I would have facing me. I could feel the nervous wetness in my armpits, and all the way to the store I rehearsed what I would say to placate John, to convince him that the story was make-believe—I would tell him I read in *Life* magazine about the marital stress of country club members, it was the Elks Club, his wife was much kinder than the woman in the story, and lots of people had drinking problems.

John stood before me with folded arms—his eyes bore into me. "Did you really think you could write about people's lives so blatantly? What were you thinking?" He set his jaw as he waited for my response.

"I didn't think, I guess." I saw my foolishness reflected in his eyes. "It wasn't about you—"

His eyes flashed, and his hands curled into fists. He opened his mouth to say something, but he closed up and his nostrils flared instead. "You were my friend. I trusted you." He took a deep breath. "The harm's done, Margaret. I'm really disappointed. You need to leave."

I gulped and stared and gulped again. "Leave? I start in an hour."

"You don't possibly think you could work here, do you?" John held his body in a formal, unapproachable posture.

I couldn't find any voice. Standing before John, with his disdain projected toward me, I wondered if my eyes reflected the fires of torture.

John stomped away. I covered my mouth to keep the crying in until I could find cover. I looked up at the mezzanine where John had his office and saw him with his head in his hands. I took a last glance at the Monster, whose yawning open door bade me a silent goodbye. I half stumbled out the back door.

I got into my car and started driving, letting the ribbons of streets and roads pull me along. I found myself in farmland, and I focused on keeping the car steady on the dirt and gravel roads. Bella's new paint became covered in dust, but I didn't care. I didn't deserve to have a nice looking car anyway.

Word would get around. People would ask why I wasn't at Graham's, and Mother... she would be so ashamed of me. Fired. Mother's cautions played over and over in my head. "The Landings don't do things like that; why can't you just be normal?"

As a car approached, I reined in my tears. As soon as I was alone on the road again, I let myself cry. If I hadn't needed to be steering, I would have been wringing my hands.

I saw a Texaco sign in what must have been a five-person town, not counting the gas station attendant, and a quick check of my gas gauge confirmed that I needed a fill-up. I wiped my eyes and pulled into the station. I drove over the cord whose dinging announced my arrival, and an old man in dirty work overalls came to the driver's side of the car.

"What'll it be, ma'am?" He had already grabbed a sponge to clean the windshield.

"Fill it up, please."

The old man stopped cleaning and studied me.

"You okay, ma'am? You look a little peak-ed to me."

"Oh, I'm fine, just tired." I let out a long breath from my empty chest and surveyed the countryside beyond the gas station. I remembered that Grams, my favorite grandmother, was buried near here. "Do you know where the Sanctuary Cemetery is? It's nearby, isn't it?"

"Sure, keep going in the same direction you were and turn left at the old house with broken windows. That's Blarney Road. Nice people used to live there, you know. Fell on hard times in the thirties. Heard the old guy kilt himself when his wife died. So sad. Say, you know someone buried at Sanctuary?" He put the hose into the gas tank, and the little window of the pump showed spinning numbers. He checked the oil while the tank filled.

"Yes, my grandmother."

"You don't say… and who was that?" he asked. He wiped the oil stick with an oily rag he had hanging out of his pocket, put it back in the engine and slammed the hood shut.

"Oh, nobody important."

"I might be able to tell you where she's buried. It's a small cemetery but big enough to have trouble findin' somebody." The pump clicked off, and he squeezed his finger on the handle to get a few more pennies of gas in.

"That's fine. I'll do okay."

"Suit yourself. That'll be $2.70…you were almost empty. Want your Green Stamps?"

"No, I don't collect them."

"Really, now. My wife redeemed hers for a new toaster. Sure you don't want 'em?"

"No, but thanks for your help." I gave him a weak wave as I drove out from under the port. In my rear-view mirror I saw him standing there, watching me drive away.

I drove to the house with the broken windows and went left, just as the old man told me. Soon I saw the wrought-iron arch that announced Sanctuary Cemetery. Sleeping cherubs were carved into the limestone pillars that held up the sign.

I slowed and guided my car through the gate and down an uneven dirt path. After fifty yards or so, I pulled over and wondered how to find my grandmother's grave. The dust cloud from the car's movement settled and revealed the weedy maze of the cemetery.

I had no recollection of the grave's location—only the memory of losing a precious confidante some twenty years ago. I missed Grams. She was the epitome of grandmothers—accepting, loving, and full of wise words that made sense to a ten-year-old girl. Maybe Grams could soothe the shame I felt.

Once I got out of the car I wandered up and down the grassy rows of graves. Barton, Cowpers, Smith, no Landings—the names were running together in a sea of limestone panels. A crow in the lone nearby oak tree squawked an annoying raspy talk, and its cawing scraped my nerves. I walked toward the bird to scare it away, but the squawking got louder and louder—punishing me for intruding on its territory. I passed the century-old tree that was the crow's perch, and the bird blessedly stopped its racket. He stared at me, its yellow eyes burrowing into mine. He refused to fly away. My skin chilled, and I looked down. At the toe of my shoe was a simple granite headstone inscribed "Carrie L. Landings."

I fell to the ground and started crying. "I'm in a real mess," I whimpered to Grams, and the floodgates of my misery opened. I had no job, I had a son I couldn't see, I alienated whatever friends I had, and I had no future. Life wasn't about getting, I thought, it was more about giving things up. I sat there blubbering, pulling tufts of grass with each sorrowful thought.

Worn out, I stopped crying. I flipped to my back and watched cotton clouds pass by. Grasshoppers jumped nearby, buzzing with each leap. The sun forced my eyes into tight squints, and I reveled in the warmth of the spring sunshine, the tears cool on my cheeks. My pulse slowed from its desperate rhythm and Grams' calm enveloped me. I fingered some dandelions with my outstretched hand, and my mind wandered to the tenacity of those stubborn weeds. Year after year they emerged after frozen winters, drying summers. If dandelions could do it, why couldn't I?

I turned my head and stared at Grams' name etched on the granite and replayed the conversations we had had—advice on boyfriends ("Play a little hard to get, Maggie"), what I was going to be when I grew up ("Let your spirit tell you, dear"), and how to get along with Mother ("You're loved, that's enough").

I lay on the warm grass a long, long time waiting for Grams to talk to me, to push some sensible advice through the garbage in my brain to some conscious level. Maybe I was expecting too much from a dead, embalmed grandmother. The sun warmed me like a quilt, and my eyes got heavy.

I woke to the flutter of wings and saw a flurry of black feathers in my peripheral vision. The crow, who had been silent since I had been at the grave site, sat in a tree above my car. Do something, the stare commanded. He cawed, "Grow up."

I stood and brushed the loose grass off my dress. "Okay, okay, I'm climbing out of my self-pity, Mr. Crow."

The bird had deposited a gift on the hood of my car as only large birds would do, but I left it as a reminder of the problems I caused by not thinking things through. I climbed into the car and headed home. I drove with deliberation—I obeyed every stop sign, used the signal for every turn. The crow was right—it was time to grow up. I started with small things, like obeying traffic rules.

The cornfields flew by as quickly as my thoughts. I played with life's maxims. Rule number one: don't use people. Lena and John were my teachers on that. It required not doing something. Rule number two: be truthful in spite of the consequences. That would be more burdensome, in spite of Charlie's patient tutorials. That rule meant I had to do something, usually painful, to make things honest. I had to trust that the pain would be temporary and would lead to a later reward—like turning down a piece of pie in anticipation of fitting into a new dress.

I had to tell Mother about my firing. What if word about my firing was the last news she heard? She deserved to hear it from me.

34

The crow's eyes and raspy caw wouldn't leave me. My fourth grade teacher had told us something about Indians and their spirit animals, but the memory was hazy, caught in a fog of passing notes to Susie and watching my nemesis Charlie Black stick his tongue out at me. I did remember swinging around in my seat when I heard Mrs. Mendal say, "Animals spoke to the Indians."

Back in town, I turned Bella toward the hospital, but seeing the library, I pulled into that parking lot instead.

"What do you have about animal spirit guides?" I asked the librarian.

She frowned. "Well…let's go see." She took off for the far corner of the library—the children's section. I had to scurry and finally caught up to her when she pulled out a book *All About American Indians*. "Do you have a particular animal in mind?"

"A crow."

"A crow or a raven? There's a difference."

"I guess I don't know."

At that, she headed to a nearby shelf and pulled out a book of birds. After checking the index, she showed me side-by-side pictures of a crow and a raven. I studied the smaller crow and the larger raven that had a thicker, curved beak. I pointed to the raven. "That's it."

"Very interesting." She motioned for us to sit at a table, child size of course, and we sat with our knees to our chests and leaned over to examine the Indian book. "American Indian" book, she corrected me.

"Here we are. The raven. 'The raven is a symbol of change, bringing light to the darkness. It appears to you when you are most upset, and guides you out of your darkness. It leads you to your truth so you can fulfill your destiny.'"

I sat stunned. *Bring light to the darkness…leads you to your truth?* No one would believe this, especially Mother. I didn't think Presbyterians catered to such notions. But it made sense to me. That raven led me to Grams so I could encounter truth. Rolling on the grass and staring at clouds probably helped also.

"You don't believe in this stuff, do you?" The librarian studied me as though she already had the answer.

"Oh, no, I…" Truth, Margaret, the truth. What was I afraid of? "I don't know."

"It's the devil's work, if you ask me," and she pushed the book back into its allotted space.

* * *

I approached Sister Agatha to get my visitor's card. She probably didn't believe in animal guides.

Mother lay in the plastic tent, which had a blue cast to it. I looked closer and saw that it was her skin. The pink radiance of life was gone, and she was still. Too still. I panicked and ran out to the hall. "Please help, my mother isn't breathing!" I could hardly breathe myself.

Adele ran into the room.

"What's happening?" I watched Adele taking Mother's pulse.

Another nurse rushed in and at Adele's nod, she took me out of the room.

"I want to go back," I cried.

"It's best you stay out here, so we can take care of your mother."

The nurse gently pushed me from the room and went back in, closing the door behind her.

I went to the door, opened it a crack, and peeked inside. Adele was stroking Mother's hair, and the other nurse was listening to my mother's heart through a stethoscope. The nurse shook her head. Adele looked upward to see me peeking through the door.

"I'm so sorry, Margaret, your mother is gone."

My hand flew to my mouth, and I stifled a sob. Adele came and put her arms around me.

"I'll leave you alone with your mother for a while so you can say your goodbyes," she said then left me alone.

I took her hand, which was cool but still soft to the touch. There was a lump in my throat, preventing any words about my misery, my longing, and my grief. "I love you, Mother." I put my head down on the bed beside her quiet body. "Are you with Daddy now?"

* * *

I left the hospital with a bag of Mother's belongings. I sat crying in the car and looked through the last things she had touched or set her eyes upon. One of the items was a photo of the three of us in 1938—Mother, Dad, and myself, grinning in front of the family home—the home I had owned since I returned to Liberty. The painful truth hit me that I was at the top of the family chain—alone and dangling there by myself with links above me and a mystery link below me.

What was my life going to be like without having a mother to hug or a mother to please? Lighter? Heavier? With Mother gone, what do I do with the daily minutiae that beg to be shared?

At home, drink in hand, I sat under the *Life* magazine cover of Bette Davis, whose gaze was locked onto some unknown object in the room. "For Mother," I said to the poster. Bette stared back like my mother's lifeless eyes.

I cried, sniffed, blew my nose and cried again. My self-pity was embarrassing, even though there was no one in the room to judge my weakness. I picked up the family photo again and commenced my own staring, my mind empty. It filled suddenly and dramatically with the image of a newspaper headline— "Local Woman Found Dead Gripping Late Mother's Photo." I went into the bathroom and threw some cold water on my face. Revived, I went into the living room. Now what?

The what appeared at the door. Kathy stood on the front stoop. She held an offering wrapped in a striped dish towel, most likely a loaf of Irish soda bread, a Celtic sign of friendship she once told me, but then I was never sure which of her stories were true or manufactured.

"How're ya doing?" She held out the bread toward me.

Her caring unplugged my emotions, and I bawled. She put her arms around me, the towel-wrapped bread at my back. The still warm loaf gave off a comforting aroma. Arms and fresh bread were the best gifts she could have given me.

"It's hard to be losing a mother," she said.

I sniffed and opened the door wider so she could come in. I took the bread, warm in my hands, and placed it on the kitchen counter. Back in the living room Kathy was holding the photo of my parents and me.

"You have your mother's eyes," she said. "She was a very kind and considerate neighbor," Kathy smiled and added, "but I've really enjoyed the daughter...you."

"When your mother died, did you feel like you had told her everything you wanted to tell her?"

"Good heavens, no," she said. "Are ya having a guilt trip, as they say, about something?"

"I wasn't with her when she died. I wanted to talk to her about something important, but she was gone." Tears spilled over, and I grabbed a tissue from the box on the coffee table.

Kathy came and sat beside me on the sofa. "Ya know, dear friend, all a mother needs or wants to know is that she was a good mother, in spite o' her mistakes. And I'm sure you told her that in actions if not in words."

I thought about the times I sat by her bed and held her hand. I told her I loved her many times, but did I tell her she was a good mother?

"Did you tell her you were glad to be her daughter?"

"Hmmm...not in those exact words, but I hope 'I love you' goes a long way."

"She understood. I was her neighbor, and there were many a' time we would talk through the gate about how proud she was of you. She would light up at the mention o' your name."

Kathy's words buoyed me.

"So, what can I do to help?" she asked.

35

My role as chief griever began at the house. Kathy and Adele took over hostess duties while I mingled with the visitors. Some callers carried items in while casting periscope eyes over as much of the house as possible. "My, this looks so different than when your mother was here." Those who carried goodwill as well as their casseroles stood at the door humbly and said things like, "I know you're probably getting a lot of food, but I admired your mother so much, I wanted to do something," and then offer up their homemade love. After two days, pies, cakes, casseroles, and salads of questionable contents filled the refrigerator and covered the kitchen counters.

Mrs. Borden even brought her signature offering—"brownies of death"—aptly named by all those who had received them whenever there was a family tragedy. The rich chocolate treat served a critical function—when conversations became too weepy, people slipped into the kitchen for their sugary solace and emerged with chocolate crumbs on their chins and faces. Kathy and Adele were appointed chocolate-face watchers—mine as well as the visitors. I would be alerted but the visitors were not. They were unwitting objects of needed humor.

* * *

On the day of the funeral, I peeked through the door of the sacristy to see who had come to the service. I immediately spotted the bridge group—including Mrs. Gibbons, seated humbly halfway down the pews. In the second row, in back of where I was to sit, were my closest friends, Kathy and her husband, Adele and her fiancé, and Charlie.

Charlie had been so patient with my grief and had assisted me with all the arrangements—the hymns, scriptures, and the eulogy. He listened when I recounted fond memories that made me cry. He was helpful when I picked out the clothes my mother would be wearing for the viewing—it was almost like having a girlfriend, better than a girlfriend. I had the company of a man. I told Charlie that I wondered if the dead know what families clothe them in for their last journey. A corpse somewhere must have muttered "Oh, no, not the blue dress, it makes me look fat." Charlie laughed at that.

My uncle, my mother's only sibling, stood beside me as we waited to emerge from our inner sanctum. I examined the empty space reserved for Uncle Roger and me—the empty space that awaits the VIP griever—the person who feels the most loss of the departed. I imagined Bobby sitting there for me someday. He would be the link beyond me.

Uncle Roger and I watched the stream of mourners making their way up the maroon carpeted aisle to their seats. "I see the town cronies have taken their seats in the front half of the church," he said. "The rows must be numbered in gradations of wealth."

"Uncle Roger," I whispered. "You are so bad. You never did like Liberty, did you?"

He regarded me with crinkled eyes. "Your father was a prosperous man, and your mother adapted well to being a big fish in a little pond, but she never took too seriously the rigors of small town society life."

"She could have fooled me. If I heard once, I heard her say a thousand times 'What will people think?'"

"That's part of small town living. You have to protect yourself." He paused. "You were smart to get away, Maggie, at least for a little while. Helps put things into perspective."

I gave Uncle Roger a grateful smile. "It's a mixed blessing, isn't it? You can be anonymous in a city when you need to be but it's nice to have roots, healthy roots at least. I can't decide if Liberty is a town to come home to or a town to run from."

"Depends if roots strangle a person or spread to give you a foundation, I guess."

"Good point." I thought about what Uncle Roger had said. My roots were both strangling and comforting me that day.

"You're more Wilson than Landings, young woman. You have your mother's spunk. Your father was a good man, a quiet man. But your mother had the energy." He patted my shoulder. "I'm proud of you, you know. And I'm glad you don't have the Wilson hiccups today, either. Only the Wilson hiccups sound like a bull-riding cowboy."

"Don't even bring it up, that's bad luck."

"If you're not hiccupping yet, you won't. I'm sure." He gave me a wink of support. He looked over my shoulder. "So that's the young man who's been helping you out the last few days, eh?" He gestured toward Charlie. "Strange he would show up after all these years. You knew him in college?"

My face grew hot. "He's divorced now. Guess he couldn't get me out of his head."

"I see."

"He was able to take some time off work to help me out."

We stopped talking and continued our surveillance of the parade of mourners.

"Oh my gosh." I took hold of Uncle Roger's arm. In the back of the church was Howard, who was tugging at his clerical collar. Next to him was John Graham, alone. By their postures and mouth movements, I assumed they were introducing themselves.

"What is it?"

"Oh nothing," I lied. "Actually, the men in my life are following me like a buzzard, smelling carrion. There are several sitting together in the back."

Pastor Engleman, who just stepped into the sacristy, cleared his throat. I asked him, "Is my nose red from crying?"

"You're fine."

When I turned back I noticed the employees from Graham's Department Store. I saw Mr. Concord wave to Mrs. Remington, and Lena gave a "hey ya" wave to Jess Barry. Everyone who was anyone in my stories was lined up as reminders of my careless literary efforts. The soft talk bounced within the stone walls of the church like a ping pong ball gone wild, but I couldn't hear the words. What were they saying?

The organist started playing "Closer My God to Thee," and that was our signal to follow the minister out of the sacristy, down the steps in front of God and most of Liberty, to our appointed seats in the "Special Mourners Row." A barrage of flower scents hit me as I walked by the bank of lilies, roses, and a sundry of floral arrangements. I walked semi-sideways so I didn't give anyone a clear view of my griever's scarlet nose.

We sat with the casket in front of us. Mother was in there, I reminded myself, and I would never see her smile again, feel her soft hands in mine, or hear her laugh. My nose blossomed more with each squelched sob.

The music stopped and the minister stepped up to the podium.

"Dearly beloved," he intoned, "we are here today to celebrate the life of Katherine Landings. I want to start with her favorite scripture, Deuteronomy 6, verse 5. She told me in the hospital that whenever she was confused, this verse reminded her of what life was all about. 'And thou shalt love the Lord thy God with all thine heart, and with all thy soul, and with all thy might.'"

I poked Uncle Roger. "We never talked about the Bible. She never told me about her favorite scriptures."

He shrugged. "Doesn't surprise me."

Pastor Engleman continued. "We've heard this so often that most of us don't even pause to consider what it means. To Katherine it meant humility, it was a spiritual goal that she strove for but knew she could never do well enough for her Lord. And we all know, that for Katherine, humility was a very real struggle." A wave of subdued giggles rippled through the church. "Yes, she is laughing with you. She had a great sense of humor...she taught me a lot. Yes, taught me, her pastor."

"I bet she taught him not to roll his eyes," I said to my uncle.

"Let us take one part of that verse and see it through Katherine's spirit. '...with all thy soul...'" He paused to look at the congregation. "The Hebrew word for soul is 'nephesh,' and it is used over seven hundred times in the Old Testament and has over forty uses. When I told that to Katherine one afternoon, she said in a not too lady-like way, 'Criminy, how am I supposed to make sense of that?'"

I heard another ripple of soft laughter, and I wanted to run up to the casket in front of us, open the lid, and ask her how she could use that word but insisted I not? Instead, I burst into big watery tears that escaped my eyes and nose and ran down my cheeks. Uncle Roger patted my hand and handed me a fresh handkerchief, always ready in his suit pocket for a moment of gallantry.

"Many times we think of the soul as the part of us that is life. When we die, the soul leaves the body and goes heavenward. But what of the saying, 'She is a good soul?' Many people said that about Katherine. What were they saying about the woman who now lies in repose before us? The word 'soul' is full of meaning: self, life, person, appetite, mind, living being, desire, emotion, passion. Doesn't that describe all parts of us? Our personalities? Our talents? Our weaknesses? So as Katherine demonstrated in the way she lived, she realized that she was imperfect and also knew that her imperfect self was good enough. Although her standards were high, she didn't expect perfection in others. She realized that each of us has a soul that is sufficient and capable for loving our Lord."

Did Pastor Engleman direct his eyes at me?

"Hee-yuauah."

Shame seared my neck and face.

"Hee-yuauah."

"Oh, no, Margaret, not your hiccups," Uncle Roger whispered.

"I can't help it. Hee-yuauah."

A twitter of giggles erupted in the row right behind me, and I rotated in my seat to see everyone but Charlie holding their hands over their mouths, eyes shut, trying not to laugh. Charlie looked at me, confused. Pastor Engleman stopped his eulogy, his eyes wide and perplexed.

Not having a paper bag, I breathed into my cupped hands. I held my breath. Uncle Roger dug the nails of his right hand into my forearm. All was quiet.

"Another of Katherine's favorite scriptures was from 1 Thessalonians 4:16. She drew great strength upon the Lord's promise to come again." Pastor Engleman lifted his chin, drew a breath for maximum volume and intoned, "For the Lord himself will come down from heaven, with a loud command, with the voice of the archangel and with the trumpet call of God—"

"Hee-yuauah."

The congregation burst into laughter, and Pastor Engleman signaled the organist to proceed to the next hymn. Through the heavy pumping of the organ and strains of "A Mighty Fortress Is Our God," the laughter diminished to a few twitters and finally to plain old Presbyterian singing. My hiccups stopped and the service continued without any more interruptions on my part.

In the receiving line Uncle Roger and I acknowledged and withstood the comforting words of friends and acquaintances. "She is in a better place" made me wonder what place that was. I grew numb with the onslaught of comments and hugs, all well-meaning.

I looked down the line. Where was Howard? There he was, standing to the side with a cup of Presbyterian punch in his hands, his ear toward Mrs. Remington, and his eyes on Charlie. Was the frown on his face placed there by what he was hearing or what he was seeing? I hoped he was jealous. The next chance I had to glance over, Howard was gone.

And no one mentioned my hiccups until Mrs. Gibbons.

"My goodness, dear, I haven't heard the Wilson hiccups in quite a long time."

"It's a gift I shared with my mother—an appropriate reminder of fun we had together, don't you think?"

She opened her mouth to say something, but nothing came out. She moved quickly toward the beverage table. She stood there looking as if she was expecting someone to talk to her. No one did, and she left the room.

Uncle Roger patted my shoulder. "Good going, Margaret. Your mother would be proud."

The reception line diminished in time to appease my full bladder. I escaped to the Sunday school floor where I might have privacy. I opened the door to the restroom and heard the sound of soft crying. I hesitated to go in but my urgency was profound. There on a slip-covered chair in the restroom was Mrs. Gibbons, her eye makeup streaked and her nose red. She quickly covered her face with her hankie.

"Mrs. Gibbons, are you all right?"

She pulled the hankie away from her face. "You hate me, don't you? Everybody hates me, except your mother and now she's gone." She started crying into her handkerchief again. In muffled words she said, "The Reverend Engleman looked right at me when he said your mother didn't expect perfection…she told me once that I was a lovable old busybody."

"I'm not sure what to say, can we talk after I go to the bathroom, I really have to go…all that punch and all."

Mrs. Gibbons sat straight, startled. "Of course, dear." She wiped her eyes.

"Hold on for just a minute." I went into the stall. When I came out, she was gone.

*   *   *

Later on, Charlie and I settled on my living room sofa, shoes off, feet on the coffee table. The evening had turned chilly, and he had built a small fire that crackled and spit its woody aroma. Mother's presence hung over the room like a gigantic warm quilt.

"I certainly entertained folks, didn't I?"

Charlie gave my hand a squeeze. "Funerals are way too sad. You did everyone a favor."

I gestured toward the kitchen where mystery casseroles sat. "We could have something to eat."

"I'm not too hungry after drinking quarts of Presbyterian punch." He took my hand. "So, what are your plans? Are you going to stay in Liberty now that your mother is gone?"

I put my head back against the cushions. "Criminy, I don't know. Bobby's here now. I need a job, but I don't think anyone will hire me if John doesn't give me a recommendation."

"I don't think you should be alone tonight. I've cleared my schedule for a few more days. I can sleep on the sofa."

"Are you sure you're gay?" I asked. "I could really use a man like you."

"Believe me, I have wondered the same thing." Charlie smiled.

"Do you think my mother is up there rolling her eyes?"

"From what I heard about her at the funeral I would say both."

I played with his hand, the hand of a friend not a lover. "It's strange how death changes things. A flesh and blood mother can trigger guilt and neediness. But the mother who's in heaven becomes… love…with a sense of humor added."

Charlie laughed. "So true."

"Remember me telling you about the raven at the cemetery? Adele told me that ravens and crows also signify impending death. If that's the case, I think it's not only about my mother dying but about time for my old self to die. Pastor Engleman made me think about what kind of soul I have."

"How do you mean?" Charlie sat forward.

"I want to rise like a Phoenix above the ashes of my life," I threw up my hands, "and somehow redeem the selfish and self-centered person I am."

"What makes you so selfish and self-centered?" he asked.

"Oh, I dunno, maybe writing about people's private matters without considering how it will affect them."

"Oh, that. You know there can't be ashes without a fire."

"I've been in the fire…I have truly already been in the fire." We both gazed into the flames that jumped and leaped before us.

36

The closet in my den was haunting me. Behind those doors was the last intimate vestige of my mother's life—her clothes. Now that Mother was gone, a coiled lariat lay in there, ready to spring loose and lasso me to the past. I was tempted to allow myself to be captured, held as a spinster woman living in her dead mother's house, carrying on her mother's life. It would have been so easy.

But I resisted. I wanted to cast off the past, to make 407 Livingston Street my home, my place to grow up. I caught myself. Stay in Liberty? The clothes would hold me back from that journey, always reminding me I was a daughter first, not a woman.

I called Adele, my supreme advisor. "Do you think it would be bad to get rid of Mother's clothes? The church rummage sale is coming up."

There was silence, then she said, "I don't think bad has anything to do with it…but you might be rushing things a little. Are you sure you're ready for that? It's only been a month since your mother died."

"It's too painful having her things here. I miss her so much, but I need to move on. When I first moved in I got rid of the old stuff that even Mother didn't want, and the best I put in the guest bedroom closet. She said to make the house mine, but I felt guilty when I pitched something. Now it's like there's a monster in there, ready to rope me into a grieving frenzy as soon as I open the door."

"Oh my." Adele paused. "Maybe keep a couple of things, in case you have the need to hug something of hers."

"Hmmm…good idea," and I hung up the phone. I went to the kitchen to fix lunch. I pulled out the pig-shaped breadboard that I had given my mother one Christmas. I remembered how she oohed and exclaimed over the uniqueness of its marble eye and curled tail. I examined the hodgepodge of knife scratches that represented hundreds of crustless sandwiches my mother had made for me.

I ate my sandwich and thought about life on my own, really on my own, as the last branch on the Landings family tree. My father was an only child, like me, and so I had no Landings cousins. My cousin Penny was a Wilson, although she didn't inherit those infamous hiccups. Life was not fair.

A lack of parents or siblings meant there was no one to hold me back, not that my mother or father ever did, but there was also no one to catch me either, like my parents did from time to time. So, I was my biggest barrier.

Back in the den, I stood in front of the closet and inhaled some courage. My hands shook as I grabbed the closet door handles and pulled. I steeled myself but all that attacked me was a subtle whiff of my mother's L'Air du Temps perfume lingering on her clothes— and the odor of well-used shoes that were piled on the closet floor. Several boxes of sweaters and purses completed the collection. I could do this, I told myself.

I began by taking the dresses, blouses, and skirts out and laying them out on the bed. Every few minutes, I would take a wad of clothing and hold them to my face to get a whiff of my mother's scent. I closed my eyes, took a deep breath, and entered a world where Mother still lived.

I surveyed my progress. Clothes lay in a heap of multiple colors, fabrics, and shapes. More still hung in the closet, and several boxes remained on the floor. My sorrow smothered me, and I wanted to flee from the room where Mother's ghost lived and seek uncomplicated peace from a gin and tonic.

Maybe Adele was right, maybe it was too soon. If I didn't finish, I may never, and so I persisted. I organized the clothes into categories like Adele told me they do with patients on a battlefield. Clothing that was ripped or wornout was put in a "do not resuscitate pile." Those that needed a little help but were salvageable were put aside for fixing. Some were in such good condition they needed no attention. They would surely be someone's must-haves at the sale.

Going to the rummage sale setup with Mother had always been fun. We would both stare in awe as volunteers tore through the contributions looking for expensive items donated by the wealthier members of the church. "Oh, look," someone would shout, holding up a treasured find. "Here is Mrs. (fill in the blank) Evan Picone suit." And several ladies who would admit to wearing that size would rush over for first dibs. Giggles erupted over obscene ashtrays, practical joke items, and risqué lingerie. It was the volunteers' pre-emptive strike for the best items.

As I stood in front of the bedroom mirror, I held up a navy polka dotted shirtwaist to my chin. My mother frequently wore that dress to bridge club. I pictured her walking out the door, waving brightly, promising to come back. And she always did.

After several hours weaving back and forth between fond memories and the pangs of loss, I gave up. I retrieved a couple of boxes from the basement, threw the whole mess—sorted and unsorted—into them. I didn't even look at the last boxes in the closet. Couldn't be anything that important, I thought

"Kathy," I said on the phone to my neighbor. "Could you help me take some of Mother's clothing to the rummage sale? I know you're volunteering there."

"Are ya sure ya want to do this so soon?" Kathy sounded a little concerned, like Adele.

"I know, but I need to do this sometime. It won't help to procrastinate."

"See ya there tomorrow."

* * *

I took the boxes to the church the next day, and Kathy helped cart them into the basement where tables of people's memories and junk were piled. Customers were already going through the treasures laid out according to category. Knowing that the clothes would be in new homes, making someone else proud, made me feel I had achieved a small step forward in my life without Mother.

Back home, the empty closet taunted me, "Now what?"

The thought of organizing my den energized me. What do I want this room to be? What do I want to be? I thought about the writing I had done there. I remembered the misery my stories had evoked, and I started to put away the typewriter—this could be a reading room—but a battle of inner voices ensued. "Keep on writing, Margaret, it's what you want to do. Make room for your creative muse." Another voice: "Your writing has done nothing but cause trouble, be done with it." After several rounds of "yes, you can" and "no, you can't" self-talk, the encouraging voice won. I decided to better organize the room for reading, *and* writing.

I kept the desk in the same place, but I moved the bookshelves so I could reach the dictionary and encyclopedia from my desk chair. I placed the chintz chair next to the window so the sun would share its brightness. I put the lady head vase next to the brass banker's lamp that had been my father's. The delicate features of the ceramic lady softened the harsh lines of the lamp's metallic finish and shape. I also hung the Bette Davis poster in sight of my desk so when I looked up I would be inspired by those commanding eyes.

Taking a break, I sat down and picked up the issue of *Forbidden Love* magazine Charlie bought and thumbed through the other stories. One story title made me jump— "Love in the Elevator" by Kaye Langley. That was the author of the banker and the blond story. As I read it, I became sick with jealousy and worry. It was written the way I wish I could write, and it could have been about me. But it wasn't. Two renters met regularly in the elevator, and everyone in the apartment building learned what time to stand in the stairwell to hear the wild antics of the lovers stopped between floors. What did Charlie say about people reading themselves into any chronicle that resembles their own lives? I wondered how the author came up with the idea. It was a very good story, and I was jealous of the author's prose.

As I sat at my desk later that evening, I sought inspiration from the photo on the wall. Miss Davis was silent and brooding.

I looked for my notebook to review some ideas

Where was it? I clawed through the desk. No, it wasn't there. I lifted the cushion of my chair. Not there. I scoured through the books on the shelves. Nowhere. I remembered that I tossed it out of sight somewhere the night Lena accused me of spying. I squeezed my eyes shut and grimaced. An image came to me of the notebook leaving my hand and landing...in the bottom of my mother's closet. The closet with Mother's clothes, the clothes that I took to the rummage sale.

I pressed my hands against my forehead and snippets from the notebook pages raced through my mind: "how Mrs. Gibbons gossips, swelling breasts, the loins of love, does Lena love Santa, the lonely manager, throbbing column of delight, women in the window, lonely men, hungry women, hot flesh, cold eyes." Oh my god, anyone could have seen it and passed it around.

I was sure I would have to leave Liberty—preferably in the middle of the night. I sank into my chair. The notebook, imagined in someone else's hands, hung over me like a personal storm cloud. I felt like I was in the bottom of a gulch, townspeople aiming their rifles, arrows, and rotten garbage right at my chest. I hugged myself and started rocking back and forth, hoping to lapse into a catatonic state. Someone would find my rotting body when the decay of my demise seeped under the doors and windows. People would be saying, "You write dirty, you die dirty." Nothing I did could get the notebook out of my head.

37

The house was my hide-away for the next couple of days. I didn't get dressed, and I barely ate, and I closed the drapes to protect me against acid public opinion. I watched television in a semi-conscious state, moving only to get up and change the channel and to take on an occasional trip to the bathroom. Bette stared down at me from the wall with eyes that said my ride was only going to get bumpier.

On the second day I checked the mailbox, and found a letter from *Forbidden Love* magazine. Great, another story published to bring me shame. Instead, there was no check, no salutation with the word "congratulations." I briefly saw the "sorry" and the title of my rejected story "The Gossip" before I threw it in the trash.

For the next twenty-four hours I moved only from the bed to the sofa, from the sofa to the bathroom, and from the bathroom to the bed, in various combinations of those motions. I had to do something. But what?

On the third day I woke up, bored and needing sun. I opened the drapes and saw there were no tanks in my driveway ready to fire upon me. Could I have been so lucky that the notebook was thrown away, unread? I showered, ate some oatmeal, and straightened the house. Maybe the gods were smiling on me, and it was safe to venture out.

I went into the local drugstore for a phosphate to celebrate my re-emergence. Wearing new navy pumps with fashionable and dangerously narrow heels, I tripped over the marble sill of the doorway. The oblivious chatter that was part of Dorton's Drug and Soda Bar came to a halt and didn't resume until I recovered and made my way to a swivel stool at the counter.

My legs were long enough not to have to make a leap onto the seat so I imagined myself being quite graceful as I sat down, swung toward the counter, and removed my scarf and gloves.

"I'd like a cherry phosphate, please," I told Billy Kling, the shop's soda jerk. His white jacket was spotless, and his paper hat angled just so on his greased and wavy hair. He gave me a wink and smiled.

"Sure thing, Miss Landings." He picked up the tip from the previous customer, wiped the counter in front of me, and retrieved a soda glass from the shelves behind him. I caught him checking his image in the mirror behind the counter, straightening his bow tie and smiling to himself before he proceeded to make my order. Another self-impressed young man—where do they all come from?

While Billy was fixing my phosphate, I became aware of the heavy quiet. I looked in the mirror in front of me and saw ten pairs of eyes peering my way. As my own eyes met theirs in the reflection, the people turned back to their booth companions and began talking again. But the chatter was not carefree or random. It was subdued, whispered with barely discernible pointing toward me as though Bonnie Parker herself had walked in and casually sat down after her last bank robbery. Using the mirror again, I tried to read their lips. I was positive mouths were forming the word "notebook."

Billy brought my drink, and I asked him, "What is all the attention about?" I stirred my phosphate and tried to act casual.

He continued to wipe the clean counter and nodded toward the women in the booths. "I hear you're famous—wrote a story in a magazine and all." He found another clean area to re-wipe. He gave me a half glance.

My appetite for the frothy pink beverage evaporated. Regardless of what Billy said, I was sure they were talking about my notebook. I wanted to bolt out the door and get into the safety and anonymity of my bed again.

A young woman came up to me. "Are you Lydia Bailey? The writer?"

There was nowhere to hide. "Yes."

She turned back to her friends and gave a thumbs up. "We've all read your stories. Can I have your autograph?" She handed me an issue of *Forbidden Love*, open to the Waltz story. I signed with a flourish; it was probably the last time a magazine page would earn my signature.

The young woman looked down and frowned. "I'm sorry, do you mind signing it as Lydia Bailey? That's the famous name."

Criminy.

The door opened, and the little bell announced another customer. I looked up to see Kathy. I signed the magazine as Lydia Bailey and then waved my friend over to the empty stool beside me.

Instead of sitting down, she came to my side and took my arm. "Finish your drink and let's go sit in the park across the street. It's nice out and there's some talking we need to do."

Forgoing my phosphate, I paid my bill and gathered up my things. We walked out, and the late summer air warmed me.

We sat on a bench and when I turned to Kathy, I noticed her frown—she sat stiffly beside me.

"What's up?" I asked.

"Everyone in town is talking about you."

"I know. Someone asked me for my autograph!"

Kathy sat stone-faced, her green eyes, menacing. "There is the matter, however, of your notebook."

"My notebook?" I felt the blood drain from my body, and I held onto the bench seat to keep from falling. "My writing notebook?" Could I not have more than a few minutes of happiness before the next anvil dropped?

"Yes." Her eyes were dark.

"Someone got it at the rummage sale, didn't they?" I could barely breathe.

"Yes." Kathy shook her head and looked back at me.

My eyes filled. "I wish I could die."

"You aren't going to die." Kathy pulled my notebook out of her purse.

The sight of the worn leather was like a rebirth for me. I reached for it but Kathy pulled it back.

"When you dropped off the boxes, I personally went through them since I knew your mother and all." She waited for dramatic effect, but I stared at the notebook, fighting the compulsion to snag it out of her hands. "And in the first box I felt something solid. I pulled it out and this is what I found. I put it in my purse before anyone else noticed it."

"Oh thank you." I grabbed my friend and gave her a hug, but she remained stiff and unyielding. I sat back and scanned her face for a clue to her coolness. "What's wrong?"

"Did it occur to you that I might read it?"

My heart dropped, as if it could drop any lower.

"I'm 'super wife,' aren't I? Is there anyone safe from your prying eyes and racy stories?"

"Kathy—"

"Where do you get off making fun o' my life because I like being a housewife and caring for my husband."

She burst into tears. "And what's worse, your story is true," she said between breaths. She punctuated each phrase with a jerk of my notebook. "I do dream of other places. I'm tired of hearing about his interesting day when mine is so, so servile. I'm tired of the drivel we talk in bridge club."

I sat there in shock, not saying anything.

"Thanks to you, I realize how unhappy I am."

"I—"

"Thanks to you, I know how trivial my life is." She spoke through gritted teeth. "And I suppose my misery is going to be another one of your stories."

She stared straight ahead, new tears threatening. Her face had changed from anger to sadness. She tossed the notebook onto my lap. I barely caught it. "Here, take the damn thing," she said.

"I am so sorry. I deserve your anger...I got caught up in writing those stupid stories." I caressed the cover. "Ow."

"What?" Kathy asked.

"I cut myself on the lever, it's sharp." I watched a teeny drop of blood fall onto the notebook and spread like a small ink stain. "That's fitting—injured by the very thing that caused you so much pain." I sucked on my finger. "Is there any way I can make this up to you? You could've passed the notebook around and made fun of it—and me, but you didn't."

"And have everyone know that I bake frozen pot pies in my own casseroles so my husband thinks I made them?"

I discerned the slightest smile on Kathy's face.

"At least you are doing something exciting, Margaret. I have to admit that I found it all very interesting until I came to the pages about me." She smiled a grin of concession at me. "You did make nice comments about my skin and hair though." Her face grew a little friendlier.

I let out a big sigh that I had been holding to protect myself from breathing in the bad feelings from Kathy. "You are a good friend, I don't deserve you."

"No, you don't," she said. "I have a question though."

"Sure, anything."

"On several pages ya have notes about a boy named Bobby and birth dates and addresses." She leaned closer to me. "Is that *your* child?"

I told her everything about Bobby, Charlie, and my firing. She sat motionless and let me talk. When I was finished she put her arm around me.

"Ya poor thing. Ya seem to be anywhere but where the luck is."

Still, I realized that the contents of my notebook had changed the relationship between Kathy and me. I had kept secrets, and if I were her, I would have always wondered what else was hidden. We bid goodbye, each knowing more about the other than we did an hour before.

38

As I drove onto my street, I saw Adele, still in her nurse's uniform, sitting on the front stoop of my house. When she saw me, she jumped up and ran to my car as I pulled into the driveway.

Waving her hands, she signaled me not to turn off the engine and to let her into the driver's side of the car.

I hesitated, but I saw the look that a nurse like Adele gives when you won't take your medicine. I moved over.

Breathless, she jumped into the driver's seat. "Where have you been? I've been calling and calling."

"Why? What's going on?" Hope mounted that Mr. Beals had finally gone to rest.

"It's Pete. He's gone. We have to go to the police department. He left a note, addressed to you."

"If he's gone, that's good, isn't it? Good riddance, I say."

"No, Margaret, he's *gone*. Dead. He hanged himself." She put the car in gear and drove.

He killed himself? My mind filled with images of Pete snarling, Pete crying over his dog, Pete putting his rough hand on mine. He's gone? By his own doing?

He's dead, and he's still controlling my life. Why am I involved, I wondered?

I gripped the door handle and fought the urge to jump out. "Why did he kill himself?"

"That's what the police want to talk to you about."

I slammed the dashboard. "Turn around. I don't want to go. Why me? This doesn't make sense."

She ignored me and sped through a yellow light, her white

thick-soled shoe pressing down on the accelerator.

I gripped the arm-rest. "Why do I have to go to the police?"

"I told you. They have a letter addressed to you."

"I don't want a letter from Pete, especially a dead Pete. Why can't they just read it?"

"They have, but there's something in it they want to question you about."

"They think I had something to do with his death?"

"No, no, it's not your fault." Adele took one hand off the wheel to pat mine. She looked at me and said, "Pete made his own decisions." The car drifted left of center.

"Holy criminy, watch where you're going!"

She jerked the car back into her lane.

I gripped the door. "How did you get involved?"

"I was getting off work when I saw the ambulance come in. They pushed the gurney by me and I saw that it was Pete, he wasn't bagged yet." Adele took a quick glance at me. "It's a small town, Margaret. The chief of police knows me, knows that you and I are friends."

I hid my face in my hands. "Stop."

Adele pulled the car over and put it in park, but she did not turn off the engine. She took my hands.

A little calmer, I raised my head. "Do you know what's in the letter?"

"Yes, but you should read it for yourself."

"You don't understand. If people see me go into the police station, there will be all kinds of rumors in addition to what's out there now."

"Margaret, grow up. What happened to all that talk about the raven and change?" Adele's eyes narrowed. "A man has died at his own hands, and his last words were to you."

"Why would I want to read how I've ruined someone's life?" I crossed my arms and stared out the window.

"You think this is about you?" Adele took in a deep breath. "No one's at fault for someone else's suicide. Pete didn't blame you. He left you some money and that makes the police suspicious."

My head jerked back to her. "Money?" I frowned. "Pete didn't have any mon—" I stopped and put my hand to my mouth. "Oh no, I wonder if he actually went through with it."

"Went through with what?"

"A long time ago, Pete 'confessed' that he wanted to get back at some people who had cheated him of some money. He worked for them, laying carpet for six months, and they promised to pay and never did."

"So?"

"He told me he figured out how to get his money, that nothing could stop him getting what was his. I was so shocked I didn't ask him how or when he was going to do it."

Adele sat back into her seat. "Wow."

"Yes, 'wow.' I have to admit I'm curious now. Let's go see what this is about."

"Such a saint." Adele pulled the car back onto the road.

"Say, where've you been the past few days? Haven't seen or heard from you," I said.

She kept her eyes on the road ahead. "I'll tell you about it later."

Neither one of us said anything more during the next few blocks to the police station. We pulled into the angled parking that lined the street in front. I got out, stood beside the car, and studied the plain brick building. An image of a vulnerable Pete flashed across my mind and a fragment of pity roiled in me, but I pushed the thought back down. I looked at the black and white police car at my side—its presence sending waves of anxiety through me. The red light on the patrol car was not lit, but the one in my memory was. The night in high school, when I was pulled over for running a red light, burned in my mind like the one on top of the police car. The policeman's face was all judgment as he wrote my ticket. My legs were water around cops.

I watched Adele approach the parking meter. After digging through her purse, she found a dime, put it into the meter's slot, and twisted the dial. A metal rod with "4 hours" stamped on it popped up in the little window.

I panicked. "We're not going to need four hours, are we?"

"A dime was the first coin I found." She took my arm. "Let's go."

A policeman pushed the buzzer beside the heavy wooden door. A metallic click answered, and the officer motioned us to follow him. My chest tightened as I crossed the threshold into the sanctum of testosterone and authority. We walked down a hall tiled with black and once white linoleum squares. Wood doors with textured and heavy frosted windows had stenciled black lettering declaring the occupant or purpose of each office: Lieutenant Rawlings, City Parking Fines, Detective Squad Room. Then the officer stopped. He opened a door and stood aside for us to go in, but I saw the name and backed up a step.

"I can't do this. We know the detective, it's Mark Walls."

"'Splice,' the AV guy?"

"Yeah, I don't want him to know about my life."

Adele gave me a little push and said, "He probably already does."

A toned and muscular Detective Walls stood up from his desk and motioned to two hard wooden chairs. He was not the Splice I knew in high school, a bespectacled teenager with a pocket protector and pimples on his neck. But he had been one of maybe two boys in school who could dance the jitterbug like a pro. His ability to swing, turn, and pull in his partner like an *American Bandstand* teen made him a popular date.

"He's not chubby and short anymore," I whispered out of the side of my mouth while still keeping my eyes on the tall and dark-haired detective.

"Have a seat, ladies. I'm sorry to be seeing you under these circumstances."

I bobbed my head but my voice and body were frozen by the atmosphere of bureaucracy. Gray metal filing cabinets lined the wall behind the chairs. A box typewriter sat to the left side of the desk, a black phone with oily stains on the receiver sat to the right. A worn writing pad adorned with unrecognizable doodling and coffee stains sat in front of Splice, er, Mark. All around him, on the desk, on the file cabinets, and on chairs sat papers and folders. Thumbtacked WANTED posters hung on the wall behind him, their unsmiling faces stared at me. "You're in deep now," they mouthed.

Once we were all seated, Detective Mark pushed an envelope across the desk toward me. Its slide across the worn oak screeched in my ears. I noticed Pete's scrawled handwriting on the envelope

"Please give to Miss Margaret Landings, 407 Livingston Street."

"He knew where I lived," I said to Adele.

Mark cleared his throat. "I'd like you to read it. I know this isn't easy." He paused. "It's a strange note, not one we usually get in these situations, but we do need your take on it."

I picked up the envelope and pulled out a piece of notebook paper. "Who found him?"

Mark straightened his tie. "He was in jail, here, you see. We picked him up for disorderly conduct. Drunk as a skunk, as they say—"

I grimaced.

"I'm sorry. Anyway, we were letting him sleep it off in jail, but he hanged himself in his cell. We found the note in his pants pocket."

Pete's face invaded my mind again, and this time he was pleading, like the night he asked if he could join me for dinner. My hands trembling, I forced myself to read the words that Pete wrote.

> Dear Margaret,
> By the time you read this, my miserable life will be over and maybe I found some happiness in the hereafter. The only person I could think of that might care whether I was dead or not was you. I know I made your life miserable, but I couldn't help myself. It made me feel better to be near you. I hope I didn't scare you too much, well I guess I did because you avoided me. I guess I deserved that. I know I didn't act like it, but your a classy lady, and I want to thank you for caring about my dead dog. The only thing I have left is that money I told you about. I actually did what I said I was going to do. I'd like you to put it to good use. Maybe to the dog pound or something. Have a good life, Pete. PS I put the money in a post office box. The key is in the dog biscuit jar on my kitchen counter. PPS I know your into that Bette Davis lady, but your smarter than her.

"I had no idea." My eyes filled, and when I looked up at Mark and Adele, I burst into tears. Adele took me in her arms and patted me until the tears subsided.

"He seems to have liked you," Mark said.

Sniffing, I asked, "Did you get the key?"

"We have it in the evidence room. We already have the money, and that's what we're investigating. It's the exact same amount that was stolen from the Vales a couple of months ago."

"Who are the Vales?" asked Adele.

"They own a carpet business," Mark answered. "I guess they hired Mr. Jordan to do some carpet laying and the business relationship didn't end so well. Mr. Jordan overcharged them, they claim, and they refused to pay the difference, and there were threats."

Adele and I looked at each other.

"Margaret, the letter indicates you had knowledge about the money and where it came from. Did he tell you about the Vales?"

In the few seconds that Mark waited for my answer, Pete's miserable life whirled before me—the loveless home, the dog he put out of its misery, his disasters with women, and his story about the Vales.

"Pete has no family, and he was saving his money so he could have some sort of legacy." I had heard detectives were walking lie detector machines, and Mark was looking at me like my printout was going haywire. "He was a hard worker, you know," I continued.

Adele put her hand on my arm. "Margaret, you—"

I ignored my friend's tactile reminder of the truth. "He was a strange fellow, but he did tell me about some of his aspirations, and…" I took a deep breath, "…Pete wanted to donate his money to the local dog pound." Mark continued to gawk at me. "Yes, the money should fund the new Pete Jordan Dog Shelter. There's enough, isn't there?" I stopped and smiled at Splice. "It's such a coincidence that the money is the same amount as that stolen from the Vales. Pete was a little rough around the edges, but he was an honest man. No, he was very adamant about saving money."

Adele and Mark both sat with open mouths. Taking advantage of surprise, I continued, "So, Detective Walls, how do I ensure that Mr. Jordan's wishes are followed?"

Back in the car, Adele turned to me. "You lied."

"You could have said something, you know."

"I was so surprised," she said. "You hated Pete and everything he stood for."

"I felt so sorry for him. And I realized that he was a person, like you, or me. And he needed a friend."

"Why? He didn't do anything for you." Adele, who was on the passenger side this time, shook her head at my unexpected behavior.

"What? Now you're the skeptic and uncharitable one? I found Pete's letter very touching. Funny, words seem to mean more from a dead person than a live person."

"That's kind of sad."

"I know, but… Pete did do something for me."

"And what was that?"

"He gave *me* the opportunity to do something good. Think of it as a raven thing."

I started the engine and backed the car onto the road. As I put the car in gear, both our bodies relaxed, and we sank into the seats.

When I dropped Adele off at her house, I leaned out the car window before she went in. "Thank you for going with me to the police station."

She came back to the car. "Sometimes friends do tough things."

"This time I'm glad you did."

I drove off, taking a last glance at my friend, who stood on the sidewalk and waved goodbye.

She looked so sad. I planned to ask her about that the next day.

39

Charlie stood at the door. "Adele called me. I canceled my appointments and came as soon as I could."

When I saw him, I fumbled with the door handle so anxious I was to see him, to share what had happened. I fell into his arms and broke into a bawling babble that chronicled Pete's suicide, my guilt, my redemptive idea for the dog shelter, and my disbelief that any of it happened. In between my garbled confessions, I thought about the goodness and strength of Charlie's shoulders and arms. My tears were about yesterday's drama, but interspersed with those tears were thoughts about what a waste it was that Charlie was gay. That only made me cry harder.

"None of this is your fault," he said as he held me and patted my back.

"I know," I blubbered. "Nothing goes right. I—"

"Hey, enough of that. Let's sit down. Let me get you something to drink."

Charlie made sure I was in a chair with a box of tissues at my side, and he went into the kitchen. I could hear him opening and closing cupboards in a confused search for glasses. That someone was taking care of me, even ineptly, was a distraction from my emotional tantrum. Pretty soon I heard the sounds of glasses on the counter, ice dumping, and carbonated soda making its fizzy way into containers. He appeared beaming in the living room with two glasses of root beer. He may have been different from most men, but he still had that maddening male quality of being overly proud of doing the simplest task.

He gave me my root beer and sat down. "From the sound of things, you really came through for Pete."

"I'm not sure it was all about Pete. Somewhere down inside came the urge to help, even if he couldn't help himself. And I have to admit that my good came from his good—he paid me a compliment in his letter," I smiled, "and in front of the detective who turned me down for a Sadie Hawkins dance in high school."

"What did Pete say?"

"He wrote that I was a classy lady."

"Ah, I see." Charlie held up his root beer as a toast. "That explains things." He looked at me. "You're selling yourself short. You saw an opportunity to help some poor bloke realize a dream. Nothing we do is pure. We're always pulled by the shoulds and wants of a decision. But you landed in the column of the right thing to do. Hat's off to you." He tipped his glass toward me.

"Even if I lied?"

Charlie nodded. "Didn't you tell me Pete was owed the money by employers who didn't pay him? It's muddy, but morally defensible. I'm speaking as your friend, not as your attorney."

"I guess." I wiped away what remained of the tears on my face. I relaxed to the comfort of Charlie's voice. "Do you think there will be any problem with the money going to the dog shelter?"

"No, they don't have any proof it's the stolen money. And the letter serves as a directive, of sorts." He sipped his soda. "I know you have the best of intentions, just like you did with Bobby."

I sat forward, surprised that a man as practical as Charlie would bring up a topic that he had told me to forget. "I thought you said I needed to get on with life and forget about him."

"I've been thinking about your need, and if I admit it, my need, to have some connection with our son."

"I'm surprised. Tell me more." I sat back, soda in hand.

"If we want some tie to Bobby's life, without being intrusive, why don't we set up an anonymous trust for him for, you know, college. I want to. I don't know if you have any money for that sort of thing. I can do it or we can do it together." He studied me for a reaction.

"I could have some impact on his life after all, couldn't I?"

"Do you want to do it together?" Charlie asked.

"Well…my mother left me a small inheritance…let's do it," I said. "It would give me purpose again."

"Great. I'll—"

The doorbell rang, interrupting our rapport.

I opened the door. My brain tried to make the leap from the plans Charlie and I were discussing to acknowledging a solemn Adele at the door.

She thrust a legal looking document at me. "I'm sorry but you need to see this. I can't keep it from you any longer."

I frowned.

"Please, may I come in? We need to talk."

"Charlie is here."

"Good…he needs to see this too."

I led her into the living room. I shrugged my shoulders and raised my hands to signal Charlie that I had no idea what was happening.

Adele sat on the edge of the chair.

He and I exchanged looks that read, "What the hell is this about?" Glancing from Adele's face to the ominous document on her lap, Charlie's face wrinkled in worried curiosity.

I sat stiff and ready to defend myself.

"I know you think I give you too much advice—"

"Good observation," I said.

"Please hear me out. I do have your best interests at heart. I really do." Adele took another deep breath. "I want you to be happy for the right thing, not imagined things."

"I've heard this story before. You think I'm too involved with Bobby."

"…that you're involved without all the right information," she countered.

"You gave me the information, dearie."

"But with a warning. There were several delivery rooms in that hospital—"

"We've been through this."

Adele leaned more toward me. "There was something not right about your connection to Bobby. Maybe it was the wild coincidence that I didn't believe, maybe it was because you and Charlie are tall and Bobby is short for his age, I don't know. I had to dig a little deeper, for your sake."

I didn't want to hear what she was saying. I saw Charlie sit forward in his seat.

"What kind of digging did you do?" Charlie asked. He rested his wrists on his knees, clasped his hands except for the forefingers that met and pointed a directive toward Adele.

She turned to me. "The information I gave you at The Office came from a friend of mine who worked at Charity Hospital. I wanted more official information so I went to the Allegheny County courthouse and looked up birth records for May 30, 1946. Bobby's is there of course, with the Taylors listed as his parents, a corrected copy for adoptions, I'm sure."

"So that's where you were the past couple of days."

"There was another birth, same day, same time…a boy. The parents are listed as Deborah and David Smith."

Charlie's fingers stopped pointing. He straightened and placed his hands on his thighs.

"So there's doubt," he said.

I shot Charlie a venomous look. Whose side was he on?

"You still haven't proven anything," I said to Adele.

"Did you look on the birth certificates to see the doctors' names?" asked Charlie.

Adele took a deep breath. "Yes. The doctor who delivered Bobby was Dr. Titus. The doctor who delivered the other boy was Dr. Schultz."

I caught myself before I slipped off the edge of the chair. "My Dr. Schultz?" The room, or maybe it was the world, tilted about forty-five degrees, enough for me to know that my life as I dreamed it was sliding out of my reach. I struggled to breathe.

"Criminy." I stood up and walked to the window. I stared at nothing while Bobby's face zoomed in and out of focus. Mostly it was his smile I saw, a son's smile for his mother, who wasn't me. Why did I so blindly agree to my parents to give my son up for adoption?

Charlie sat frozen, not yet comprehending that his fatherhood was once again a mystery.

"I guess we don't need a trust for Bobby's future," I said to the window. I leaned against the pane and moaned.

"Are you all right, Margaret?" Adele asked.

"No," I answered.

*   *   *

Charlie and Adele left about an hour later—an hour in which each of us tried to say anything only to give up and say nothing. After I closed the door behind them, I wandered into my den and studied Bette's face. It was just a face on glossy paper. What had I been thinking that a person in a movie could shelter me from the battering of reality, that makeup could cover up the scars of my life's decisions and indecisions? I had no job, no mother, no child, no husband, and an imaginary friend who was an image on the silver screen and a photo on paper.

The emotional rumbling started deep down inside and erupted in a mad clawing at the poster. "I hate you, I hate you, I hate you," I screamed as I ripped through first her mouth and then her eyes. In less than a minute, all that was left of Bette Davis lay in shreds at my feet.

I sagged to the floor and settled amid the remnants of the poster. I sat splayed like an open book. So, my life had come to this. Pete's letter came to mind and I heard his Appalachian twang, "I know your into that Bette Davis lady from the movie, but your smarter than her." His grammar wasn't great, but his words touched a chord in the strings of my life. Was I smarter than her? I didn't feel like it. I wasn't clever and biting, and I certainly hadn't given up anything for the love of a good man.

I picked at a ragged piece of the poster and when I flipped it over I saw one of Bette's eyes—the lid closed partially over the pupil, the iris dark and aimed directly at me, the arch of the eyebrow and the lashes framing that sultry orb. Out of the context of the poster, the eye wasn't Bette's anymore but the eye of Every Woman—daring me to do something. But what? Exasperated, I tossed the paper eye away from me but like a boomerang it circled back to my lap, eyeball side up. Every Woman stared at me, and Adele's cautious words drifted into my consciousness. "Maybe Liberty was just a stop on your journey, Margaret."

The thought struck terror in me, and yet I considered the possibilities. What's to keep me in Liberty? Well, yeah, the few friends I've made, my mother's house that I've turned into my home.

I got on my hands and knees, gathered the paper bits and stood to throw them in the waste basket. Walking to the kitchen for a gin and tonic—a weak gin and tonic, I told myself—I saw myself evolving from a child to a fully functioning woman.

I took my drink back into the den and sat in my comfort chair. The cocktail disappointed me, so I set it down and sat thinking with my hands in my lap. Why would I stay? Be the Margaret Landings that so many had come to connect to tawdry romance stories? Run into John Graham whom I couldn't have? I still ached when I saw him—I could spot him a block away by his familiar gait, pick out the timbre of his voice in a crowd of a hundred. Bobby. Mourn the son who wasn't mine? Work. Spend the rest of my life in a small town with small possibilities?

What would my mother say? I dug into the reservoir of Mother's voice, some helpful, some hurtful. Uncle Roger had said at her funeral that she was practical, that she protected herself by not fighting the inevitability of small town living. She adapted and lived the good life. My thoughts went back to an afternoon years ago when I sat on Mother's lap while she read Black Beauty. After reading the last page, she caressed the print, closed the book and patted the leather cover. She looked quite content and said, "You see, darling, we eventually get to where we're supposed to be."

I looked up at the wall that no longer held Bette's face. Without the poster, the wall reflected nothing, only my thoughts. A moment's panic slammed into me but I let it dissipate. In its place came energy, and it had no strings, no expectations. "Margaret, meet Margaret," I said aloud. The walls in the room became a garden fence, protecting its contents and hiding the outside world. I hungered for the outside.

So that was it. I needed to leave Liberty, to start again, somewhere, doing something new. Could I do this? Another move in so short a time. Would the roulette wheel of fate make me a winner or a loser?

40

I stretched my head from side to side to loosen the kinks of a restless night. "Meet me under the clock at Kaufmann's," I told my cousin Penny on the phone, "I need to talk to you."

"What, has it been a year since I talked to you? I bet it's wedding bells," she said.

"Not even close. You can't believe what's happened. I'm sorry I woke you, but if I leave now, I can get there about noon. Please?"

She was silent a moment. "This doesn't sound good."

"I need my level-headed cousin to help me make a decision."

* * *

I arrived under Kauffman's clock as the large iron hands jumped to the half hour. A loud single "bong" announced to Pittsburgh that the next o'clock was thirty minutes away. The large city icon had two naked brass men, one on each side, who seemed to struggle under the weight of time they held between them.

I had an insatiable hunger for affirmation, but my choices were limited. I had decided to leave Liberty but so many doubts were eroding my decision. When I ripped Bette Davis off the wall, I had torn her out of my repertoire of advisors. Adele talked herself blue about fate and destiny and following your dreams until I couldn't take it anymore. She was definitely in the middle between "stay" and "go." I sensed that Kathy was envious of my freedom, and her advice would be biased toward staying.

I had great hope in my cousin Penny. She was a "lighthouse friend"—someone who stood ready when I needed her. She witnessed the ocean of emotions I went through during the first months of my pregnancy before I went into the Crittendon Home, and she was a silent spectator to my family's pressure to give the baby up for adoption. She also knew Charlie.

I saw her waving madly from the shopper-filled street.

We made our way into the Tic Toc Restaurant and sat down in a corner booth. The waitress brought us water and plastic-covered menus. I took off my gloves and waited for Penny to do the same.

"I'm sorry I couldn't make it to your mother's funeral," she said.

"You missed an exciting show of the Wilson hiccups."

"You didn't."

"I did."

Penny grinned and picked up the menu. "Let's see what's for lunch before you tell me the news."

I took a deep breath. "Turns out you led the father of my baby straight to me."

"I what?" She set the menu down.

"You worked with Charles Robertson, didn't you?"

Penny looked at me. "Oh my gosh."

"When you were telling him about your hypothetical friend who had a baby out of wedlock, he was able to put the pieces together, and he came looking for me."

My cousin nodded, speechless.

"This green and white car always seemed to be where I was. I thought it was this creepy guy, at least I thought he was creepy. Anyway it turned out to be Charles, who was trying to get up his nerve to talk to me. He was following me when I had a car accident. Evidently injury and mayhem break down barriers between people. We really connected."

Penny jumped forward in her seat and put her elbows on the table. "How wonderful."

"Don't get too excited," I said.

She sat back. "Why not?"

I looked around to reassure myself that no one was within hearing range. "Turns out he's a homosexual."

"A queer?"

"That's another story, but there's more."

I told her the whole saga about John, Bobby, Howard, Pete,

Charlie, and Lena. Several times I had to wave away the waitress who would periodically come to take our orders. Penny's eyes never left mine. She seemed to sense when the waitress was approaching and without losing eye contact with me would wave her away too. The waitress became more hesitant in her approaches, slowing down as she neared the zone of wave-a-ways.

Finished, I sat back and looked down at the menu in front of me, but all I saw was incoherent type.

She took my hand. "Not to state the obvious, but you have a big decision to make."

"No kidding." I picked at a loose thread on the binding of the menu. "I don't know what to do. All I know is that I have to do something. I thought that doing what was best for me was the answer, but I wasn't considering other people. I have choices, and I'm scared I'll make the wrong one, again."

I watched the waitress draw near our table, hesitant as though she were expecting the go-away wave. I smiled at her instead and she came over with pad in hand and curiosity in her eyes.

"What'll it be, ladies?" We ordered cheddar melts and fruited Jell-O salads. The visibly relieved waitress slid her pencil into the hair over her ear and headed back to the kitchen.

"What am I going to do?" I asked Penny.

"This is a good opportunity to find out you're stronger than you think you are." She paused. "What do you want to be doing ten years from now?"

"I want...I want a family." I braved a glance and she was studying me with her head cocked. "Isn't it ironic," I continued, "that I would have to adopt?" My eyes burned.

"Someone would be returning you the favor. You gave a child and a family a wonderful life. It'll be your turn. But in the meantime, before you have a family?"

"I guess I have to work."

"Are there jobs in Liberty?"

"Women in Liberty are sales clerks, teachers, or nurses, but I want more. I don't mean to have illusions of grandeur—"

"I'm picturing Napoleon with his hand in his waistcoat."

"I can dream, can't I? Am I that weird to feel as though I'm destined for something?" I looked at Penny. "Don't I get some sympathy?"

"Hmmm, not much. You've been given a little detour on your road to greatness. We can learn invaluable lessons from the unexpected sights on a detour, you know."

"A ten-year detour? I'm ready to get back on the main road."

"Funny. Do you think you could get your old job back? I heard the company wasn't too happy with your replacement. I have a friend who works there."

"I really liked that job. I was good at it." I took my water glass and drained it. "The writing I did for *Forbidden Love* was okay, but the magazine rejected my last two submissions. I think I'm a better editor than a writer."

"I have to admit I read one of your published stories."

"You did?"

"Buying the magazine was, shall we say, a little embarrassing, and I had to hide it from my husband."

"I see a 'but' in your face."

"There was no heart. Plot, but no heart. I wouldn't give up on writing yet."

"It's given me nothing but trouble."

"Maybe you are writing about the wrong things. Have you thought about writing mysteries? You know, kill someone off in the first chapter. It could be Howard."

"Tempting."

"I do believe you have stories to tell, but maybe you're looking outward for inspiration rather than inward."

The waitress brought our lunches, and I dove into my food with the energy of a person who had given a last confession and found out that she wasn't going to die after all.

Penny interrupted my ruminations. "You have packing to do."

41

Kathy looked at the roadmap and said "Wow, you're going back to Pittsburgh. How did ya get your job back?"

"It's always helpful when your replacement isn't as good as you." I looked past her at the stacks of boxes piled on top of one another, representing hours of sorting, debating, and folding. There were piles of clothes as well as boxes of mother's mementos that insisted on taking the journey with me. Bette Davis and her trappings were in their new home already—the Salvation Army donation box.

"And are ya going to keep writing?"

"Full of questions, aren't you?" I swirled the coffee in the cup I had poured.

"I'm sorry—"

"Actually it's good you brought it up. After my last rejection and the take-off of Lena's career, I'm not so sure."

"Lena's career?"

"It's kind of embarrassing." I glanced at a *Forbidden Love* magazine peeking from a stack not yet packed.

"Seems Lena had the last laugh. She took my idea about writing stories based on people in town. Only she was more masterful than I at hiding the sources of her inspiration."

"I don't understand."

"You've heard people talking about this new author Kaye Langley?" Kathy looked at me, puzzled. "That's Lena."

She jumped out of her chair. "Ya effin' me, are ya?" Kathy was as surprised as I was by her outburst, and we laughed.

"I'm not effin' you," I said when I got my breath back.

"How did ya find out?" She sat back and leaned toward me.

"I went to the post office to close my postal box, seeing as how I wasn't getting published anymore, or least that's how it felt. Anyhow, who should be there getting mail from *her* post office box but Lena. She was surprised to see me, and she dropped a letter that I saw was addressed to no less than Kaye Langley."

"Jesus, Mary, and Joseph."

"She bent down to pick up the letter. When she stood up, victory was written all over her face. She told me the Santa story propelled her to try it herself, and she found out she was pretty good. 'Studied yours to see what needed improving,' she said."

"Jesus, Mary, Joseph, *and* the wee donkey."

I laughed. "Hadn't heard that one before."

"I save that phrase for the really big surprises."

"So," I said, "maybe things work out for the best."

"Destiny, Margaret, destiny."

"You and Adele still have me confused as to which is destiny and which is fate. Was I *fated* to fail as a writer? Does my *destiny* lie in Pittsburgh?"

"First of all, you haven't failed. Maybe you need a different path to your goals."

"My goals historically become mistakes."

"Speaking of mistakes—"

"Oh, the men. Charlie is happy in Pittsburgh doing his lawyer thing. But I'll probably see him from time to time. We are friends, you know. I never want to see Howard's pasty little face again, and as for John Graham…" My voice trailed off.

"Yeah, what about Mr. Graham," Kathy asked, "…your unavailable soul mate? Good riddance. He should never have pursued you."

"I should never have given in." Lost in thought I twirled the coffee cup by the handle a couple of times, the ceramic scratching of the cup on its saucer momentarily entertaining me. "I still have a child out there somewhere, too."

"As Charles would say, 'He's not yours to have.'"

We sat in silence for a few moments— Kathy looking at the map of Pennsylvania and I blinking away Bobby's image.

* * *

The next morning I stood in the driveway of my locked-up house. The moving van had pulled away, carrying my possessions to another adventure. Mother and Daddy were smiling on me, the sensation was so sure.

I had put Mother's wedding ring on my right hand as a reminder to wait for a guy who, in her words, "picks up after himself." Good looks and selfish needs hadn't worked out as criteria for finding a suitable match, so perhaps a more objective approach will guide me through the interminable maze of men.

Adele drove up, got out of her car, and walked toward me with a practiced smile. She looked at the SOLD sign and gave me a thumbs up signal. Suddenly she burst into tears, and we grabbed each other. "What if I don't see you again?"

"You will, and often," I said. "I'm just five hours away. Let's cry a few minutes and hug, and then I have to go." Finally we both wiped our noses on our sleeves and laughed at our grossness.

"Later, alligator?" I held up my hand with my little finger crooked.

She put up her hand too and curled her pinkie to interlock with mine.

"After a while, crocodile."

I took a last look at the house in which I grew up, both physically and emotionally. I gave Aqua Bella a pat and climbed in. I had packed Bella nearly to the windows with clothes but made sure I could still see out.

Adele handed me something black and soft. It was a stuffed toy, a raven. "That's for reminding you to be open to change."

I examined the toy's yellow bead eyes. "Are you expecting me to caw?"

"No, I'm expecting you to become an independent woman."

Pulling out of my driveway, I waved to Adele, to Mrs. Eisling peeking through her window, to my neighbor Kathy, standing on her porch and looking like she was going to cry any minute, and finally to my house. I set my jaw for courage.

I could see Adele running after the car and waving. She eventually stopped, panting. Wow, what a friend.

Once on the main road I turned on the radio to hear Doris Day singing "Que Sera, Sera." What a great song for starting my new life. *Whatever will be, will be.* I increased the volume and sang along.

Speeding by cornfields tall as King Kong, I headed toward my rebirth in Pittsburgh. I thought about Kathy and Adele telling me that, maybe, I had been writing about the wrong things from the wrong sources of inspiration. I glanced at the plush raven on the passenger seat, its golden plastic eyes set on the road ahead.

All was well with the world, and I coaxed Bella to a comfortable, but slightly rebellious speed. I looked in the rearview mirror for a final peek at the past before I dedicated myself to the future. What I saw instead of retreating countryside was my purse hurtling from the top of the car, through the air, and bouncing on the highway, only to be squashed by the tires of the police car following me with flashing red lights. Criminy.

An Interview with the Author

How did you get interested in department store elevators as a stage for Miss Margaret Landings' personal journey?

Elevators have always been fascinating to me. Operating one was my first job in my grandfather's department store. I learned that the elevator gave an excellent vantage point for observing what was happening in the lives of the customers and the employees. At the time, I was too young to understand what I was seeing. It's the looking back that gives us glimpses into the truth of human drama.

How did your life influence this view of the Main Street merchants who populated the small towns of the Midwest and all over America in the mid-20th century?

John Graham is not a typical Main Street merchant! He was created for dramatic effect as were all the other characters. I have a great deal of respect for the retailers and clerks who provide goods and services for a community. They know their customers, and they know their merchandise. My grandfather was known to give loans to struggling families who had a hard time paying their bills. One woman who was raised by a single mother told me that my grandfather would let her pick out a new school dress whenever she brought in a grade card full of As. That wouldn't happen at the big box stores of today!

Does coming from a small town still influence your life and values today?

I think that living in a small town helps people realize our interconnectedness and opportunities to make a contribution to others' lives. But everyone is different. We all have to decide what is important to us regardless of where we live. Margaret struggled with the expectations of living in a small town, but she also knew that the anonymity of a city had its drawbacks. Perhaps we are at best advantage when we have experienced both worlds.

You have several themes in your novel: self-deception, woman's role, secrecy, mother-daughter relationships, redemption, homosexuality, and so forth. Did you write to the themes or did they emerge?

The themes emerged as the characters developed. And it's true—characters take over a story. Pete, for instance, was going to be a "bad guy" all the way through, but he had a redeeming side that begged to be revealed. Margaret, Kathy, and Adele all speak to the theme of woman's role—about to be turned upside down in the sixties by Betty Friedan's *The Feminine Mystique*. The image of a happy suburban housewife in the 1950s was used to sell products, but women began to question the message.

Do you plan to write a sequel?

Oh yes! I plan to take Margaret through the seminal decades. *The Ups and Downs of Miss Margaret Landings* focuses on the iconic fifties and Margaret's personal journey. The next book, *Margaret's War*, is about the 'sixties. The Vietnam War will be a major factor in Margaret's life, and she will learn the pain of making decisions that have an impact on many people, not just herself.

You can ask Patti more questions about her books at her blog http://www.margaretlandings.com or email her at patti@pattialbaugh.com.

If you've enjoyed this book, please consider leaving a review on Amazon or Goodreads (or ideally, both). Many thanks.

A Reading and Discussion Guide

1. Margaret Landings is the protagonist and narrator of the story. How do you think Margaret changed over the course of the story? If you were able to interview her, what question(s) would you ask? Whom would you cast as Margaret for a movie version?

2. The 1950s and a small Midwest town setting are central to the story. How does the setting function as a character in the novel? How do the characters interact with the setting?

3. One of the themes of the book is loss. How did the characters in the story deal with the losses they experienced? Do people have to have similar experiences to understand someone else's loss?

4. The mother/daughter relationship is another theme. How would you characterize the dynamics between Margaret and her mother? What was typical or atypical about their relationship?

5. Adoption procedures are very different in the 21st century. Charlie said to Margaret, "Maybe in the future birth parents will have contact with their children, but not in this day and age." Are open adoptions better than the closed adoptions of the 20th century?

6. Bette Davis' place in Margaret's life is central to Margaret's journey of self-discovery. Do most people have some illusionary person or attitude that helps them deal with life? Who are some of the persona you (or someone you know) use?

7. Margaret is frequently confronted by the words "fate" and "destiny." Adele says to Margaret, "Don't assume that fate is the same as destiny. Fate gives us lessons and can lead us astray. Destiny is what we are meant to do." Another time Margaret asks herself, "Was I fated to fail as a writer? Does my destiny lie in Pittsburgh?" What do you think the different is between fate and destiny?

Rudin Press
2013

Made in the USA
San Bernardino, CA
13 December 2015